MONUMENT

Tyler,

I love you man! Thanks for holding my hand while I pooled.

Patrick.B

MONUMENT,
a novel

patrick blennerhassett

N_1 O_2 N_1

CANADA

*Publisher's note: This book is a work of fiction. Names, characters, places and
incidents are either the product of the author's imagination or are used
fictitiously, and any resemblance to actual persons living or dead
is entirely coincidental.*

Library and Archives Canada Cataloguing in Publication

Blennerhassett, Patrick, 1982–
Monument : a novel / Patrick Blennerhassett.

ISBN 978-0-9739558-4-2

I. Title.

PS8603.L46M66 2008   C813'.6   C2008-902616-0

Printed and bound in Canada on 100% ancient forest-free paper.

Now Or Never Publishing Inc.
11268 Dawson Place
Delta, British Columbia
Canada V4C 3S7

nonpublishing.com
Fighting Words.

to whom it may concern

Monument

Destroyer

The moment his body crashes through the restaurant window, I realize how drunk I really am. This wasn't supposed to happen, I think to myself. I didn't throw him that hard. I watch the glass shatter, each shard seemingly so significant, spraying out around his fallen body in a widening electric halo. A crowd gathers instantly, though I'm hardly aware of their presence, busy as I am hammering this guy with one fist while pinning him against the windowsill with the other. The following day I'll learn, via the usual backchannels, he needed thirty-eight stitches to close the ragged gap in his lower back. I won't feel bad for him at all.

He starts to corral my face with his hands, forcing my head up. All I can hear are shouts from behind. And there, in front of me, I see three Denny's waitresses staring at me with that look, that one of fear, excitement and astonishment I've seen so many times before. Smiling, I just keep throwing punches, flinging shards of glass everywhere.

By the time the police arrive we're long gone. I can't really remember anything, not immediately, but as the four of us flee the scene everybody is talking furiously at me, filling me in painstaking detail. I feel like vomiting as the memory of what just transpired overtakes me. Still, it was nothing out of the ordinary. Just some guys outside a Denny's looking for a fight, and our condescending to oblige them on this particular night.

Either way, my hands are the most mangled part of my body, a sign I won the fight, which is probably a good thing.

I throw up in the backseat of the car, and realize it's my own car I've just thrown up in. I stick my head out the window and let the wind calm me down, while Vancouver's buzzing lights stream by in a blurry mess. Cancer and I head back to our apartment, the one we've been living in for close to three weeks and have yet to put anything in except for a TV and some towels stolen from a hotel during our last hockey tournament. Our place is in earshot of East Hastings. It overlooks the parking lot in the alley and off in the distance you can see the Woodward's W, a beet red letter hanging over the area like an asterisk.

I check my wounds in the bathroom mirror. My figure appears—scattered tattoos, fresh scars and hockey hair, with lean sculpted features resulting from sports and labour, not some downtown gym. Once in my bed it's a mere minute or two before I pass out into a deep, noxious sleep.

By the time I wake up, some eleven hours later, I'm reasonably late for my first session with the court-ordered psychiatrist. I speed through Vancouver, knowing full well being late or missing this appointment might land me in jail.

I open up the mahogany door to an office packed into the corner of the tower's third floor. An empty waiting room contains a standard receptionist behind a standard desk, with business cards that match the office's contemporary interior design.

The receptionist looks up from her computer. "May I help you?" she asks.

"I've got a three-thirty appointment with Mr. Gustafson," I tell her.

I sit down, and then glance over at the dated stack of MacLean's, Reader's Digest and Time magazines. I'm too tired and far too hungover to read. Instead I sit and stare at the receptionist, thinking how good she might be in bed, or atop that desk, otherwise allowing my body and mind to rest. I'm pretty sure I'm going to throw up again sometime today. I've got a bad headache and an excruciating amount of pain in my upper neck. My knees and calves are sore, a dull sore, and my lips are dry and chapped. I feel dirty because I haven't had a shower yet and I've got day-old gel in my hair.

I'm exhausted, sick and sore. My knuckles, splattered with dry blood, are held together with band-aids, and I continue to find little shards of glass hidden in the various cracks and creases of my body like little razor-sharp grains of sand.

Before I know it I'm in the doctor's office, sitting in a dark blue leather chair, quite obviously his patient chair. I glance around at all his credentials framed in glass, and at all the pictures of his kids and his wife and his dog and think to myself, *Who takes pictures of their dog?*

I wonder if he cheats on his wife. I'd maybe like it if his wife cheated on him—with me—and meditating on this I zone out completely by the time the conversation starts in earnest. The first ten minutes are a blur of disconnected sentences and bad answers I regret as soon as they leave my mouth. I felt uncomfortable as soon as I sat down, but he didn't even seem to notice, or care, so now I've decided to return the favour.

"So what do you think that means?" he asks after a time.

"What means."

"What does that mean to you?" he attempts to clarify.

"I guess it means what my view of life is. I guess it means maybe I'm not looking for what everyone else is looking for."

"How so?"

"I think this searching for meaning is doomed to failure. I think we need to look beyond the question. You can't expect an answer to a question that doesn't truly exist."

My hands are now moving around with my words, spelling them out in the air. He can tell I'm trying to focus when I do this, and I can tell he can tell.

"So you're saying there's no meaning to life."

"No, I'm saying there's no question, 'What's the meaning of life?' It doesn't exist."

He looks perplexed.

"Okay, if you really think about it," I continue, "we structure our life on the erroneous assumption that life is a means to an end. Something that has a form, a structure—a beginning, a middle and an end. We think life's purpose is to find the meaning to this question of the end."

"But you're saying the 'question' doesn't exist."

"Only in our heads."

"But doesn't that make it real?"

"Nothing the human mind creates is real. It's simply a creation of thought. If I think life matters, I'm convincing myself of that even though it's not possible, or at least highly unlikely."

He contemplates this a moment.

"So what are you getting at," he says eventually. "You're running in circles here."

"I dunno," I shrug, "you're the one who's supposed to have all the answers."

He studies me over the ensuing awkward silence.

"So do you have any questions?" he asks at length.

I lean forward momentarily, and then lean back into my seat. "Yeah . . . well, I just hope this works, you know," I say, rubbing the stubble on my chin.

"Why's that?"

"Well it's just that nothing's seemed to stop me so far. I've been drinking and driving for ages, and this just happened to be the first time I got caught, that's all."

"It's up to you, Seth. It's always been up to you. The decision will come from you. But I think your being here is obviously a step in the right direction, and really what more can you ask for right now?"

I sigh.

"Yeah, true, I just hope I'm right this time. I'm getting tired of being hungover all the time—it sucks. It's expensive and it's tiresome. And I'm sure it's not good for me in the long run."

"Look at it this way," he replies, leaning back in his chair. "You've got everything to lose, and even more to gain."

I burp under my breath, and blow it out the corner of my mouth. Another long uncomfortable silence arises that I decide not to break.

"Are you hungover right now?" he inquires in all serious-ness, and and I just shrug at him like he should know full well.

Afterwards I hit McDonald's on the way home for some of the best hangover food I've ever had. Then I hit the sack only to be woken up by Cancer barging into my room in a too-small grey suit complete with white shirt, yellow cuffs and a baby blue tie. He looks awful and he knows it. He's just returned from one of his many cousins' weddings, an event I had to bail out on because of my psychiatrist appointment.

He jumps on me, and then proceeds to dry-hump me ferociously. I try to squirm out from underneath but he's much too big, and I can feel his crotch grinding into my stomach. His sheer mass disgusts me.

"Oh Seth, I love it when you talk dirty to me," he wheezes, and I can tell he's drunk. I try to reason with him, half laughing, half gasping for air. Finally he lets up, stands up, and I see he has two beers in hand, one unopened.

"Dude," he says, trying to appear serious. "Get this. You're still allowed to come to the reception. And guess what, they have my two favourite words there."

"Open bar," I say as he drops the beer on my nuts.

"It doesn't start for another hour or so, so get your ass in the shower, throw your suit on, and quit being such a fucking pussy."

I sit up and crack open the beer. I feel much better now that I've had some food and a nap, but I can feel the

McDonald's already trying to escape my intestines, grumbling all the way.

"I need to take a shit," I say.

By the time we get to the reception I'm already drunk. We hit the open bar hard, and Cancer explains to the poor little Hispanic bartender that if his hand is ever empty, even for a moment, he's going to use it to shove the bartender's face through the refrigerator door.

We get so loaded the two of us eventually find ourselves on the dance floor with some forty year-old women who look like they might watch *The View*. Or maybe host *The View*. Either way, I end up hooking up with some other girl, a roommate of Cancer's latest conquest Samantha. Cancer brought Samantha as his date, but the bastard didn't say a single word to her all night, and proceeded to hit on everything else that looked like it might have a vagina. Poor girl.

We all end up back at this Samantha's house, and I end up losing my favourite black tie. I have anal sex with the girl, whose name I never take the time to discover, and then we come back upstairs to find Samantha verbally assaulting Cancer. So we go.

We meet up with Caleb and Ryan and some guy named Sol, who looks like some metrosexual faggot who works at the Gap. But he turns out to be a pretty good guy, sharing his Special K, buying us drinks and not being a clown, so he manages to escape unscathed.

Sometime during the night Cancer gets the idea that we should head back to the golf club in Kerrisdale where the wedding was held. Rumour has it they leave the keys in the golf carts overnight. All one would have to do is break in, he explains, unlock the chain link fence by busting the lock with a shovel and voila, fresh horses for the men. Before anybody realizes this is a very bad idea, we're parked a few blocks down from the golf course snorting the last of the K and cramming beers into our suit jacket pockets.

Cancer is the first to find a plausible spot to hop the fence into the enclosed yard where they keep the carts. The only light, coming from the clubhouse, is hidden from view by several massive pines lining the first hole, a par five it turns out. There's dew on the ground but it's warm out, warm enough that I'm sweating by the time we scramble over the fence and gather ourselves up.

Cancer is so drunk he gets into the first golf cart he finds and drives it right through the chain-link gate, smashing open the lock in the process.

"Weren't we supposed to find a shovel?" asks Caleb in all seriousness.

"Change of plans," I tell him, hopping into a cart and driving out onto the course. Cancer nearly T-bone's me as soon as I get off the cart path and onto the fairway. He speeds by, beer in hand.

"Watch where you're driving," he yells, shaking his beer furiously at me.

It's a great time. Something inside the Special K is making me sweat, while at the same time imbuing each sense with a new vibrancy. I snorted a bunch of it, and the wind rushing past my ears as I speed around the course in a golf cart is only making it better, or worse.

Caleb spends most of his time tearing up the eighteenth green, trying to Tokyo drift his cart. Ryan rips up and down the fairway playing chicken with Cancer, and ends up having to swerve out of the way at the last second, clipping Sol's cart and sending him onto his side at high speed. I run Cancer with my cart but miss him entirely, and head instead straight for a pond. As soon as the cart hits water I bail out, only to have Cancer plough into me from behind. I try to jump out of the way, but get knocked head over heels anyway. Cancer comes screaming around as I get up. I can see he's got his pants around his ankles and a wire driving range bucket over his head as he drives, beer in hand.

"Get the hell off the grass," he yells, throwing the last of his beer at me. "You're ruining my short game, fucker."

A Priori / A Posteriori

On October 15TH, 1982 at 8:44 A.M., a pureblood golden retriever made his way onto the three thousand-square foot lawn of the White House. He'd wandered away from nearby Pershing Park where he'd been playing fetch with his owner. White House secret service agents proceeded to chase the dog around the lawn for a good twenty minutes while he playfully dodged and weaved his way amongst their black ties and utility belts, tongue flopping, tail wagging excitedly.

TV crews started rolling as people gathered to watch these several highly trained and athletic men attempt to catch one wily canine. In the meantime, the retriever continued to dodge amongst the suits, setting off alarms all over the property. After many furious attempts to capture him failed, one distraught agent pulled out his issue weapon and put a bullet in the dog's brain.

Afterwards, it was revealed the owner's name was Jonathan, the dog's name was Fitzy, short for Fitzgerald, and the agent's name was Kennedy. I was born that day.

I discovered this story one day in a newspaper clipping at the Vancouver Public Library. The story hit me hard, like a fist in the gut. The funny thing is, I've never told anyone about the strangely curious happenings of October 15TH, 1982. I've never mentioned it to my parents, never brought it up as something to diversify myself from the masses or as a way to get laid.

One of my most poignant memories of life back on the family farm in the Okanagan is of deer-hunting in the woods. Losing sight of my father, I chased a wounded stag for a good fifteen minutes, accompanied only by the dogs and a single-action bolt rifle. Eventually we caught up to the deer I'd shot earlier just along the hairline of its backbone, ripping open a giant wound that now bled heavily down its backsides. The dogs circled, barking furiously as the deer stumbled, backing down awkwardly into the snow.

As I slid the action back to throw another bullet into the chamber, the deer fell forward onto its knees. As it settled down, the dogs slowed, huffing violently at the end of their long unexpected sprint. Unlike them, I'd never seen a live deer up close, its skin and fur still pulsating and steaming with sweat and heat.

I studied its eyes as it looked at me not with intent, but with a simple acknowledgement that it was not concerned anymore. It knew it was going to die and didn't particularly care how close I came at this point.

With the dogs circling in to sniff and inspect this dying animal lying there massively in the snow, I watched its eyes turn off like a dimming computer light. That was it. This is death in all her beauty, I thought to myself. Not some furious rage, some monumental music. Just a fading of light into darkness.

I tell my father, in plain English, if he slaps me like that again I'm going to hit him back a hundred times harder. He looks at me like I'm thirteen, but I'm not. I'm a six-foot-three, two-hundred twenty pound man and I'm angry with him.

I stare directly into his eyes. My father, a tall man, thick and barrel-chested with dark hair, dark eyes, and a thick beard never longer than half an inch, says, "You talk to me like that under my roof and I'll do whatever I want to."

We just stand there like statues as the air quickens with impending violence. I'm not sure how this argument started, but maybe it was the divorce. It's usually the divorce.

"Things are different now," I say. "You just can't intimidate me anymore."

I know he thinks this is bullshit. He's a correctional officer, and he's easily handled men like me before. But I'm no kid
now, though the thirteen year-old inside me is screaming, 'Hit
the motherfucker! Hit him for me!'

"Pack your shit," he tells me. "I want you out of here now.
I knew this was a mistake from day one, letting you come
here."

"Fine," I say, stepping past him on my way out of the
kitchen, but he doesn't move aside. I bump into him with my
shoulder, shoving him off balance and into the refrigerator. He
comes back at me, but before he can get his hands up I've
grabbed his head by the ears and rammed my forehead into his
nose. Then something odd happens. Something inside me gets
excited. And suddenly I'm firing hard rights into his face, my
fist pumping back and forth like a piston. Again and again I
connect as he goes down to one knee. Blood splatters across
the white linoleum floor, but I don't stop. Stopping now would
just invite retaliation, a chance for redemption. No, I keep
pounding away at him, my hand ricocheting off the top of his
hard skull.

He tries to wrap his hands around my knees to take me
down, but I throw my hips toward him, cornering him, corralling him, and he loses his balance. He goes down sideways,
exposing a flash of unprotected cheek. My fist rams his teeth
into their gums, and rips the jaw tendons from their founda-
tions. I feel his cheekbone collapse. I cock my fist back again,
but he's gone limp. So I just stand there a moment, towering
over his unconscious body, my right hand loaded, ready to
strike.

"Now I'll get my shit and go," I tell him.

I learned to skate and play hockey like most Canadian kids
did, on a backyard rink made with a long garden hose
wielded by a very patient father. It's true he'd been a good

father, at times. For one, he was extremely stringent in his teachings, showing me the basics of crossovers, stopping and skating backwards. He showed me how to properly receive and cradle a pass, and how to skate with the puck, eyes always up. He taught me the fundamentals of the game, probably the one thing I'm grateful to have received from him. He was a former semi-pro player himself, having skated in the IHL a few years, winning their minor league version of a cup a couple of times with Michigan's Port Huron Flags in the late '70s. But he didn't really talk about those days, or anything else concerning life before my sister and I arrived to further complicate things. He never talked about why his career just kind of dried up after a while, other than the fact that he did too, by all accounts remaining sober to this day. Regardless, he did know exactly what to teach me in order to make me a proper hockey player.

The small one-acre chicken farm we lived on allowed us to keep a pack of mutts, Appenzell Mountain dogs mostly. They didn't have names, they were simply called "dog." As in "Get out of the way, dog," or "C'mere, dog." Their short grimy coats were chocolate brown mixed with patches of white and black. I remember their floppy ears flying all over the place when they ran. My buddies and I spent hours on the rink with them, manoeuvring through their splayed legs as they tried desperately to navigate the slippery ice.

One of the younger pups, sometimes referred to as Mutthead, had a bad habit of barking at the puck whenever it was touched. One day I got so frustrated with him I wired a puck at his ribcage, sending him scampering up to the tree line. He remained up there for hours, licking his wounds and howling about the mistreatment. Finally, around dinnertime, my father went up and found him, and killed him on the spot. When he eventually returned, stepping into the light of the kitchen with dead dog in hand, he informed the family the farm had started to lose money. And before it went under entirely, he said, he would pawn it off to one of his friends and move us to the city, end of discussion.

Backstage, at a convention centre, somewhere near the Main Street Skytrain station in Vancouver. I'm both excited and nervous, two feelings that have been further enhanced by the large amounts of cocaine and nicotine in me. I'm sweating profusely inside my pieced together black suit, recently purchased from Value Village. I can feel the sweat in my pits, in the creases of my elbows and knees and in the crack of my ass. I wipe the beads from my eyebrows with a napkin. I remove the bottle of vodka from my pocket and take a long hard pull, then chase it with some cranberry juice.

It's dark and warm backstage, and I'm basically alone back here. Out front there are speeches and conversations and laughter—drinks clinking and knives cutting into food amid all the friendly banter. I take another pull from the bottle, tilting it up quickly, this time without a chaser. The alcohol is working its magic, smoothing me out, warming me up. I take another pull, this time maybe a little too much, and I quickly guzzle some cranberry juice in an effort to keep it down. But it's too late, and I end up scurrying over to a garbage can to the left of the stage to heave up Caesar salad and rare steak behind some sound equipment. I also vomit what looks surprisingly like blood, but is in fact the bottle of Syrah I ploughed through on the car ride here. I throw up again, dry-heave for a while, then wipe my face clean on the curtain. Then I hit the bottle again.

Now I'm out on stage and everyone is waiting for me to speak. They want me to speak about my father, for this is his retirement party, his final reward for all his fine work as a correctional officer these many years. Unfortunately he just recently divorced my mother, leaving her and my sister alone, and I'm not feeling too pleased about it. However, I'm both surprised and impressed I didn't fall down on the way to the podium, and I mention as much to the audience. No one laughs. "I had this big speech ready," I say, tasting the remnants of vodka and meat as I hiccup loudly into the microphone. I glance to the table on the left, my family's table, and then make the conscious decision to embarrass both my father and myself even further.

"My Dad," I say. "Wow. What a guy. I mean thanks, Dad— for everything. You've been a real role model."

The crowd offers up a few sporadic claps.

"It's funny," I continue, "work like this. . . . 'Correctional' work, I guess you'd call it. . . . I mean for fuck's sakes, you could've beaten on the prisoners all day long, couldn't you? I mean I'm sure they probably deserved it. At least *some* of them must have deserved it. More than your wife and son, I mean. You know," I say before anyone can interrupt me, "somebody once said to me, 'Seth, your Dad's an asshole'—oh wait, that was me."

I see the host, one of my father's co-workers, rise from his seat and begin to make his way towards the stage.

"On a different note, what the fuck was up with those steaks?" I say. "I mean, c'mon people, you work for the provincial government, couldn't you have taken a fuckin' flex day and picked up some decent steaks for the occasion?"

My father just sits there staring at me, his face a blank cast of stone.

"You know, we could've been like—like, say, the Hulls," I laugh. "It's true though. It wouldn't have been such a stretch, if you think about it. I'd be the lippy little shit who gets cut from the Canadian team and ends up selling out to the Americans, and you'd hit the bottle hard and start wailing on your wife. Oh wait, you did that. Well way to hold up your part of the bargain, Dad."

The host, now on the stage, pulls me away from the microphone.

"Cheque please," I say, holding up a finger in a flurry of feedback and jostling. Then I steady myself, and with one quick move drive my palms into the chest of the host. He staggers back, out of reach, and I leave the stage in search of that garbage can again.

From the Okanagan, the family moved south to Langley where my father eventually started work at the local provincial prison. It was right around this time he started getting physical with me. First it was the occasional slap across the back of the head, then one time he punched me hard in the face. For the longest time I thought this was normal, for a father to physically dominate his son, and it took me many years and a lot of persuading to be proved wrong. Still, after a while I developed a wicked mouth in response to his beatings. And the bigger and tougher I talked, the more heated the confrontations became as a result. Eventually, though, I started to fight back. I'd use kitchen knives, a lamp, anything I could get my hands on to defend myself against his ever escalating attacks. One time I knocked him clean off his feet by whipping a basketball at his head.

My mother and sister remained distant to me, mostly by my choosing. I felt as if something inside me was my father, and could lash out at them uncontrollably at any moment. I'm positive he hit her on more than a few occasions, but I never found out for sure, and my mother would never fess up. She was always projecting outwards with either depression or stress, always shallowly fishing for compliments she could no longer get by shaking her ass in some bar or club, an act that had carried her much of her youth. Now she was a retired looker, an aging starlet for whom the spotlight no longer shined, and it was slowly eating her to death.

Meanwhile, my sister was already off making her own tragedies with young men, jumping from one boyfriend to another seeking trust that would never come. But she was still smart, still intuitive like I was, and so I knew someday she might walk from this nightmarish slumber into something more stable, but she would have to do that on her own.

The fights between my father and me were just that, between the two of us. I tried to keep my mother and sister out of it as much as possible. This was my punishment, I thought. I'd brought this upon myself and needed to bear the burden alone.

He was a very organized man. He had to be in order to run both a family and a farm. You could set your watch by him—bastard didn't even need an alarm clock—he'd just wake up at six in the morning, every morning, without fail, like a robot.

Life was divided up into tasks to be completed in order of priority. He always kept a thin black notebook with him, with a list of things to do: fix engine, do taxes, take out garbage, retile roof. Right from day one he tried to instil these qualities in his son, but unfortunately for us both I had more of my mother in me. I was unorganized and unpredictable, and I quickly became a nuisance to him. His days at jail were not discussed much, other than who was retiring or when the next Correctional Officer/Police Force Hockey League tournament would be held. I suspect maybe it was life amongst the inmates that drove him to be so hard on me. Maybe he was hoping discipline and organization would keep me from becoming one of them eventually. But after a while I became a prisoner of his just the same. After a while I gave up trying to decipher why he did the things he did, and simply started to spite everything my father stood for. I began to hate him.

There are various encounters and memories I have that still haunt me. Dinner was one. Dinner was to be eaten to its expected conclusion, or else the diner would sit at the table all night. Sometimes I'd bang my head against the table until it began to bleed all over my mother's brand new linoleum floor. Or sometimes I'd get so angry I'd bolt to my room only to be dragged back to my seat by the arm or the leg or, occasionally, the neck. Then there were the dishes afterwards. Dishes were to be washed and dried in a certain way, and in a certain sequence, and sometimes when they weren't washed right— like if I'd done the plates before the cutlery—my father would take the clean dishes out and make me wash them again. Sometimes those episodes would become so extreme he would actually pin me to the counter, occasionally even holding my body up as I let it go limp, pleading for escape. Or he would grab my arms and force my hands to wash the dishes, all the while screaming obscenities into my ear. Still, I'd find it funny being his marionette. But then my laughter would inevitably result in a firm grip around my neck, his big bear hands squeezing so hard I could feel my tendons separating beneath my skin.

Then there was the day he tried to teach me to drive stick shift. I couldn't get the ambidextrous aspect down—I was a dedicated lefthander, and my right hand was there simply for support, not to function with any type of agility and aptitude on its own. I stalled his truck until the gearshift dislodged, and we went at it right there in the cab. I never tried to learn to drive stick after that. Never.

As I grew older, I spent more and more time away from the house. Not to do drugs or smoke weed or drink in an alleyway like so many of my friends, but to play hockey. If I wasn't playing or practicing for the rep team, I was playing road hockey. I'd often play so hard I'd make myself throw up, releasing all my energy and all my frustrations into every slap shot, every hit, every game. The hockey rink became a battleground for me. And I became my campaign's own worst critic. I demanded nothing but perfection from myself and, in turn, my teammates, and would dress them down if they weren't playing up to their capabilities on any given shift.

The bigger and more powerful I became, the further up the run-ins with my father were ratcheted. The police were called in a few times, but not much would happen once they arrived. They'd take down our personal information and chat with both of us, separately most of the time. I'd never say anything, really. These guys weren't going to save me. Most of them knew my father from jail or hockey, and any prospective police work would be scrapped in favour of plans for the next big tournament coming up.

One time, though, things did get seriously out of hand. I'd come home with another average report card: A's and B's in PE and English, and D's and F's in pretty much everything else. My father spent hours trying to teach me math, but I just didn't get it. I didn't have the same type of brain he had. That night we worked on an assignment for what seemed like hours. Eventually I'd had it for the night, but he insisted I finish. I don't remember how it started, but somehow he pushed me down the stairs, and then accused me of embellishing my fall. Accused me of diving, in essence. I turned and bolted to my room, and as soon as I heard his footsteps coming down the stairs I hid around the hallway corner. His face met my fist, and the fight was on. We destroyed the downstairs den, ploughing through a bookcase, then the coffee table, then the television, before ending up with him on top, pinning my arms to the floor. I spit in his face, cursed him repeatedly, and wrestled until I was exhausted and ready to vomit.

My mother and sister came to bear witness, but neither of us would let up. After ten or fifteen minutes of fighting, during which time I managed to struggle to my feet, we had each other tied up, with both our shirts ripped open and our faces smeared with blood. I knew the longer the fight went on, the more my youthful stamina would win out, so I kept up, taking punch after punch until finally I found myself on top. I went to work on his face with my fists and elbows, my knees practically puncturing his chest and stomach.

By the time the fight reached its inevitable conclusion, my mother and sister had escaped to a nearby motel. My father and I were home alone for the night. I won't say what happened next, but with no one left to call the police in a frantic bout of fear, and living in a neighbourhood where the sounds of siblings shouting and families fighting were simply ignored, things got much, much worse.

Sitting in my car, parked in a dark lot alongside a strip mall amongst a few scattered cars obviously abandoned for the night, I'm hyperventilating. My left hand is rubbing my left thigh furiously, making a quiet sound of friction against the fabric. I'm ever so slightly bobbing forward, looking straight into the dark. All I can do is wait for the pills to take hold. I pick up the lit cigar from my ashtray, take a long pull, and then rest my head against the windshield and try to close my eyes and shut my brain down before something goes seriously wrong. I am having the panic attack of all panic attacks, and don't know if I can take it this time.

Sarah, this girl I've been dating, is off travelling Australia for six months, taking a year off from her Psychology undergraduate degree at the University of British Columbia. She booked the trip mere days before we met. I can't blame her for going, but it doesn't mean I can't be pissed off about it. Either way, our meeting up proved to be a rather powerful thing, and we've spent the entire last two months at each other's side. Sarah has a quiet beauty. A short girl with a tight figure, her brown eyes never show concern. Optimism perhaps, or something else I can't quite pin down. We've been utterly inseparable, two young friends so attached to one another they develop their own language. All I wanted was to be with her. She became my addiction, and as a result I curbed most of my drinking and stopped popping pills—for a time anyway.

It was easily the best two months of my life, and the most beautiful thing is I have no idea why. Sarah simply fit my world, the perfect prescription for all the terror I'd been through. She tested me, but never teased. A psychology student, she saw me as something to be studied—she wanted to perform surgery on all my troubles, but was always careful enough to sedate me, seductively, before pushing the blade in. I became her patient, her case study, her chance to put her growing knowledge of the mind to good use. She became my doctor, and I became addicted to her prescriptions in the most poignant of ways. She even took the time to try to teach me to drive stick after I told her about the episode with my father. But I couldn't. I couldn't even get her car out of the goddamned parking lot. But at least we tried.

Six months apart will only make us hungrier for one another, I've decided. I'm taking classes at UBC, somehow showing a sliver of drive and determination, which is both unexpected and encouraging. But I'm drinking away my student loan, and will be lucky to make it through my first semester without going broke.

Now I'm standing outside my car in the parking lot of a strip mall. I've decided to walk the circumference of the mall counter clockwise in an effort to calm my nerves. I walk fast, my head tilted slightly downwards to the left. I peer inside the windows, presently black and empty after what I assume was a busy day. I extend my right hand and run it across the concrete wall, the rough surface scratching my skin. I walk trying to calm my nerves and keep my mind preoccupied, battling this nasty anxiety attack I'm currently embroiled in.

Back in the car, I open both front windows and sit silently in the secluded lot. The banks of lights high overhead spotlight each section of the asphalt. They hum audibly while flies and moths swerve through the light and bounce off the glass—like something out of a Radiohead video. It's so quiet. I'm still rocking slightly back and forth, still rubbing my jeans like a madman, but the motor inside me is finally starting to decelerate, thank God.

Now it's close to one o'clock. Driving home I still feel anxious, but I'm improving, and that's all that matters. As soon as I get into the apartment, I head straight to my room and lie down with my clothes still on and pull the sheets up over my head. I curl up, knees to my chest. Silence surrounds me, and the only light coming into the room is the small sliver from under the door. I focus on the sliver, and a quick rush wells up in me. I turn over, away from the light, and another wave washes over me. I stay still and try to breathe normally. I breathe, and I wait, and I try to remain as still as possible so that my mind won't well up again. Still, my body is heating up. I try to keep my mind from flooding, and from leaking out into the world. Then another wave, a large one, and I sit up in bed. I put my face in my hands and say aloud, "Fuck this."

I head into the living room and flop down on the couch. The remote is nestled between empty beer cans and stale McDonald's fries. I turn the TV on, but there is no signal. I turn the TV off. Ambulance and police sirens wail in the distance like mechanical coyotes. I sit back and try to calm myself, but that just makes me feel worse. I feel out of control. I feel helpless. I decide to take some Ambien. In the bathroom I open the medicine cabinet and pop two in my mouth before leaning into the faucet and washing them down. Then I decide to take a Valium as well, just for good measure. I head back to my room and lie down, curling up in the blankets again. I feel better already for some reason. The placebo effect, I'm guessing. And so I lie there, curled up in a tight little ball, waiting for the drugs to kick in.

The only fond memories I have of my Langley days are those of street hockey. As soon as my family arrived in town I was out on the concrete, slapping a ball around, and before long I'd been taken in by a group of local kids who always seemed to have a game going in a quiet cul-de-sac about a five minute jog from my house, just past the power lines. I can still remember the hum of electricity as I sprinted beneath those towers, stick in hand.

We'd play all summer—after school, in the rain, whenever—we were warriors and we just didn't care. The sound of wooden sticks with super blades crackling together like a campfire was something that, from a distance, felt like a calling. Almost as if you were missing the most important game of your life.

The cul-de-sac we played on was located in a typical lower middle-class suburban neighbourhood, where neglected lawns divided rundown houses with cracked and faded paint. It was the kind of place where you'd wake up to the constant drone of lawnmowers and fall asleep to the hysterical wail of sirens. It was our home rink though, and I'm sure we drove every resident crazy with errant orange balls bouncing through yards and off the sides of cars. The rink was drawn out with coloured chalk stolen from someone's younger sister, complete with goal creases and faceoff circles we never seemed to use.

At home, when I had to be there, I'd spend my time shooting pucks off the garage door. No goalie, no goal—I became obsessed with fine-tuning my game against an unseen opponent. It was the only way to ignore the daily horror my father seemed intent on putting me through.

Being younger than most of the kids, I learned to watch rather than speak. Michael and Dusty, two brothers with short brown crew-cuts and uni-brows, were the natural leaders, though perhaps for no other reason than the fact they owned the only two nets and goalie equipment. As they were the oldest and most skilled, they would always play on opposite teams, creating a vicious rivalry I'm sure still separates them to this day.

The brothers battled hard each game, running each other at every opportunity. Their desire to win drove the rest of us to compete even harder. I learned how to take my licks, and how to be a gracious winner and a quiet loser. But I was different than most of the kids in Langley. They all had enormous extended families living in the area—English, Irish and Italians, with massive barbecues and watermelons, red plastic cups stacked on end between boatloads of soda bottles, and coolers stuffed full of beer for the adults. We'd gleefully crash these backyard parties between games, running through to fill our bellies, sticks still in hands. Unlike myself, most of the other kids would have to stop and talk with what seemed like long lost aunts and uncles from foreign countries, but who in actuality lived just over the bridge in New Westminster.

My family was different. My father's brother was long gone, dead in his twenties, nothing more than a name now. Grandparents alive on only my mother's side, along with a few aunts and uncles and cousins in Halifax I really only met once one Christmas long ago. Our German heritage almost seemed like something to hide, and I formulated early on that we were descendents of Nazis, but never did find out either way.

It was almost better this way, being such a small family unit, rather than have my father's abusive ways surface for discussion at some backyard barbeque or weekend getaway. I didn't really want to be the center of attention unless I was out on the ice or the street, stick in hand with play underway. Years of hiding from my father, quite literally sometimes, made me want to be invisible most of the time. That is, until the ball or puck dropped, at which point I became a little mass of fury snatching up all available attention like one's first gasp of air after minutes underwater.

Once in Langley, I was quickly enrolled in Atom ice hockey, and took to the game quite naturally. Cutting across the ice
just inside the blueline on a rush or anticipating passes before
they happened, I was a natural, as much a spectator of my own
talent as I was a practitioner, almost in awe of my own capabilities at times.

I broke records, and all the goals and assists attracted scouts
years before most prospects. I carried teams to trophies with an
almost insane drive to win.

Then something was taken. Possibly a chance or maybe
just a dream. One night, midway through a pick-up summer
basketball game, I tore my medial collateral ligament in my
right knee. It was a harmless play. I simply pivoted before my
leg was under me. I remember the blinding pain, and the sudden realization that filled my heart with dread. I remember
the cold hardwood floor against my face as I lay there grasp-
ing my knee. Then the frenetic squeaking of sneakers as the
play came to an abrupt halt and everyone circled in around
me. But mostly I remember the feeling of robbery, the feeling
something had been taken without consent, and quite
unapologetically.

This happened mere weeks before I was to be suiting up
at my first camp for the Western Hockey League's Seattle
Thunderbirds. I'd been drafted second overall at the WHL
Bantam Draft, and was now property of a Major Junior team.
Rumour had it they wanted me in the line-up right from day
one, right after I finished playing in the U–17 Provincial Cup,
playing for the same team Joe Sakic and Paul Kariya had once
suited up for. I'd just come off an intense summer of training
camps all over the Greater Vancouver area where I'd been
working out some kinks in my game, mainly compensating for
my lack of size by hitting the weights and doing plyometrics
and other dry-land training. I was heading towards a professional hockey career, I was convinced of that, so "devastated"

is probably the best way to describe my emotional state at the time. Though for a fifteen year-old devastation of that magnitude can't really be put into words for others to understand.

I was out the entire season. After Christmas I stopped keeping tabs on the team. That winter was one long dreary grind, stretching out into weeks of depression split here and there by sudden bouts of anger and anxiety. Something broke inside me that winter, something essential and unexplained. The war inside my head began as I watched what would have been my teammates carry on without me. Except for the occasional sporadic call from a coach or a trainer checking in on my status, I was virtually ignored. Where I once was a spectator of my own talent, I now watched as my aspirations and confidence slowly drained away.

My comeback, after close to a year, was even worse. Following a full summer of gruelling rehabilitation in a bulky robotic knee brace, I decided to climb back through the Junior levels, heading north to suit up for the Junior B Sicamous Eagles in a league known locally as "the Jungle." It was almost required for the teams to brawl if the score got too out of hand. The score almost always got too out of hand. We were pack mules pushed to extreme lengths by gruelling practices, spastic coaches, too much ephedrine and speed, and early mornings filled with high school girls and cheap liquor. I did however meet Cancer, both of us being rookies at the time. He had a similar story as I, with the one notable exception of his abundant size proving a hindrance rather than a blessing. He was a solid consistent defenceman who could contribute at both ends of the ice, but he was just too slow to compete at the higher levels. We never talked about it, but that sort of shortcoming seemed to me as if it would hurt even more.

Halfway through that first season in the Jungle I got slammed headfirst into the boards, resulting in my first concussion. Tempted by all the headway I'd been making, cracking the power play and playing more minutes than most of the team, I rushed myself back, taking only a week to recover. That first game back I got in a fight and fell hard, slamming the back of my head against the ice.

I went home for a month, got a CAT scan and returned to the team against my parents' wishes. I was stubborn and intent on going down in flames. It only took me a few games to get there, ending up in the hospital with a Grade 3 concussion, bleeding from my left ear. My coach told me he wouldn't sign my consent form to suit up anymore. And that was it, I was done.

Sarah keeps trying, but I always seem to miss her calls. Before she left for Australia she told me I was free to see anyone, and when she got back we would see where we were at. I wasn't okay with this at all, but what could I say. Now all I can think about is some Australian bastard having sex with her on some beach, wooing her with his ridiculous accent.

She sends emails and pictures, and we do catch each other on the phone from time to time, but it's just not the same. I can't feel her when she touches the small of my back to let me know she's behind me. I can't smell her while we sit together and watch TV. I can't watch her comb her hair in the mirror, towel wrapped around her chest as she leans in to check her teeth.

I feel awkward, like half of me is turned off and the other half is trying to compensate. I count the days on the calendar, hoping things will be exactly the same with us when she returns. I hope we can pick up where we left off, spending Sunday mornings in bed together, walking around downtown on Robson, browsing through all the shops and giggling at the Asian tourists who take pictures of themselves in front of every available monument. Acting like a normal couple might act. What are the chances.

My first year out of high school life really started to unravel. After I played my way out of Junior, I bolted to Vancouver like I always said I would, leaving the backwater that was Langley behind as quickly as possible. But Vancouver had problems all its own. For one, it didn't really seem to have a soul. Perhaps that's because it's such a young city, filled with immigrants who mostly keep to themselves, but with some who don't. People always tell me there's something about Vancouver they can't quite put their finger on, can't quite describe. Such a lonely city, for one. It's something that can't be defined in words, but you can feel it in the air. The people on the street rarely make eye contact. Vancouver was seen as one of the best places in the world—a brochure city, with natural beauty everywhere—but just like every city it had its denizens like me, the ones living on the fringes, existing in the underbelly we all know exists but most choose to ignore.

Not long after arriving from Langley, I found myself toiling away at some mindless warehouse job under the Cambie Street Bridge. No benefits and long hours that never seemed to get booked as overtime marked that time of living between homes, and drinking and fighting with each of my parents over nothing and everything. Trying to land a job up north to get the hell out of the city for a spell and make some much needed money. Friday would arrive after a mundane week that may or may not have been bridged by weekday binge drinking. The phone would ring, words would be exchanged, plans would be made, and drugs and alcohol would be purchased and consumed. I was simply spinning my wheels and pissing away the days, longing for something significant to happen.

Old Stock was a popular choice. Not because we wanted to be black, but because it was the cheapest beer you could get at the time. Forty ounces of malt liquor, available warm or cold. Cold was more expensive of course, by almost a buck-fifty, which was somewhat prohibitive. One forty of Old Stock was perfect before hitting the bar, but the ensuing hangovers ranked right up there with wine. Still, it was all we could afford at the time.

Sometimes someone would come into some coke or some ecstasy, and occasionally something slightly more exotic. But those times were few and far between. We weren't prosperous enough to get addicted to all those Hollywood drugs that get glamorized in movies. No, it was just beer for us poor kids.

I have memories of staggering around Vancouver, loaded, starting fights with anyone and everyone who was willing to bite on our baited tongues. Vandalizing automobiles, urinating through open sunroofs, stealing whatever appealed to us from the 7–Eleven after the bar. Everything was fair game—every night something epic would happen and it would be all we'd talk about—until the next time we were out gallivanting around like assholes. My conscience was nowhere to be found. My sense of right and wrong had been conveniently left behind.

I really didn't give a damn about anything. Sure I had goals, ambitions, but they were always too distant, always too out of reach for whatever reason. I was convinced the cards had been stacked against me since day one, and my luck obviously wasn't about to change now. But looking back, those days, for whatever reason, were some of the best of my life. I was untouchable, not because I was motivated, but because I honestly didn't care about anything or anyone besides myself. I was completely self-centred, consumed with only my own well-being. Starving Africans? Fuck them. Treating women like whores? What's your point? Beating the shit out of some guy for no apparent reason? Why the hell not. When it came right down to it, I really didn't care about my friends whatsoever, a feeling, or lack of feeling, that was mirrored in each of them as well.

If I had the money to get drunk, I did. If I could get my hands on drugs, I would. And in this way life pretty much left me alone. I hid myself in the comforts of alcohol, and what I found there was intoxicating. As soon as you stop caring, everything changes. As soon as you completely give up on life, you find your freedom. That, to me, was a revelation. And so it was that alcohol became my fuel for an unscrupulous kind of redemption.

Sometimes I'd have up to ten people stuffed in my white '89 Chrysler Dynasty, oftentimes cramming a couple in the trunk, on top of my hockey gear. And most of the time I was more intoxicated than any of my passengers, resorting to closing one eye in order to rid myself of double vision.

I remember being so drunk at times I'd have to throw myself out of whatever bar I was in. I'd get a stamp from the doorman, walk as straight as possible to the parking lot, locate a secluded area to throw up, and bail everything out of my stomach, sometimes dry-heaving for fifteen minutes afterwards. Then I'd collect myself, wipe the puke and sweat from my face, and head back into the bar to start drinking again.

Ashley is with me out on the balcony, disturbing both my peace and my quiet, as usual. I just want to smoke and be left alone to think through some of the stuff that's been bothering me of late—I'm trying, but she keeps talking and interrupting my solitude. Right now I could really go for some solitude. Even more so with her chatter cultivating what feels like a tumour inside my brain. She follows me inside, eager to argue, just like how we met in class. She's my filler, my stopgap, my poor excuse for a Sarah still half a world removed. But I'm a weak man, and the attention I was receiving from Sarah has disappeared, so I've settled for this Ashley with her designer curves, push-up bra and upper middle-class desire for bad boys who treated her like shit. I've settled for simply taking in enough air to sustain my life, nothing more, nothing less.

"So what's the problem with that?" she's asking. "See, I'd like to point something out, especially since now that you've shared something with someone you're probably already regretting it."

"I don't want to talk about this," I tell her. "What I do regret is even telling you about that shit in the first place."

"No, answer me. I don't fucking care if you regret telling me. *Answer* me. You owe it to me. Because that's what I've been saying about you all this time. You have this fear of getting exposed if you share too much. There must be people, if not me than someone else, you trust enough not to feel exposed with. And while it hurts that you don't consider me trustworthy enough—"

"Ashley—"

"—I don't get why," she continues. "Because one, I don't judge. And two, I'd never share it with anyone else."

I yawn a sarcastic yawn, and she frowns.

"I think you're harsh, Seth. And seriously misguided. People who love you won't turn their backs on you when you royally fuck up, you have to believe that. Your story is in safe hands. But then again, hey, if you choose not to believe me, there's nothing I can do about it. I just know what I'd do or wouldn't do and that's enough for me, but whatever. Life's about taking risks. And trusting someone *is* a risk. And you choose to take those risks because the ends justify the means. And that's the point. The risks make life worth living. They make you feel alive. Something to get you out of bed in the morning."

I return to the balcony, trying to formulate a reasonable response I know won't work. Arguing with Ashley is like eating rocks—stupid, pointless, and extremely painful the whole way along. I decide to go. I put my coat and shoes on and grab a beer from the fridge as I leave—she tries to stop me, first with words and then by blocking me—but of course I'm much bigger and simply shove her out of the way.

I get in my car and drive. I feel much better now, just driving with nowhere to go for an hour or so. Maybe I'll stop for

some food. I could really go for some food. I think of Ashley
crying—it makes me snicker a bit, but also makes me feel
shameful. I'm sure the guilt will pass. After all, it always does.

In the university parking lot, in the rain, I cram my car
between two SUVs, the immense size of which sickens me.
I decide not to pay the meter as I'm only going to be here a
few minutes. I'm pretty sure I'm somewhere behind UBC's
Henry Angus Building, but then again I might not be. I could
be lost completely. I pull out a map and start navigating my
way across campus on foot, and by the time I find the building my map, my course outline with the location of my professor's office, and my face are drenched with rain.

I ask some guy the time. Three o'clock, he says. It looks
like I'm right on schedule then. I make my way into the
Buchanan Building and take the elevator up to the third floor,
to room 311A. I cut down a side hallway, narrow with orange
doors on the right. The wall is covered with pretentious
political cartoons, long essays from *The New York Times*, anti-
war rally pamphlets and yellowed newspaper clippings about
anything and everything a second-rate philosophy professor
might deem worthy enough to hang outside his office.

I pass Steve something-or-other on the way. Steve's in the
same class I am, Introduction to Logic and Critical Thinking,
and obviously just finished seeing the professor himself.
Students have each been allotted times throughout the day, at
fifteen minute intervals, to collect their final essay papers and
chat with the professor about the semester, if they want to. I
really don't want to. I've already dropped out of university in
theory, and will be officially dropping out in less than a week,
I've decided.

Steve and I exchange the usual handshake and chat briefly
about plans for the weekend. He's off to some hip-hop con-
cert in Whistler, while I'm doing the usual, getting drunk and

heading downtown to see what kind of trouble I can stir up. I ask how he did on the assignment, the one in which we were asked to look into a decisive category of like-minded philosophies and compare them, seeing how they fit into modern society. He pulls a thick essay from his backpack, bound in a flimsy black binder with an opaque plastic cover. As he flips through each page, he tells me how Dr. Mike Atrivowsky fucked him over for lack of citations and, in his opinion, a rather lackadaisical set of arguments. Steve finds the professor to be a bit of a cunt apparently. I agree with his assessment, and tell him as much.

"So what'd you get?" I ask.

Steve flips to the back page littered with scribbled red writing. He got a 69 which, according to the professor, wasn't all that bad in terms of class average. I cringe to show I feel his pain, but I really don't. I just want to talk to the professor and go back to bed.

Steve and I say our goodbyes as I head into the office. Inside, the professor is standing with his back to me, rearranging some folders on a second desk. The shelves are stuffed full of books and, not surprisingly, photographs of the professor himself rock-climbing and kayaking. He's an active west-coaster, and wants everyone to know it. He senses my presence and turns around, then glances at his sheet.

"Seth, right?"

"Yeah, that's me."

"Have a seat. Perfect timing."

I sit down and wipe some rain from my face. The professor rifles through one of four large stacks of essays with a smile. I'm not sure why he's smiling.

"Why are you smiling?" I ask.

He doesn't answer, but continues to rifle through the essays instead. I'm not sure if he's simply ignoring me, or somehow testing me. Doing something I'm supposed to be picking up on. How cunning. Eventually he finds my paper, bound in similar fashion as all the others. He casually tosses it across the desk, and I catch it before it falls to the floor. He looks at me, and I just stare blankly at him a second. I really don't want to see my mark because, even though I spent a hell of a lot of time on this paper, I realize it will probably be lower than expected. Life is like that, I'm finding. It's amusing, in a way.

"Absolutely excellent paper is all I can say," says the professor, running a palm down his beard.

I flip to the last page. 92. I flash him a look of genuine surprise, then look at the number again to make sure I'm actually reading it right. "Wow," I say.

He smiles. "It's too bad you haven't shared any of your perspectives at some of the smaller seminars. I don't think I've heard you say a thing. In fact, until you walked in that door a minute ago, I couldn't even put a face to your name."

I flip through the pages—there are plenty of red exclamation points and checkmarks—though I don't bother delving too deeply into his critical analysis as, to be honest, I'm still a bit stunned by the grade.

"This was the highest grade in the class, Seth. You nailed what I was looking for in the essay outline. Taking philosophies and deconstructing them rather than constructing them like arguments. I don't think anyone else got that except you."

"Yeah," I say, and I can see he is waiting for more. Probably trying to determine if I simply stole this essay from the internet. *You fucking faggot*, I want to hiss, but say instead, "I knew I wanted to take the two ideologies and break them down into layman's terms, but also show at the same time that if people choose not to abide by or follow a certain philosophy, that choice itself doesn't categorize them entirely. I totally object to people who say having no philosophy or religion is a philosophy or religion in itself. It's categorical and branding."

"Compelling, to say the least," he says, swivelling around in his chair, turning his attention to the class list. He ponders the list a moment, then swivels back to me.

"I've been looking at the in-class tests," he says. "Not quite the same marks, I see."

"Yeah I'm not big on tests. Essays are more my strong point."

"I can see that," he replies. "Your two essay marks are substantially higher."

He pauses a moment, waiting for me to respond, and when I don't, he eventually carries on.

"I think that, with this type of quality writing, you've definitely got the tools to excel at the subject of philosophy. Judging by this paper, I can see you're quite good at taking an existential approach to philosophy, rather than simply an argumentative one. I've had plenty of students argue with me until they're blue in the face, both in here and at the lectures, and I just sigh inside because I know they're missing the point. They're taking philosophy and trying to turn it into a concrete subject like, say, biology or geometry."

I have no idea how to respond to this, so I just nod. He looks me square in the eye, sensing my reservation. I'm not sure if I should tell him I'm dropping out of university because I'm broke and a drunk. I decide not to, for the moment at least, to see where it gets me.

"Thanks," I say. "Philosophy has always been something that's interested me precisely because of its *lack* of concreteness, and I've been trying to take a fresh approach to it."

He swivels around in his chair again. "Anyway, I'd highly recommend you keep going down this path. Have you picked your courses for the fall?"

Nope, I think, because there's not a fucking chance I'll be returning, unless of course I win the lottery or someone pays off all my massive debts and I get a decent job and quit drinking like a fish. I lied my way into UBC in the first place anyway, so it's not like I really deserve to be here, and now I'm too poor, too immature, and too proud to ask for help.

"Yeah I think I'm pretty much set," I say.

"Excellent," he says, standing up to shake my hand. "Well enjoy your summer, Seth."

"Thanks, I will," I say.

Back at my car, I call Cancer. He's at some party and has been trying to get a hold of me for the past two hours, but my ringer has been on mute. He answers by yelling, "Answer your fuckin' phone, faggot!"

"I had a meeting with my professor," I tell him.

"You have a meeting with *me*, boy. Now get over here."

"Cancer, I'm fuckin' broke," I tell him, hearing female voices in the background.

"Fuck, you're always broke," he says.

"You can front me tonight, can't you?"

"I front you every night, Seth."

"No you don't, and you know it. Don't be like that."

He pauses, and I can hear some girl call out to him in a sexy voice.

"Fuck it," he says. "Get your ass over here. You got ten minutes or I'm looking for some other loser to bankroll. And there's plenty to choose from, believe me. Your generation is like a plague on the world."

When I arrive, people I don't know are scattered all around the house. I head out onto the deck to find the boys leaning against the railing, high on some terrible substance, lashing out at passers-by like a pack of ravenous wolves. When Cancer sees me, he holds up his beer in mock salute, and the others look over and do the same. I don't know whose house this is but it's very luxuriant, and therefore I'm sure we're uninvited, but the rain has stopped, the weather has warmed up, and nobody seems to care one way or the other. Things are looking up.

Cancer is dwarfing everyone as usual, with his massive
6–foot–6, 280 pound frame. His white T-shirt is already stained
here and there, but he doesn't care, unlike Caleb in his customary Polo shirt with collar up, and his spiky brown hair with
frosted blonde tips. He's got a smoke hanging from the side of
his mouth that dances and dangles when he speaks. He tends
to speak a lot. I've known Caleb since Langley—he was one of
the road warriors, and our fathers had been friends, if it can
indeed be said my father had friends. Caleb and I hooked up
again after what was probably five or six years when our Div
1 team picked up both him and Ryan for an exhibition tournament in Seattle—to which we'll all be returning this year.

Seeing him here, I remember the time Caleb head-butted
some poor sap outside the Stone Temple club on Granville.
The guy was talking shit to a whole group of us, no doubt
fresh from a few hours of drinking and wrestling at the frat
house, and Caleb knocked the jerk out cold. We joked about it
for weeks afterwards because Caleb, to that point, had always
taken more of a pragmatic, political approach to confrontation.
He's happy–go–lucky by nature, but he did have a chip on his
shoulder that night. We joked about it, saying the guy must've
insulted his views on the "modern socialist's economic plat-
forms concerning Latin America's lower middleclass labour
force," and stupid stuff like that. But in actuality the guy made
fun of his hair.

Speaking of locks, Ryan is here, sporting those and his
standard stoic look. Tucked into one of five shirts he owns,
with a beer hanging from one hand, he looks like a cross
between a white running back and a pro surfer. He's got the
best hockey hair in the world though, and he knows it. Wings
you'd think would pick him up on the breakout, aiding his
stride as he flies down the ice. Ryan and Caleb work together
as landscape architect assistants, planting little trees between
well-groomed streams in the backyards of mansions in West

Vancouver. They smoke weed on the job. You can tell they smoke weed on the job because they come over for drinks after work sporting these massive life plans that make literally no sense whatsoever. Then the weed wears off and they're plunged back to reality, only for a short time though before the alcohol saves them from any sort of chronic downward trajectory.

And then there's Chris, who's been hanging out with us a lot lately. He played with Ryan for the Junior A Centennials up in Merritt, and decided to quit halfway through the season and move down here. I don't know him well, but he's a quality guy. He doesn't gel his hair or pluck his eyebrows, and he's played Junior, so I know he's quality. Even so, the five of us represent pretty much everything that sucks about living in our society. Cancer works as a drywaller for some rich contractor in Burnaby who builds houses for richer people, mostly in West and North Vancouver. He's big and physical, and that's what makes him good at his job. But he hates it, even though he's part of some union and has the paycheques to prove it. He bitches all the time, but otherwise never really seems to do much about it. The money's too good and besides, I think he feels as though he has some sort of obligation to the rest of us, as if having a decent job and bankrolling his friends' alcoholism is exactly what he's supposed to be doing with his life.

Ryan and Caleb are no different. All they ever do is bitch about their jobs as well, but neither of them has parents wealthy enough or successful enough for them to go to school and get real ones. They're stuck. We're all stuck. Stuck building rich people's houses and manicuring their lawns while pissing in their birdbaths and shitting in the bushes out behind their guest homes. Chris is no different. He quit Junior A because he was riding the bench, and moved in with Ryan and Caleb after their third roommate moved out. Chris has no job per se, but has a few bucks left over from some small inheritance he came into. But that's dwindling fast, and it won't be long now before the poor bastard is planting little bonsai trees alongside his two roommates.

I'm not there twenty minutes before Cancer has put a serious dent into someone else's beer stock. He's decided it's his right, once again, as once again he's been forced to pay for all his friends. I'm soon so drunk on someone else's beer I'm having trouble standing up. I've missed Sarah's call again, and have thus decided to get as fucked up as possible. In about an hour the five of us are supposed to be heading to the Arts County Fair, the annual end-of-school-year festival, but I'm not sure I can do it. What with all those rich hooligans from North Vancouver who think they're Jim Belushi from *Animal House* hanging about, I'm not sure I can handle it. I couldn't fight a kitten right now, and they'd know it.

"Just think about the theory a second," Cancer is saying.

"What, that alcohol impedes a man's sexual performance?" I pipe in, cutting him off. Cancer looks at me with a dead glare. I'm referring to last night when he couldn't seal the deal with some Asian girl he'd picked up. Ryan, Caleb and Chris chuckle a bit, but not too much, lest Cancer take offence.

"You done?" he asks me presently.

"Yeah, I'm done. Go for it."

He pauses, and then resumes his diatribe. "So the reason we have so many good black athletes is because, way back when, all the smaller slaves were killed off. Culled, if you will. Therefore it was the bigger athletic slaves that were allowed to live and breed, giving us guys like Michael Jordan and Donovan McNabb," he says, holding his beer bottle by the neck, pointing the bottom at me, awaiting my endorsement.

"So what you're saying is, we have white rednecks to thank for the Chicago Bulls' dynasty."

"Basically, yes."

"Basically you're a racist," I say.

"It's not that I'm racist, it's just that I don't like black people. And Natives, don't even get me started on Natives," he
says, drowning out the others' laughter. "I mean yeah, we came
here and took all your land and turned you all into drunks, but
geez, c'mon, do something with your life other than build
fuckin' casinos, all right?"

We proceed to get violently drunk and make it to the fair,
and somehow I end up at Ashley's place later. Still intoxicated,
I break into her apartment and ravage her like an animal. She
pretends to protest, but in reality she loves that sort of thing,
except for the part where I curl up like a cat and fall asleep
immediately afterwards. I get up the next morning and crack
my first beer around ten. Ashley gets up shortly thereafter and
makes us sandwiches for lunch. I end up watching TV for a
few hours, flipping back and forth between *Heat* and sports
highlights. Usually after an hour or so I get so sick of the com-
mercials I have to turn the TV off. I don't though, and end up
drifting off on the couch instead. I can hear Ashley in her
room, tapping away on her laptop, working on God knows
what. Soft music is wafting into the living room, carried in on
the incense she's burning. I finally turn the TV off to sleep. I'm
still nursing the tail end of my hangover, though I've had three
T3s and one Valium and can feel it. I nod off.

When I awake, I'm coaxed into going out for a drink and
a bite to eat at some Italian restaurant down the street. I end
up putting back six double vodkas before they cut me off, and
then make a big scene when the waitress charges me for seven.
Ashley pays the bill out of frustration and demands we leave.
We decide to go home and relax a bit. I make another scene
while walking home, trying to fight some bum by kicking his
shopping cart out from under him. Ashley says I'm worse than
Hitler. "Who's this Hitler?" I ask her.

Back at her place, she watches me take my shoes off. I
look up at her as she shuts the door and drops her purse to

the floor, and then proceeds to take off her jacket with quick aggressive movements designed to show she's pissed off. I know she's pissed off, but then again, I also know she's pissed, which means I can get away with a little more than usual.

"That argument is so tired," I say, picking up the conversation we'd dropped just prior to the shopping cart.

"Fine."

"It was a fucking *shoe* commercial."

"Whatever."

"They're bloody *shoes* for Christ's sake."

"Yeah, well, be glad I like yours, that's all."

"Now if a woman says it's the *brain* that makes the man, that'd be sexy," I tell her.

"Well of course it is. If a guy has great shoes but is dumb as a post, he wouldn't stand a chance."

"Because that's what really matters. *Brains*."

"No shit. I'm not that shallow, Seth."

"See, you just negated your whole argument," I say, jabbing my index finger into her sternum.

"I'm saying shoes are *part* of the deal," she explains.

I back off and take a seat on the couch in the living room. *Cosmopolitan, Redbook,* some flowers and one of those little Zen sand jobs with the rocks and the rake take up most of the clear glass coffee table.

"Cheer me up," she says, flopping down between my legs, forcing me to readjust my position on the couch. "Something not idiotic," she continues, interlocking our fingers.

" 'Entertain me,' " I reply. " 'Find me a nickname.' 'Fuck me.' So demanding, this Ashley."

"Go fuck your*self*," she says, turning around to glare at me. "I *demand* the right to be demanding."

A silence develops as she plays with my hands, running her fingers over the various nicks, cuts and scars.

"I'm pretty sure every word that comes out of my mouth pisses women off," I say. She looks at me.

"Is this your way of starting a fight so you can get up and leave after we have sex, just like you always do?"

"Don't patronize me," I say.

"*Patronize* you? Fuck off. You can't talk your way out of this one, asshole."

"You know what? Fuck you, Ash. I've got nothing to explain to you. I owe you nothing."

"Oh that's great, Seth. Nice."

"Fucking horseshit," I say. "It's all fucking horseshit. You pull me into this game and shit all over me, and then expect me to put up with it."

"That's what you think this is? A game?"

"Well it sure as hell feels like a game. It feels like I'm being yanked around, regardless of what I do, of what I say, or even whatever the fuck happens on any given day. You're always testing me, poking at me and pointing out my faults, and I'm sick of it. You need to get a grip on reality."

"Don't talk down to me like I'm a child," she hisses, which seems more childish than anything she said previously.

"You are a child. You're very immature. Think before you open that fucking trap of yours, will you?"

"Fuck you."

"Blah blah blah is all I hear anymore, Ash. All the words you speak to me have lost all meaning. I don't care what you say anymore, because it's all so personal and vindictive."

I get up, grab my wallet and car keys, and leave. She says nothing, which is unusual, because she loathes when I get the last word in.

North of 63

Rummaging through my closet in search of my philoso-phy textbooks, I end up ripping through box after box in frustration before it hits me. I sold my books for beer money. I decide right then and there it's time to get my act together. I need to leave now more than I need to wait for Sarah to come home, so I decide to jump ship from my mother's house and temporarily move back in with my father. The goal, if it can be said I actually have a goal, is to see if he can hit up my uncle for a job on the oil rigs up north for four months until Sarah comes home from Australia. I'm not sure how living with him will go—we'll probably end up arguing or fight-ing—but what can I do. I'm rotting from the inside out down here, and I'll die if things deteriorate any further.

The father-son reunion goes swimmingly, for about a week or so. We even go out for dinner at a pub one night and talk like a normal father and son might talk. In the meantime he calls my uncle, and it looks as though I have a job if I can get my ass up there—to Iqaluit that is, which is located on Baffin Island up around the Artic Circle. But it all falls apart the next day when he comes home to his new kitchen filled with my dirty dishes and empty beer bottles, with his son passed out on the couch with the TV blaring and all the lights on. We end up getting into the long overdue fight, and I end up leaving early on account of it, spending a couple of nights in a local motel before catching the long flight northeast to Iqaluit.

As soon as what passes for the airport comes into view through the airplane window, I realize I'm a long way out from anything I've ever known before. A beet yellow colour, the air-port looks like a Lego shack from this height, and not a very inviting one at that. But before long the rest of the town slides into view, brightly coloured housing complexes—red, blue, green, purple—and a massive, flat, two-storey building that looks like an upside-down ice cube tray, which I later find out is the one and only elementary school.

My first instinct is to simply stay on the plane and make my way back to Vancouver, tail between my legs. But I'm long past turning back now. The people on the plane look like they're all part of the same fucked up gang as I am. Businessmen with thick five o'clock shadows, local Inuit coming back from what must have been serious culture shock down south, and various white males who all look like they've come up for work—surveying, construction, engineering, environmental studies, mechanics, whatever. We're here, and we've all banded together because of it.

The Inuit guy from the Nunavut Power Corporation that is supposed to pick me up ends up being a half hour late. When he finally arrives he's short, speaks infrequently, and has one of the ugliest moustaches I've ever seen. He notices all my belongings packed into a Bauer hockey bag.

"You play hockey?" he asks.

"Yeah, I play hockey."

He nods slightly and we make our way to his truck outside. I throw my bag in the back and we set off into one of the world's ugliest cities. Dirt roads, dirty snow, dirty dogs wandering the streets in packs. We pass an Inuit carrying the head of a Caribou, antlers and all, over his shoulder. About ten minutes later I see another man carrying two hind legs, the stumps wrapped in garbage bags, blood dripping onto the dirt.

"You smoke pot?" asks my host, opening up the ashtray.

"Yeah, sure," I say. "What's your name by the way?"

"Gary."

Gary proceeds to light up the rest of a joint he probably smoked on the way here. He turns the CD player on, and

Cypress Hill fills the truck. A trio of dirty snowmobilers rip across the street, cutting off the car in front of us. Gary slams on the brakes.

"Fucking kids," he says, passing me the joint.

I try to inhale as little as possible. I really don't think getting stoned right now is a good idea, after all.

Having arrived on a Monday afternoon, I head straight to work the next day. I'm bunking with a Newfie named Sean. He greets me with a slew of words spoken in some dialect I can barely comprehend. About all I can determine is he plays hockey too, he just returned from Jakarta, and is from a place called Marystown, Newfoundland. The housing situation is completely set up and paid for by the company. But there isn't much inside the duplex we're splitting except a huge TV, a fridge and the stench of dried meat.

Sean explains how this has been his life the last few years. Working four-month stints with the company as a mechanical assistant, then "fucking off" and travelling the world all winter. He especially likes Southeast Asia—Thailand, Singapore, Vietnam, Malaysia—and wastes no time in explaining why.

"Mutherfuckin' pussy so cheap there, eh," he says, cracking a beer and handing me another as we sit down on the chairs that serve as the living room couch. "I mean, fuck, you's best watch yer ass, but fuck it, eh. I says to this guy who's scared to go there, 'Fuck it.' I mean fuckin' Yankees beat their ass in Vietnam, so why the fuck should I be worried, eh."

I learn quickly the best thing to do when conversing with Sean is nod whenever he says something that sounds like a statement, and laugh when he smiles and chuckles after a sentence.

Still, the man is surprisingly easy to live with. He does his own dishes as well as mine most of the time, never really argues or gets angry, and spends pretty much all of his downtime parked in front of the television, which offers almost a thousand channels. He just sits there, beer in one hand, joint or cigarette in the other, flicking for hours. He's got a penchant for the British comedies *Fawlty Towers*, *Are You Being Served?* and this crazy puppet show called *Spitting Image*. Whenever I come out of my room and he has *Spitting Image* on, the house reeking of codfish and pot, I feel so far from normalcy, almost as if I'm inhabiting a delirious parallel world.

Work ends up being much easier than initially expected. Still it's no picnic. It takes me about four or five weeks to completely understand my role, and where everyone else fits into the pecking order. I quickly earn a reputation as a hard worker because, well, I am, it turns out. The Newfies work hard, but in their own way, meaning they'll bust their asses for four hours then take an hour-and-a-half coffee break as reward for their efforts. The Inuit barely work at all. One electrician named Joe simply plays *Age of Empires* all day long on his PC, and sometimes sorts through his electrical supplies. But I also learn the Inuit are "fire-proof," meaning their Native status prohibits their being let go no matter how much they fuck up, or how bad they slack off. This pisses off the Newfies to no end, who bitch behind their backs in response, calling them "niggers of the north" and other such pleasantries.

The job itself is extremely physical, and exactly what I was looking for. A smaller man would have great difficulty in my position, as most of my shift is spent unloading 55-gallon drums of oil from trucks and muscling them around. It's a diesel power plant, with four massive Wartsila engines, each about the size of a school bus, and two smaller ones that together power the entire town. They operate in cycles, the sequencing of which is controlled by computer. Maintenance is the human side of the operation. We clean massive cylinder heads the size of washing machines, and pistons taller than a man that require an overhead crane to move around.

On the floor it's all hand signals. 'OK' is not thumbs up—I learn that quickly—but the other stuff is pretty much self-explanatory. I'm basically a surgeon's assistant, except the doctors are drunk Inuit mechanics and the blood is waste oil and gasoline. But I learn the system quickly and keep mostly to myself, speaking only when spoken to. The fact I dwarf most of the other workers, and my various tattoos scare the hell out of the Inuit whenever I change in and out of my coveralls, also keeps confrontation to a minimum. Still, for all that, it's surprising how easy work can be when you're making tons of cash.

And the money flows. I end up working ten to twelve hour days, seven days a week, whenever Wartsila mechanical engineers are flown in to fix the engines, which happens fairly regularly. I make just under twenty-five dollars an hour, with an additional thousand a month for living expenses. I'm eventually reimbursed for my plane ticket as well. But it's the overtime, time-and-a-half, double-time on holidays and triple-time after five on holidays when the real money is made. And there's not much to do up here other than work and sleep anyway.

Sean and I get along fine. The duplex we share is massive, with tall ceilings and cathedral-like windows overlooking what passes for a bay. The entire house is painted in faded beige, both inside and out, but it's only about a five minute drive from work, so I don't have to go far when I need to get out.

Sean seems to take a liking to me, and why not. I buy beer all the time, I chip in for pot—always this brick stuff that barely gives me a body stone—and I never really give a damn what we watch on TV because I truly don't. We're the ultimate odd couple—a lanky BCer and a stout Newfie—almost like the number '10' we decide one night while stoned and drunk on rum. We head to the Legion on weekends, as Sean has membership, and most of the time, to get him home, I literally have to drag his drunken ass into a cab. He picks up my penchant for vodka, and absolutely loves the fact I attract women the way I do. The man will screw anything with the audacity to come home with him, and on a few occasions actually manages to. One time some Inuit woman takes him up on his offer, and then proceeds to steal two hundred dollars from him when she leaves in the morning. And the next time Sean sees her at the Legion he busts a beer bottle over the head of the Inuit guy standing next to her, then punches her in the face. But because we're white and they're not, and because I'm bigger than the bouncers, they leave and we stay. Such is life, I'm beginning to find out.

Hours turn into days, and days into weeks, as I live paycheque to paycheque watching my bank account soar. Sean cooks fish almost every night, or pizza, or else these strange potato things I've never seen before. We watch movies rented from the local department store, and the Coke or Pepsi we purchase there is always flat.

At work Sean usually runs the incinerator, two massive pipes that look like concrete garbage cans. They're hooked up to a pump that spews in waste oil, which burns out the top in miniature fire tornados. To light these things is a tricky business however. You stand on a ladder and drop a burning rag into the spinning circle of oil, then get your ass down before the flames come shooting up. Every once in a while Sean comes loping into the break room covered in oil, his eyebrows singed from a faulty start.

The town of Iqaluit itself is littered with errant kids, stray dogs, drunken Inuit and spare parts from snowmobiles in seemingly equal parts. It's ugly and it knows it. Ramshackle buildings covered with dirt, their windows covered with tinfoil to keep the sun out—which comes up around three in the morning, I soon find out—are the norm. The only high-rise, if you can call a five-storey building a high-rise, is smack in the middle of town, and the only decent restaurant is the one run for the federal government workers who come up on official government business at odd and seemingly arbitrary times.

The tide is absolutely insane—sucking in and out of the bay all day, dropping and rising about fifty metres—the second biggest in the world apparently. When the tide washes out, cargo ships come barrelling in to purposely beach themselves, at which point massive forklifts scamper in to unload all the cargo before the tide washes in again. There is a road on the outskirts of town where we go to dump waste oil from time to time, or to burn extra wood from the holding boxes the engine parts arrive in. The road is called "The Road to Nowhere" because, well, after a while, it literally goes nowhere.

The white news is usually the same. Who's in town from down south. Who committed suicide this week. Who beats their wife routinely and manages to get away with it. All the Inuit talk about, though, is hunting. Killing Caribou with high-powered sniper rifles from 150 yards away, pumping bullets into a Beluga whale out in Frobisher Bay, or how hunting seals is like those carnival games where you whack gofers that pop out of holes with a plush mallet, the only difference being the seals peek their heads up out of the water and the Inuit shoot them with .303 calibre bullets.

The best part of my summer turns out to be, not surprisingly, ball hockey. Each Saturday and Sunday afternoon is taken up by the weekend ball hockey league organized by white people and played mostly by Inuit. The ice has been taken out of the rink for the summer—only God knows why—and skates become tennis shoes, with soccer shin-pads, gloves and helmets being the only other equipment required to play.

To put it bluntly, this league is mine. The little 5–foot–6 Inuit guys who previously dominated the league are no match for someone my size. Sean and I are on the Power Plant team, and we wreak havoc on anything and everything we come up against. Sean played a bit of Junior back home too, so he knows how to go to the net and slice his passes nicely. A lot of the little Inuit guys can stickhandle like demons though. Short sticks, quick hands, wicked shots much better than I would have expected beforehand. If only the league wasn't full contact, they'd be in business. Poor bastards. My 6–foot–3 body, filled now to capacity with cod and beer, crushes them like juice boxes against the boards. And whenever I want to, I simply stand in front of the net, wait for the orange ball to come my way, and power myself to a garbage goal, making them all look like infants in the process.

But I can run with the bastards too, and sometimes, coming down the boards, they'll simply give the ball up rather than get ploughed into Plexiglas. It's nice to dominate a league again, as much as this is a league. Every once in a while the game gets cancelled because a goalie doesn't show, always some Inuit dude who didn't call or tell anyone he wasn't coming, and then neglected to give his gear to someone else to suit up in his place. He simply doesn't show, and none of his stupid little friends seem to know where he might be found. No matter, next time the fucker does show up, I pound little orange balls at his face until I crack his mask or shatter his throat shield. In this way tardiness and absenteeism are minimized.

The only time I get to talk to Sarah on the phone is when I work late at night. No one is around and I simply call her long distance, usually waking her up from an afternoon nap or catching her just returning from some exciting Australian excursion. Sometimes we talk for hours before I grudgingly hang up and drive the company truck home. She sends me emails almost every day, which I check on the electricians' computer, always replying immediately. We talk about her plans for school, her friends, her life, and whenever she asks me about life up here I smoothly shift the conversation back to her. The less she knows about this place the better, I've decided.

Still, the four months end up going by rather quickly. Sean leaves a week and a half before I do, heading home to Newfoundland for a few weeks before meeting up with some English guys he knows in Japan. Chances are he'll find his way back to Thailand after that. The house is quiet with my room-mate gone, and it's weird to have the remote at my disposal. I check his room to find he's left a load of clothes and stuff behind, simply abandoning an $80 electric razor and a nice pair of work boots, which are now mine.

Before I know it I'm back on a plane to Vancouver. I get held up in Edmonton for six hours, most of which I spend in the airport bar drinking with some jerks from Toronto who consider Dominic Hasek a shitty goalie. "He's European," I point out, "but not shitty. He's won the Vezina like how many times." But they don't listen. Guys like that never listen. Too much of a chore somehow.

Sarah is waiting for me at the airport when I return, all tanned and toned, having just returned herself from Australia a few days ago. It's the first time I've returned from somewhere, anywhere, to have someone like her waiting for me. Now that I'm back on familiar turf, even with twenty grand sitting in my chequing account, the whole Iqaluit experience feels like a dream. A four month dream. Images and impressions have already begun to fade. The whole summer seems to have happened in one giant breath, and I've already finished exhaling and am about to breathe again.

Mercaptan

A car crash is little more than a vivid string of moments—of pain, fear, panic and utter loss of control. It's nothing like in the movies, where everything is slowed down and exaggerated. No, by the time you realize you've been in a car accident it's already over. In fact, things speed up to a numbing reckless blur. The force of the vehicle's rotation, in a seemingly absurd direction, detaches you from your body, and for a few brief moments you lose touch with the physical world. Control of your bodily functions becomes something of a crapshoot. You see flashcards of scenes, shuffled together like a slide show. Your hand bracing the roof as the car flips, the floor mats coming loose, the windshield shattering in your face. Pieces of car, once so comforting and unobtrusive, jam their way into your body, penetrating your flesh with ease. And throughout it all you hear that awful crushing and ripping of metal, and then all of this confusion, all of this chaos, is suddenly over.

Then an awful silence kicks in. You're still strapped into your seat, still alive and in one piece, even though the frame of the car is crushed and bent to a fantastic degree. You feel microscopic pieces of glass on your tongue. Your gums begin to bleed, and the salty taste in your mouth is communicated immediately to your nostrils. You feel dirty. Soiled. The bits of glass force you to keep your mouth open, which oddly enough isn't so bad, as it allows the blood to drain from your mouth rather than pool under your tongue and around your gums. The intoxicating smell of spilled gasoline is your only comfort, and you can still hear the wheel humming furiously on the right rear axle.

The CD player is skipping frantically, so much so the song is indistinguishable. The flickering green letters spilling across the display read FULL COLLAPSE—TRACK 02. Guitars and voices are ripped, cut and pasted together in a psychotic confusion of sound. You get so fed up you kick the dashboard until it stops, only to realize your left leg is broken. The pain is new and sharp, something you've certainly never experienced before, and yet it's simultaneously numb and dull. You can feel your tibia shifting around inside your tendons and muscles immediately below your kneecap, scratching soft tissue, collapsing arteries and veins, filling pockets of torn muscle with blood and crushed cartilage.

You sit there, wracked with a pain you can manage only if you remain perfectly still. But you can't. The tension of the seatbelt strangling your intestines forces you to adjust yourself. The headrest, ripped apart, exposes its sharp metal skeleton to your skull. You contemplate yelling, but don't, for two reasons. One, you think you may do internal damage by doing so, and two, some other driver on the highway must have seen the accident and called 911.

You think to yourself, in some odd form of realization, "I was just in a car accident." And then you shift your head, slowly, watching with a sort of detached interest as the blood from your mouth streams all over the collar of your shirt, and check behind you. Half of the backseat is outside the door, and the back tire on the driver's side is partially exposed.

You try to cry in order to feel some sort of normalcy, but the adrenaline and oxygen are still pumping, and your blood is still speeding, forcing your veins and airways open so that all you can accomplish are deep staggered breaths of an inhuman nature.

You see a bottle of vodka on the floor by the gas pedal—the one Sarah and you split earlier—that somehow didn't break. You get a flash of a MADD commercial, the one where the cop stops the kids for a suspected DUI, only to be hit by another oncoming drunk driver. You realize you're really not all that powerful a creature. A 4,000 pound car has power, but you do not. Death is now a lot closer, and you examine it with a newer deeper sense of dread and wonder.

You look over to your left. Sarah is beside you and she is dead. There is blood all over her. Her neck must be broken, her spine shattered. You realize you are sitting beside a dead person. Someone who was vibrantly alive mere moments ago. You were intimate with this person. You were inside her. You were as close to her, physically, as anyone ever was or would be in this world. You think of her mother and her father and her brother and her friends at her funeral and all of them crying at the fact she is dead. It hits you hard, but you are beyond shock, and eerily calmed by your realizations.

Her body is slumped over the steering wheel, which reminds you of a twisted bicycle wheel run over by a truck. You see the keys in the ignition. Her blood—and possibly yours—is splattered all over the dashboard and speedometer. She will be remembered for this mistake. She will not have a chance to make this wrong a right. Her family will remember her as the daughter who killed herself, and possibly yourself, while intoxicated. They will remember her as little more than a drunk driver.

But I am a drunk. And with that realization set firmly in mind, I unbuckle her seatbelt, then mine. My body feels like a collection of broken toothpicks jammed into a slab of rotting ham. I can feel bones shifting, grudgingly, to places they're not supposed to be. Blood begins to pour down Sarah's neck, and I realize there is a large hole in the back of her head. With one giant thrust I pull her atop me. She's a heavy, lifeless doll with limbs that frustrate. Her blood is all over me—I can feel it run down my pants and into my crotch—and I can still smell her perfume. Once she is against the passenger's window, I shuffle into the driver's seat, breaking my arm in the process. I've never seen so much blood. It's surreal and somehow humbling in the worst possible way.

I place her in the passenger's seat with my one good hand, carefully fastening her seatbelt before fastening mine. My hair is wet from what must be blood and sweat, but could possibly be alcohol, gasoline and rain. The rain is everywhere, an impossibly loud percussion. My head starts to rush as I settle into the driver's seat, and when I push against the steering wheel to adjust my position the car crinkles and settles on a slant with a scraping sound of metal. I begin to breathe heavily. I begin to panic. I look over at Sarah and I look behind me, and then I faint into a world of black.

Hallucinations. Not dreams, not nightmares, but hallucinations as my mind tries to rewire itself around a bleeding swollen brain. I spend the better part of two weeks drifting in and out of a medically induced slumber. And every time I wake up thinking I'm somewhere else, somewhere unbroken, the smell of disinfectant drags me back to my recently shattered reality.

I'm lying in a hospital bed on the third floor of Vancouver General. It's dark outside but I really have no clue what time it as the TV has been broken for two days. There is a tray table on my lap. My face is still heavily bruised, and the stitches running down the bridge of my nose and across my eyebrows are dried and crusted. I dare not pick at them, though I want to desperately.

Someone has brought me photographs—I can't remember who—in an attempt to jog some of the memories I've lost. There's one of Cancer and me, his enormous bulk beside me as the two of us blow smoke into the air. My cowlick of hair and his shaved head. We're both dressed in snappy bar shirts, with the collars up. We look like assholes and we know it. Best friends too, it turns out.

Then there's a picture of the four of us, the boys, with Cancer and I on the left, and Caleb and Ryan on the right. Then a few out-of-focus shots of Ryan holding Chris on the ground, both of them wrestling around, covered in dirt and grass.

The next couple are action shots of a hockey game. I'm a blurry figure in full stride screaming down the wing, the number 16 emblazoned on my back. We were the Top End Construction Sabres apparently—Cancer's boss owned the team—that's how they knew to pick us both up in the draft that year. The next is Cancer and I after the game, looking slightly up, sweat beading all over our enormous grins.

The last picture is of Sarah, in her room, a reflection in her dresser mirror. I can see photographs of me tucked into the corners of the frame, and written backwards on the mirror in lipstick is *Sarah + Seth* with a giant heart around it.

I had just returned from Iqaluit. And recently returned that is, as in a little over two weeks. I'd come home with too much money and no actual plan to return to university. I hadn't signed up for any classes and hadn't told my parents. I'd wanted to come home, go on employment insurance, and drink and play as much as possible, positive it would be my last chance to live so frivolously before settling into a long and sanitized adulthood. Instead I am to be charged and plead guilty to Driving under the Influence, section 253(a) of the Criminal Code of Canada. I will be given a year's probation, fined $600 dollars, and required to do 20 hours of community service. My license will be taken away for six months, most of which I will spend in a hospital bed, and upon release I will be ordered to see both a drug and alcohol counsellor and a psychiatrist. In the end I will think the judge takes pity on me however because I'll have been on suicide watch the previous few weeks, let alone the fact I'm not actually to blame for the accident. And the fact I broke my left leg, my right arm, sustained minor internal bleeding and a Grade 3 concussion, plus over fifty stitches, will not go unnoticed either. Perhaps he feels any further punishment wouldn't fit the crime. He doesn't say and I don't ask.

They never do find out the truth either. They only find out what I want them to. Sometimes I wish they would find out the truth. I often regret what I did. But now I'm stuck with it and nobody would believe me anyway, so what's the use. Everyone looks at you differently after something like that. With pity, intrigue, and mystery. You become their cautionary tale told when they want to move someone else emotionally.

Even so, the accident was far from press-worthy. It was just a case of too much rain. Besides it wasn't an accident so much as a mistake, something to be covered up rather than exploited, featured and delved into. I was not a marketable enough tragedy, I guess, and all I am left with is myself and that telling looks on peoples' faces. Friends, family, anyone I knew who knew what happened, they wonder what I must be thinking. Wonder what must be going through my head. But I just want to forget. I don't want to talk about it or explore it or try to resolve the issues and pain it created. I just want to bury it, and that's exactly what I do. I want to bury it so deep it will be completely wiped from existence.

It's raining again. I'm outside the back of the courthouse in my black shirt and white tie, and my dress pants and black dress shoes that give me calluses every time. I pull out a cigarette and do a token search for a lighter I know I don't have— a stout security guard with a moustache offers me his instead. My eyes squint as the flame nears my face. I pull back and take a drag and let the creamy, coarse formaldehyde drift from my mouth. I hold the cigarette like a pen, down and away, between thumb and index finger.

"So?" says the guard, placing his lighter back in his shirt pocket, breaking the silence I was quite content with. "Good news or bad?"

I grin my crooked grin, looking at the ground as I let a gob of spit fall from my mouth. I look up to see him checking out the partially healed scars on my face.

"Neither."

I notice him looking at the cast on my right arm, half hidden by my dress shirt, defaced with black felt marker. I explain to the security guard, and his moustache, that this is what happens when you pass out with a cast on your arm at some all-night keg party. He chuckles, and I turn and walk the other way. By the time everyone else has come out of the courtroom, I've gotten in my car and left. Left all the questions and the uncomfortable stares and silences behind. Left all the unfinished business behind. I'm tired of this, and everything else for that matter. I'm tired of caring. And I will not, not for a long time.

I really don't want to be here at all. I say it again in my head. I really don't want to be here at all.

She stands up and makes her way to the front of the auditorium. It's quiet except for a few whispers way in the back. When she finally reaches the podium it gets even quieter somehow, the only noise being the crinkling of the one piece of paper she holds in both quivering hands. She wipes her eyes and steadies herself in front of the microphone stand, soft feedback crackling from the speakers. There must be at least four hundred people here in this auditorium, but I am not one of them. I am calm, motionless and blank, and I am not here. Then she makes eye contact with me, locking eyes briefly, silently questioning me and bringing me back. I can't decipher what she's thinking. All I know is she's looking straight at me. Then she begins to speak, but I can't follow the words until I hear, ". . . and you realize this is no game. And there is no turning back."

And then silence. Excruciatingly uncomfortable silence. I try to cry, but I cannot. I'm locked out. She leaves the stage and makes her way back to her seat amongst the hush and muted sobs. She thinks I killed her best friend, and I cannot tell her otherwise. I sit motionless in my chair, my toes curled tightly into the soles of my shoes. Fingernails digging into the backs of my legs. I am dead to these people just as Sarah is dead to her. I am now the monster who will forever inhabit the basement of their lives.

Syncopic

Div 1, as we all call it, and my second season in the Greater Vancouver Senior Men's League. It's the place where all the guys who played semi-pro or Junior but never made it anywhere higher inevitably tumble down to. They have jobs and lives but still want to play a decent grade of hockey, so this is it. This is our new reality. This is our predicament.

Last season, before the accident, I was well on my way to winning Rookie of the Year. But that's way behind me now. At least I'm healthy again though, relatively, and this is already shaping up to be my year.

I've learned much from hockey I'm sure translates into the real world, but I'd rather not try to formulate it—quite honestly, I feel like an asshole whenever I do. It's a game, a good one, but still a game. You don't play hockey to learn about life. You play hockey to escape from life, even for just a little while, to simply get the hell away and think about something so specialized and isolated it can't be touched by anything or anyone. And all you have to do is enjoy it, occasionally nurse it and care for it, and it becomes the one thing, the one place where you really know who the hell you are.

The first game or so back is always tough after the off-season, and unless you've been on the ice all summer, you've got some serious rust to shake off. Guys are simply trying not to look silly that first game back, trying to feel comfortable in their gear even though they don't.

Your legs are always the first to go. The quads and calves start burning, and every stride becomes more difficult, as though the ice is softening into quicksand. You come off the ice and, as soon as you hit the bench, you can feel the fire. You don't know if you'll ever be able to take another shift, but you take a drink of water, rest, catch your breath, and get your ass out there again.

Your passes always seem a second or two off, and every once in a while the puck does a back flip over your stick and leaves you skating away from it like a fool. Guys "blow tires" as they call it, or trip over the blueline, going down as though they've been shot by a sniper in the stands.

But when you're in the groove, healthy and in game-shape, there's nothing better than hitting top speed or wristing a perfect shot right into the mesh. As for me, having recovered somewhat from my injuries from the accident, I've started the long search to regain my game, which I know will return to me bit by bit, shift by shift.

Any good hockey player stresses over his equipment. You're essentially wearing a full suit of armour, and sweating like a fat chick on a treadmill inside it too. The skates and stick are the most important pieces of gear. Without a good stick you're little more than an idiot in a bunch of padded plastic out there. If the stick's got too much flex, pucks fly all over the place, and you look like you're dumping the puck in when in reality you're trying to take a shot on goal. Different blade curves make passes and shots leave the stick at different times, and a stick too long or too short will seriously hamper your stick-handling.

If your skates aren't sharp enough, or else too sharp, you can't get a proper stride going or turn at the appropriate time. If they're too tight, every time you hit the bench your feet flare up, leaving you pussyfooting around like a fool.

You can always tell a guy who's played his whole life, since Peter Puck or Atom. He knows the subtle nuances of the game and the unwritten code, and most of the time he knows how to keep his head about him and not take stupid penalties. He knows when to dump the puck in rather than carry, when to take the man and when to simply shadow him. And he's got his eyes on you whenever he's checking you. You meet this guy face to face and you know he's going to do everything in his power to beat you.

With experience he develops a sort of sixth sense out there, knowing an opponent coming down on his off wing is going to have a tougher time shooting the puck with any power or accuracy. And if he's on his good wing, chances are the shot is going to go wide, wrap around the boards and start a breakout the other way.

This guy also knows if he stands in front of the net long enough with his stick on the ice, he'll score goals, perhaps even a lot of goals. And he knows the stat sheet doesn't have an asterisk beside garbage goals. A goal is a goal, but he knows not to show off when his team is up by a bunch. And when it's an empty net, he just calmly shoots it in, he doesn't get pretty and he doesn't rub it in. If a guy dishes a suspect hit and gets away with it, he's fair game for a calculated measure of retaliation. Basically, if you're going to dish it out, be prepared to take a return shot at some point during the game. These guys know what it feels like to be on the other end of things.

And anything that happens on the ice stays on the ice. Once the final whistle goes, it's over, drop it, leave it there and don't take it to the handshake or the bar or the hallway out-side the dressing rooms.

Yes, I've learned a lot from hockey. But very little of it have I managed to translate to the real world unfortunately. I'm pondering this while sitting in my psychiatrist's office. Back with his neatly trimmed beard, his family, his fucking dog and his golf clubs. I wonder if he golfs at the club we visited a few nights ago, joyriding around like escaped monkeys, and I won-der if maybe a probation officer would've been a better option than having to sit and listen to this guy tell me my life is going to be okay if I just keep my nose clean and work hard.

He wants to know about my hockey career. The one that had so much promise. He wants me to harken back to the year I should've been suiting up for the Thunderbirds in Junior. Some of the prospects I trained with that year are now fulltime employees of the NHL. Some of the guys I would've been suiting up with are now playing professional hockey, whereas I'm sitting here with him, staring out the window just to spite the bastard.

Then I decide to stare at him. I'm tired and I don't have time for his questions seemingly ripped straight from the Diagnostic and Statistical Manual of Mental Disorders. After a while I slide my attention to the window again, suddenly awestruck by my ability not to give a damn about anything.

"Seth?"

I continue to stare out the window, completely ignoring him. I'm off in some other place, and not coming back any time soon, it seems.

I feel like I've been hit by an ice cream truck. I feel so terrible in fact I decide to quit drinking and smoking and engaging in unprotected sex right there on the spot. But this newfound wholesome attitude fades away almost immediately once I leave the office and get some McDonald's cheeseburgers and fries inside me.

Two days later we're in Seattle for an early season exhibition tournament, Cancer, Ryan, Caleb and I all travelling together just like last year. It's the second day of the tournament and we've split our first few games, landing ourselves in the consolation final. Of course I had to get special permission from a presiding judge in order to cross the border, which still turned into a four-hour ordeal filled with paperwork and uncomfortable questions like "Sir, do you have any drugs on you?"

"What, like in my pockets? Of course not."

"No, sir, do you have any drugs *in* you, is what I mean."
And stuff like that.

Once we get back to the hotel, the guys decide to take the fifth of whisky and leftover beers from last night and get wasted in the pool. I head back to our room to dry out my gear for tomorrow's game, and to find a saw to cut my stick down. Afterwards I find out Cancer and Caleb threw some plastic lawn chairs in the pool in political protest of the pool's closure due to a high chlorine count. At this point Cancer proceeded to take a piss in the pool, only to be one-upped by Caleb who took a dump in the hot tub before security chased them both from the area with clubs. Off they went, breaking beer bottles and pounding on doors as they rumbled down the long carpeted hallways, laughing and hiding in the rooms of some of our more well-adjusted teammates. Nice group of guys I hang out with, I know.

The following morning, as soon as I get up, I know something is wrong inside me. I head for the bathroom at about noon, at which point I begin to sweat and feel sick. I sit down and lock the door—I'm going to be in here a while, I can tell. Binge drinking throws the consciousness through episodes, drifting in and out, where days become hours and months can feel more like minutes. Right now time is moving very slowly, churning my stomach one tick of the nausea clock at a time.

Chances are, during my drunken wandering and stealing of other people's drinks at this Seattle club last night, I swiped some chick's beer spiked with GHB. This has happened before, whereby I inadvertently imbibed the date rape drug, and the feeling is pretty much the same as I remember it, but then again I'll never really know for sure. Cancer and company could have raped me with a carrot and I'd never know. And don't think they wouldn't do it either—I've seen it done before.

It's been four hours now and I haven't so much as moved from the vicinity of the toilet bowl. Every once in a while I crawl up to the sink and suck some tap water down my throat, only to throw it up again at once. I'm no longer thinking, I'm surviving. Sweating and constantly adjusting my position, I've thrown up countless times over the last four hours. Every time I do, I wait for blood. But the blood never comes, and now it's just water. And when I do throw up the water, it makes me want to drink more.

My head resonates with a dull pain that started in my temples and crawled all the way back to my neck. I feel so weak. I wouldn't be able to walk more than a few meters if asked. My whole body hurts with a pulsating yet mundane ache. The bathroom floor is sucking me down, a harsher gravity pulling me into the very ground. My hands jerk and slide across the thin layer of sweat on the linoleum floor. My shirt is covered in vomit of an inhuman nature. I haven't had the energy to clean the sink or the mirror, all over which I threw up when I first made my way in here. There's still piss in the tub from when I got onto my knees to urinate into it, because the toilet was covered in too much puke.

I try to clean the floor in the vicinity of my head with toilet paper, wadding up the used sheets and tossing them in the toilet, but when I flush it starts to rise. I scamper back as chunks of vomit from hours ago resurface and spill over the rim onto the freshly wiped floor. The water and puke and toilet paper are now flooding the bathroom, filling it with an unholy stench. I crawl to the door, open it and drag myself out, knocking over a few empty bottles on my way across the floor. The maids will have a fun time with this one, I'm sure.

Lying there on the carpet, employing a wet towel as a pillow, I curl up into a ball and try to get some sleep before calling housekeeping. I've never felt this bad in my entire life, I think to myself. Is this rock bottom, finally? But for some reason I know I'll be going out tonight. It's our last night in Seattle and we've only got one game left in the tournament tomorrow, and for some reason we've yet to be kicked out of our hotel. Maybe I'll take it easy tonight, I tell myself. Yeah, sure.

Some time later, Cancer, Caleb and Ryan come barging into the room, dressed up and smelling of cologne and booze, eager and ready for the bar and all that that entails. Cancer nearly breaks my kneecap opening the door, and they all laugh hysterically when they see me lying there. I let them know, with a half-hearted series of grunts and gestures, the bathroom is out of order. Ryan pokes his head inside the bathroom door anyway and laughs uproariously, at which point of course they all have to have a look and laugh and fuck with me some more. Now I'm on the bed with my shirt off and I feel a little better. I can't help but laugh as well.

"Jesus Christ, it looks like a crime scene in there," Ryan says, returning from his tour.

"What exactly are we dealing with in there?" asks Cancer from around the corner.

"I think it's just puke, but I can't be sure."

"Quite a piece of artwork there. I'm proud of you Seth, this is fine work. We should take a picture."

"I don't know if I can go out tonight," I say to no one in particular.

Cancer pops his head out from around the corner, looking horrified. He's opening a small bag of cocaine. "Look, wipe off your vagina, do some coke, and get in there and take a cold shower."

I turn over and bury my head in the pillow.

Later, after eight hours of drinking in and around Seattle, we find ourselves locked out of our hotel rooms, the doors having been bolted with padlocks. No matter, we paid cash up front, and we'll be heading out early in the morning for our

last game, and then straight for the border. Cancer ploughs
through the door like it's wet paper, and we end up having a
few girls over. They do a striptease for us, and then the one
goes down on the other while we all watch. Cancer and Caleb
eventually join in, at which point Ryan and I head off to
7–Eleven to get some hot dogs and Chiquitas, sensing our time
here in the room may have reached its logical conclusion. By
the time we return, the door is jammed closed with towels, so
we crash in the other room, climbing in through the window
that looks out over the hotel parking lot.

   In the morning, the other team doesn't bother to show up
for the consolation final, so we're stuck in the parking lot,
somewhere out here in the suburbs of Seattle. All the remaining warm alcohol gets everybody good and drunk again, and
Cancer and Caleb tell all and sundry about their foursome in
excruciating detail. Apparently they switched halfway through,
and then switched back, but then one of the girls started getting weird after she passed out, twitching and talking in her
sleep like an oracle, prompting these two gentleman lovers to
toss them out shortly thereafter.

   At the border, by the time we realize Canadian Customs
has me and my accomplices pegged as drug smugglers, it's
much too late. I spend another four hours filling out paperwork and answering questions while my three friends sleep on
their hockey gloves on the lawn out back. Meanwhile the cus-
tom officials turning my car inside out. They find a bunch of
beer bottle caps but nothing else incriminating, so we're let
free with little more than a "Here's your keys, boys. Welcome
home."

I'm in the bathroom shaving for the night, ignoring my
thoughts as they bounce around trying to claim my attention, all for naught, because the Valium is now doing its job.
After Seattle my body went through its customary period of

detoxification. Over four days I consumed large quantities of ephedrine, nicotine, caffeine, cocaine, Valium, alcohol, possibly some GHB, and greasy fast-food, all mixed in a hurricane of physical exercise and serious lack of sleep. My body tried to shut me down into hibernation with the shakes and sweats, screaming, pleading with me to stop the abuse.

Then my brain started to hum furiously with these substance-induced panic and anxiety attacks, like an internal siren going off. My thoughts began to bounce around frenetically, so I took the Valium to quell the alarm.

As soon as I'm done shaving it's time to hit the bar. Cancer and I have put a serious dent into a flat of Canadian, and that bastard has been blasting through some Cuban cigars his Dad brought back from Pinar del Rio. The whole house smells like a dirty tavern. Even the food I've been eating the past few days tastes of cigar. It's disgusting.

We park the car in a handicap stall just off Granville. There's no line-up at the bar, and we meet up with some guys from our team. I get fucked up quickly on whisky purchased by our affable goalie Glen, who happens to be a rich chiropractor, or so he maintains. The pulse of the music is almost as intoxicating as the liquor. The rumble and eruption of conversation pulls you in. You go deaf and then, quite miraculously, begin to hear everything. The booze tastes better, the women look better, and your buddies are closer to you than they've ever been.

While outside having a smoke I meet some chick and we show each other our tattoos. I go back inside and have a look for something better, but can't find anything, so decide to settle for her. She buys me a bunch of candy-flavoured shots, and I make her do a tequila or two. Then I make sure her drink is full and that she keeps drinking all night, because I'm planning on having my way with her.

At some point I proceed to lie to her about everything— myself, her appearance, my overarching ambitions in life—so much so in fact I'm having trouble keeping up with them all after a while. I'm not sure if I'm currently taking engineering at UBC, or if I just started playing for the Burnaby Bulldogs. I lose Cancer at about one o'clock, and before I know it I've fended off the chick's overly protective fat friend and made it back to her house where we playfully wrestle on the bed, then make out, at which point she gives me head and I immediately pass out. Most of the time I have trouble sleeping beside women, but not this time, and before I know it it's eight o'clock and I'm wide awake and needing to get the fuck out of here before she wakes up. I can't even remember her name.

In the bathroom I realize just how hungover I am. And in the shower, on a whim, I hold the shampoo bottle to the tip of my penis, patiently allowing a squirt of urine to enter, then another, until the bottle finally foams over. Success. I replace the cap and proceed to the conditioners, repeating the feat meticulously. When I finally return to the room, she's still passed out, partially covered in her pink bedspread. I take a quick glance at her exposed breast, ponder fondling it, and then get dressed as quickly and quietly as possible. I collect some change from her dresser, just enough for a cigar and Slurpee, then leave the room and creep downstairs to a congested student-like living room littered with posters of bands I've never heard of, let alone listened to. There's a murky neglected fish tank in the corner, and it's there, while staring into the abyss, I'm confronted by her roommate, all two hundred-plus pounds of her. Our eyes meet over the tank as she sits there at the kitchen table, smoking. "Where you off to?" she inquires with a hoarse voice.

"Out to get a pill."

"Pill? You didn't use protection?" she asks, seemingly intrigued at the prospect, which scares me.

"Nope, no protection. She insisted I cum inside her for some reason."

I open the front door and walk to my car. Once the engine
is warm I shift into gear, glance over at the roommate running
across the lawn yelling profanities at me, and drive calmly away.
I catch a glimpse of the girl I just spent the night with standing in the upstairs window waving at me, bedspread wrapped
around her like a giant pink cloak. Then I drive faster, looking
for Grouse Mountain or any sign of water, trying to get my
bearings here. Eventually I realize I'm not far from Cancer's
girlfriend's house, which is where I think I heard him say he
might end up if nothing else panned out. I stop at 7–Eleven
where I purchase a Pepsi Slurpee and a Blackstone Cherry
cigar with my recently stolen funds, and ask the cashier for
some matches. They don't have any matches. They never do,
the bastards. Back in the car I search for matches, and stumble
upon a lighter instead. I light the Cherry and blow smoke all
over the interior of the car. Then I pull out my cell phone and
scroll down to Cancer. I call five times before he finally
answers.

"Hello?"

"Yo," I say, taking a drag off my cigar.

"Yo."

"What's up?"

"Fuck, man, I'm at Samantha's."

"You okay?"

"I don't think so. I'm on the fuckin' couch. Bitch."

"How come?" I ask.

"You tell me."

I take another drag, and slowly remove my white tie. I've
got to get a new tie.

"So come and get me," he says.

"I'll be there in like ten."

"Pick up a Blackstone—"

I hang up before he can finish, and by the time I arrive at
Samantha's house I'm officially wide awake and completely

hungover. My lips are dry, I have a soft steady headache, and I feel like shit. The Slurpee, however, feels good, and when I get to Samantha's I call Cancer again. He answers from the front deck as he's putting on his blazer and wrapping his black tie around his neck. Both his shoes are in one hand. I hang up when he reaches the car, whereupon I catch a glimpse of Samantha standing in the window. I finger her, smile, and glare into her eyes, and she calmly returns the favour.

"Morning, sunshine," Cancer says as he loads himself into the car, plucking the Cherry from my mouth. He takes a drag and huffs a cloud of smoke towards the windshield.

"So why'd you sleep on the couch?" I ask.

"Don't ask me. She was going on about you when we got back. Something about you sleeping with her cousin and not calling her after."

"Oh yeah. What else she say about me."

"Oh, the usual. Bad influence and shit like that." He mimics a mouth flapping open and closed with his hand.

"And you said?"

"I said she was right. You're a cocksucker," he says, and we both laugh.

I hand him the Slurpee. He takes a large pull, licks his lips and holds the dashboard as we pull a tight corner onto the highway.

"Fuck I'm hungover," he says. Then he stops, looks at me, and turns around and slips his hand under the seat, pulling out three cans of Budweiser. "Still cold," he says, pulling off two and handing one to me. "Cheers, you cocksucker."

We both laugh and chat about the night a while, and then Cancer drifts off into space, his head resting against the dashboard. We drink and drive and smoke in silence. Finally he snorts and turns to me. "So what do you want to do tonight?"

I make my way to the edge of the dance floor, positioning myself between two muscle-bound East Indian guys reeking of CK One. The lighting in this club is terrible, and the music is far too loud, but the women here are usually worth the annoyance and besides, everywhere else had a line-up. I find Cancer resting on a stool with Caleb, Ryan and Chris staggered off to his left, chatting up a group of girls. Cancer glances over at me, a big smirk crawling across his face. I sit down beside him, and he leans into my ear and yells through whisky breath, "Look to your far left on the edge of the dance floor. Past the pillar."

I lean over and scan the crowd. Two girls catch my eye, the same ones we met earlier at a Petro-Can in Kitsilano. We told them to meet us here. The one is wrapped in tight faded jeans and a baby blue spaghetti strap top. Her face isn't her best feature, but she's clean and cute, so she'll definitely do. The other one is slightly larger, like a plus-size model carrying a few extra pounds under her girdle.

"Which one do you want?" he yells, his face too close to mine. Whatever whisky it is, it's cheap that's for sure, which comes as no surprise.

"Let's not get ahead of ourselves," I say, sitting back down on my stool.

Cancer peeks back beyond the pillar and returns with another smile. I realize this isn't a sure thing yet, but then again I'm not really drunk enough yet either.

"Let's go do some shots, strategize, then go dance with them," I suggest.

"Kay," he says. He stands up, flicks my nuts with his fingers, then starts walking towards the bar. I tend to my injury a few seconds, looking constipated and pain-stricken, before eventually following along as nonchalantly as possible.

Sometime later we dance with the girls. I get the thinner one. We have drinks and hang out with Caleb, Ryan and Chris, all three of which are too drunk to speak. Ryan can barely stand up, let alone prop up the chick clinging to his belt. A guy I met ages ago remembers me from some long forgotten house party. He's got a face full of acne and a platinum chain around his neck. He stands about five-foot-six. He wants to know where I got my "macking skills." He wants to know the "secret to the great unknown, the key to the pussy." I tell him I'm sorry, but most of it's just looks, which is at least partially true. He seems momentarily shaken by this statement, but still buys me a couple of beers in exchange for the insight. So then I proceed to tell him how I've slept with more women than he's probably seen in his life, having spent some time backpacking around the world learning all the tricks of the trade—Cairo, Ibiza, Europe—yeah, suddenly I'm a jetsetter compared to this guy.

We eventually end up back at the girls' place, who happen to live with some dude who wakes up and seriously weirds us out with his pale complexion and shifty eyes. He's half something, and all creepy, and obviously a basehead to be avoided at all costs. Either way, Cancer gets laid and I get the couch, as the girl I was after doesn't feel right about sleeping with me on the first night. She gives me her number and email and says we should go on a date next week. Yeah, right. After she goes to bed I try to crawl in with her and orchestrate a few cheap feels, at which point I get tossed out again like a bad dog. I crumple up the note with her number on it and stomp on her cell phone while I'm outside having a smoke. Then I doze off on the couch. Eventually Cancer wakes me up. He wants to go, so we go, heading to Denny's for the token late night dine-and-dash. Then we head home to bed, as we have a hockey game in a few hours and desperately need the sleep to be at all effective.

In my room, a small stack of photographs sits on my dresser, partially buried by paper. I pull them out carefully, so as not to disrupt the intricate pile I've carelessly created here. The film is still slightly sticky on the photos and most of them are stuck together. I see a picture of myself and Sarah, me nestled in behind her. I turn the picture over to read the words written diagonally in fine black marker:

I'm at a loss for words with you. You are the most important thing I've ever come in contact with. I'm in love with you.

Sarah

Memoirs from the Gutter

This strange bar I'm in has wooden floors and long rectangular windows. It's dark outside and I don't recognize anyone. Dark figures drift in and out of my peripheral vision. Then one of my cousins comes out of nowhere and asks me if I want to order some pizza. Weird. I tell him I'm allergic to tomatoes. Then a cell phone rings and everyone in the bar stops and stares at me. I am instantly frightened and awake not knowing where I am.

I sit up in bed and look over at my cell phone blinking and ringing on the nightstand. "Hello," I say, my voice hoarse and my eyes half shut.

"Hey, Seth."

"Dad. Hey. How's it going?" I ask.

"Good, how are you?"

"Good."

"Were you sleeping?"

"Um, yeah."

"It's two o'clock in the afternoon. . . . Have a late night last night?"

I don't answer.

"Sleeping in till two o'clock in the afternoon, Seth. Very productive," he goes on.

"Fuck, Dad. I'm really not in the mood for this."

I stand up and throw some jeans on.

"You never seem to be in the mood for something like this."

"Yeah, well, can you blame me?"

I hear him sigh. "You're really good at avoiding these things now," he says, and a long silence ensues.

"What things, Dad?" I finally ask, despite myself.

"Last time I phoned you I wanted to talk about your finances and you said it wasn't a good time. So is it a good time now?"

"Sure. Go for it. Let's talk cash."

"First of all, your employment insurance is going to run out in a few months and you seem to have no job leads whatsoever."

"Actually, I told you I had a *lot* of job leads, and I explained them to you the last time we talked."

This is bullshit of course, but I throw it at him anyways. I really don't care whether he believes me or not.

"So do you have a job?"

"No, I don't have a job."

"So you could just be lying to me. How am I supposed to know differently?"

"Well I guess you're just going to have to trust me, Dad."

"What about college?" he asks. "Wasn't that the reason you went up north to work?"

Silence.

"Wasn't that the reason you went up north to work, Seth?"

"You want me to answer that, really?"

"Yes, I do."

"Yes, that's the reason I went up north to work. I went up north to work to pay for college, Dad."

"And now you've decided *not* to go back to college, is what it seems like. Is that right?"

"Yeah, sure. Whatever you say."

"And now it's been well over a year, and what have you accomplished since you went on employment insurance?"

"Nothing, Dad. Is that what you want me to say?"

"Well I'd sure like to think otherwise."

"Yeah, well, it's not easy when, as soon as you get back, you get into a fucking car accident. And your girlfriend—"

"Seth, people tend to use situations like these as crutches, and then simply hobble along on them the rest of their lives. They blame everything that happens afterwards on this single event that happened long ago, having convinced themselves of that fallacy somewhere along the line."

I pause. "Well that's a penetrating insight, Dad."

He sighs. "You went through a very tragic thing," he says, "and your mother and I both supported you and paid your bills for as long as we could manage. And then we said it was time you moved on, and yet you've simply continued on with the exact same lifestyle that landed you in this mess in the first place. No job, living off money lent to you by your friends, borrowing money off your parents in hectic spurts whenever your friends fall short—it's pathetic."

"Dad."

"I'm serious. What did you spend close to fifteen hundred dollars on—in six days—a few weeks ago?"

"I told you, I went to a hockey tournament in Seattle."

"And you spent fifteen hundred at one hockey tournament?"

I don't answer.

"How do you spend fifteen hundred at one hockey tournament, Seth? What happens if I'm not willing to lend you the money to carry you through to your next employment insurance cheque?"

"I dunno."

"How will you pay for rent?"

"I dunno."

"How will you pay for food and gas? Do you think Cancer will lend you the money for food and gas? Do you think your landlord will let you not pay rent?"

"No."

"Well where does that money come from then?"

"It comes from you, Dad. I know that."

"No, I don't think you know that. Because you say that, but then I get these calls demanding I lend you more money because, once again, something crucial has come up."

"Yeah, well, I dunno."

"I dunno is right. You haven't a clue, do you?"

"No clue, Dad. Clueless."

"How much money have you borrowed from me in the past six months?"

"Don't know, Dad. How much?"

"You tell me. You should know this."

"Kay, I'm done."

"You're done?"

"Yeah, I'm done."

"Soon you won't even have any income coming in. What are you going to do then, Seth?"

"Join the circus, kill myself, sell my organs for money, get a job—the options are literally endless."

"Get a job. That would be a good idea, don't you think?"

"Okay, Dad, I'll talk to you later," I say, hitting the end button and turning my cell phone off.

I'm so tired of my father, and of my mother, and of their weary world of money. Every argument my parents ever engaged in seemed to stem from money. Everything revolved around money. Vacations, food, entertainment, sports. Anything I wanted or wanted to do had to take money from something else. Someone had to lose something for another member of the family to gain something else. Everything was fucked up because we never had enough money. We never had enough of the one thing that makes life easier and uglier at the same time. I'm sure money was the actually reason they got divorced, or at least a primary factor.

My parents will never heal. They are completely beyond repair. They've argued and yelled and screamed at each other so much their throats are permanently sore. You can hear it when they speak. They're too tired of life to care anymore, but not desperate enough to bring about the appropriate drastic change so urgently required. They've fucked themselves over, and they'll never know why because they can't listen to anyone or anything other than their own diluted complaints about the world.

Still, I gotta get a job.

Sometime during our next night out, lost between bars, Cancer takes a disliking to a Vancouver cop with a French accent. It's best not to mess with Vancouver cops. Many a time I've driven through the East End and watched them beat some junkie senseless in broad daylight. Either way, Cancer and his francophone-hating ways manage to piss this policeman right off, and he smacks the 99 cent pizza out of Cancer's hands. As I and the cop's partner do our best to calm these two would-be combatants down, parts of the pizza somehow end up on the French cop's face.

I end up catching most of the ensuing pepper spray, and then the two of us are carted off to the drunk tank where we are recorded, lectured, strip-searched and placed in a holding cell for the night.

And that's where the silence kicks in. And then it's just you and your thoughts. You begin to think way too much in a place like this. You think about everything you've ever done wrong. You remember all the times you've lied to your parents. You try to remember all the good times you've had, but somehow always end up back at the bad ones. You never really remember the times you wronged someone and got away clean. You only remember the times you messed up and got caught.

"How about this one?" I say at one point while sitting on the floor. " 'There is no knowledge that is not power.' "

"Mortal Kombat?" says Cancer.

"Correct. When you turn the game on, that's the first thing that hits the screen."

"Yeah, I remember. For Super Nintendo."

"For Super Nintendo, yes. So?" I ask.

"Well what about all the information that's useless. Like, say, how much an average apple weighs in milligrams."

I ponder this a moment.

"Okay, let's say that's a question on your SAT."

"That would never be on an SAT, fag."

"You never know, that's the point."

"How's that power anyways?"

"Higher SAT score equals better prospects, better job, better life and whatnot."

Cancer spits on the floor, then coughs.

"Kay, I've got one," he says. " 'What goes around comes around.' "

I shake my head.

"Why not?" he asks.

"Just because you do something bad doesn't increase your chances next time around. There's no such thing as luck."

"Of course there is. What about that fucker that won the lottery twice?"

"It's still just odds. Luck doesn't exist, think about it. No matter how many times you roll the dice, the odds, regardless, are always one in six."

This conversation has taxed Cancer's already overly taxed brain. He leans forward, head between his knees, and sighs tremendously. I lean my head back against the concrete wall. It's uncomfortable, but it allows my neck to rest. My spine has become compressed, my tailbone moaning a dull ache.

The walls in here are a benign beige. The toilet is stainless steel. I look over at Cancer, who's now resting his face in his hands, obviously still stinging from the pepper spray, much like myself. He seems more tired than drunk. I think I am too. But the only way to fall asleep in a room like this is to pass out, and we're both not drunk enough for that oddly enough.

The bruise on my left shoulder blade is no more than a mundane sensation now, a quiet reminder of where I am. Room temperature is slightly below normal, which may or may not be on purpose. I would commit actual murder for a blanket and pillow. It's interesting how something so trivial and practical could make all the difference in the world, could make such a depressing situation bearable.

Every time I end up here in the drunk tank I make the same proclamations. "This is it," I say. "No more. I've hit rock bottom, and I don't like rock bottom, so I'm not gonna carry on with this rock bottom lifestyle no more." Shit like that. Yet for some reason—perhaps the company I keep—I know this probably won't be my last time here at the hop hotel.

"What time do you think it is?" asks Cancer.

I just shake my head. This feeling of being oblivious to time is quite frightening when you're actually confronted with it. I'm both scared and disturbed—it could be any time in an eight hour period, I have no idea. They could let us die in here. There is no way we could possibly escape. We could bang and scream and yell for days, and it would make no difference.

"I'm so fucking hungry," says Cancer to his feet.

We're approaching the final hours of our incarceration. Most of the drunks have departed, or else their voices have run dry. Either way, my body is telling me I need sleep—now, preferably, or else it might shut down. Waiting in here is like waiting for a bus. You never really have anything to help pass the time, so you just let your mind wander out there amongst the traffic. Then your mind starts to get tired and you find yourself playing games. You start to pace around like a caged tiger, knowing the cameras catch everything you do. You mimic some Bruce Lee chops and high kicks a few times knowing someone, somewhere, might be watching. You take a piss by standing and facing backwards on the toilet, anything to occupy your mind. If you're alone it's worse, though a companion isn't often much help. Neither of you have the power to make time speed up, or make this misadventure more bearable. Conversations become sparse and disjointed. The more you dry out, the less verbal exchange becomes helpful, or even rational. Your mind is at its worst. It begins to rot. You're too tired to think, and your thoughts become irrational, almost non-sequential. Gibberish. The fact you've been forced to look at the same beige walls for the last eight hours doesn't help either. There's no stimulus for your senses—your brain has been placed in a coffin, and now it's simply waiting for burial—and you truly feel lost. Then the depression sets in, like a slow gas leak from under the door. You're no longer drunk but hungover. Going through this transition while awake is something I'd wish on no one, not even Cancer.

I remember back when I was sixteen, and got so drunk on cheap red wine the cop had to drag me by the arms into the back of his patrol car. I remember my father showing up, and the ensuing blank look on his face. I remember the clammy taste of bad wine in my mouth, the hangover, and the throwing up in the kitchen while being lectured by both parents. That was one of the worst, by far. But there were other times of course.

The second time he showed up, I wasn't as drunk. I'm sure the cops just threw me in because I was so disrespectful, and rightfully so. It took my father a little longer to show up too, disappointment now replaced by frustration.

The third time, I watched and waited by the door only to realize he wasn't coming. The bastard had gotten up and answered the phone in the dark, and then decided that was enough, and gone back to bed in a huff. That was far more difficult then the first two times, I remember, because I knew what he must be thinking. I knew sooner or later I would have to return to his home, to his lecture, and to his anger, and that frightened the hell out of me.

The only good thing about my present predicament is I'm of age. They let you take the full ride when you turn nineteen. So at least I don't have to drag my father into this tonight. At least this time the poor bastard will get a good night's sleep in, if nothing else.

There's always some foolish fuck who gets thrown in around dusk. He thinks if he yells and swears loud enough, and long enough, they'll let him out. This guy always has some weird excuse too as to why he should be let out. Usually it's so elaborate you can't help but smile. This morning he needs to be let out because his golden retriever was grazed by an errant bullet off Hastings during a drive-by. Well of course it was. But then all he gets for his trouble is a jail full of deaf ears and the occasional "Shut the fuck up or I'll kill you" courtesy of Cancer.

The only thing to do now is to stare—at the wall, the roof, the socks of the guy next to you. Your eyes become fixated on the simplest of things—your fingernails, a crack in the wall, a drop of water by the toilet. You study the object, examining it to unfathomable depths. You wonder how drops of water stay round, retaining their shape.

"What do you want to do today?" I ask instead.

"Well, I'm gonna sleep till like four or five," Cancer answers, now lying in the prone position with eyes closed.

"You wanna get a movie maybe?"

"Maybe."

"Cool. I kind of want to see *The Thin Red Line* again."

"Seen it."

"I realize that. But do you want to see it again?"

"Naw. I don't like watching a movie more than once unless it's really good."

"So *The Thin Red Line*'s not a good movie?"

"No, I didn't say that. I said it's not worth watching again."

"And what movie would be worth watching again, Cancer."

"A really *good* movie," he says.

The morning shift has arrived, and they've let most of the drinkers free. The anxiousness animates your body, and you pray every time you hear footsteps they're for you, for your cell, and they're going to set you free.

You wait. And then you wait some more.

And then it happens, usually taking you by surprise. After you've given up all hope, hunched there like some piece of rotten un-refrigerated fruit, the door rolls open, and the world that seemed so distant three seconds ago is suddenly back, slapping you in the face.

We both stand up, and the officer takes us one by one to collect our shoes, our wallets, our necklaces and everything else taken from us when we first checked in. Avoiding eye contact right now is a key component of liberation. Just get your shit and get out—don't talk, and respond to questions only when absolutely necessary.

One of the desk clerks recognizes me, long after I've figured out who he is. He says he remembers coaching me in basketball in elementary school, which is correct unfortunately. I want to slap him, but I just grin and say I don't remember. Each of his words is delaying the contact of my head with my pillow, and it pisses me off.

"I really don't remember," I tell him, even though I do remember him, his name, and the fact he gave me a ride home from practice one time.

"You were a good little player back then. You still play?"

"No, I don't play."

The clerk smiles, routinely examining my file. "So you had a little too much to drink last night, did you."

"I don't drink," I reply.

He smiles again. "I see."

When you finally get outside you realize it's light out, which strikes you as something of an epiphany. People are heading off to work, filing into Starbucks for lattés and low fat muffins, and the only thing you want to do is get inside a dark room and sleep your life away. It feels like midnight but it's actually a lot closer to noon.

Cancer and I begin the long march back to our apartment. We're too broke to pay for a cab, and the walk is tough on the body. The legs don't function properly and the knees are constantly sore. You walk with a one-track mind—bed, bed, bed, bed, bed. Conversation is sparse at best, and you walk in stoic silence most of the time.

Eventually we arrive home, and climb the two sets of stairs to our apartment. Cancer drops his keys at the door.

"You cunt." I say, and open the door with my own.

We walk in, slipping off our shoes on our way to our rooms, ignoring the pigsty that is our home. I close the door to my room, emptying my pockets straight onto the floor. Loose bar change flies everywhere, twoonies and loonies and quarters. I throw my wallet in the direction of the dresser and then collapse like a felled tree onto my bed. Muscles begin to relax for the first time in over eight hours, screaming with relief. The quiet ecstasy I'm feeling right now almost makes it all seem worthwhile. Almost. And then like a snap of the fingers, I'm out.

I have this dream where I can't get back into high school to finish an exam I never completed. I walk around the school grounds and find there's a graveyard where the field used to be. I meet one of my old English teachers. He tells me to call a number from a payphone to get into the school. I walk through the graveyard and end up getting lost. Then the dream ends and I wake up.

I get up sometime in the late afternoon, perplexed as usual, and make my way to the kitchen feeling somewhat refreshed, despite the circumstances. The smell of day-old Bull's Eye steak sauce and cigars is looming like a cloud. So are the fruit flies. I open the cabinet above the fridge, pull out a Chocolate-flavoured instant breakfast, mix the powder in a glass of milk, and stir it up with a spoon. Then I take one forty of Celexa, one Ativan, two multivitamin pills (one an Omega-3 fatty acid), two extra strength acetaminophens and a Claritin. I down the concoction in a few quick gulps, then peel a banana and stuff it in my mouth. Then I drink a glass of water, gag slightly, taste the banana coming back up for daylight, and hit the sack once more.

When I awake again, Cancer, Caleb, Ryan and Chris are playing GoldenEye on our N64. It's six o'clock. Chris greets me in the kitchen after the latest game finishes in a barrage of yelling, screaming and a slap to Caleb's face courtesy of Cancer.

I can hear them arguing now, Caleb and Cancer. "Fuck off, I'm Odd Job this time. One-on-one with you, faggot," says Caleb.

"Fuck you. You can't be Odd Job," barks Cancer.

"It's the only way anyone can beat you, you fucking cunt."

"Wah, wah. Don't be jealous because I play like Jesus. How many times do I have to tell you guys, no fuckin' Odd Job in my fuckin' house."

"The only reason you play like Jesus is because you play this fuckin' game all the time."

"Not all the time," says Cancer in a calm and suggestive voice.

Caleb looks at him.

"For instance, sometimes I'm fucking your sister," he goes on.

"Motherfucker!" Caleb screams, at which point I hear the contents of the coffee table spill onto the floor. It's well known that Cancer made out with Caleb's sister one night at a UBC dorm party a few months ago. All is well now, though Caleb is still a bit touchy on the subject, and rightly so. Cancer is a leg-splitting womanizer and Caleb's sister is nothing if not a nice girl.

"What's up, buddy," says Chris, inspecting me. I'm still dressed in my clothes from the night before, and my hair is an absolute mess. "Heard you spent the night in the tank."

"You heard right."

"How many times is that now?"

"Six, I think. Maybe seven. Eight."

"Fuck."

"Yeah, this one was tough because I wasn't even that drunk."

Chris opens the fridge and passes me a beer. I mess around in the kitchen a while, cleaning up and organizing what little we have. Then I get tired of cleaning and wander back into the living room where another heated game of GoldenEye has started. Cancer truly does love this game, and plays it incessantly. He barely graduated from high school on account of his obsession with it, but he's virtually unbeatable at it, so it all worked out in the end.

I watch them play a while, then head back into the kitchen for another beer. When I return, they're all standing there in the middle of the room, the game over and all the controllers down. Cancer and Caleb are talking about chugging a bottle of whisky. Apparently Caleb did it last New Year's Eve in Whistler at some timeshare party nobody else we knew attended. It's quite obviously a lie, but Caleb seems quite willing to do it again, right here, right now, to shut us all up.

"I'll fuckin' do it, you cunts," he blasts. "Don't push me."

Caleb stands there in the living room with the small bottle of whisky. He unscrews the top and raises his hands in the air like he's leading a prayer meeting. A moment of quiet respect befalls the crowd. But then Ryan flicks him in the nuts and he collapses immediately to the ground. We all laugh as he gets up with an impish grin on his face.

"Okay, Ryan, how about this," he says. "If I can chug this whole bottle, you have to drink a shot of my urine."

Ryan looks puzzled. "Okay," he eventually responds, "what are the rules?"

"Rules?"

"Well, for instance, are you required to hold this whisky in for a certain amount of time?"

"Nope, all I have to do is drink the whole thing in one go, and then open my mouth to prove I've swallowed it."

"Deal," says Ryan.

"Urine versus whisky," I say. "How epic."

"This is for you, you fucking albino," says Caleb, pointing at Ryan. And with that he raises the bottle to his lips, clears his throat, and takes three long deep breaths. He looks extremely calm. Almost Zen-like. He stands completely still, breathing slightly through his nose, and flicks the bottle up. We start to cheer. He's pounding it down in big long gulps, each terrible swallow bringing him closer to dubious victory.

He reaches the three-quarter mark, and seems to stall. He hiccups, and we all cheer a little louder. Then it comes up, all the whisky and a stomach's worth of vomit, splashing out onto the carpet. We're sent reeling back by the spray, the puke flying everywhere. Enormous laughter erupts.

Caleb bends over, continuing to vomit. He bolts to the bathroom and just manages to get the second rush of puke into the toilet. We all follow along eagerly. Ryan is laughing so hard it's almost deafening. Cancer is on his knees in tears. Caleb tries to reprimand us but ends up throwing up once more, this time all over the toilet seat.

"Motherfuckers," he manages to yell as he comes back up for air. He steadies himself on his knees, looking like he might actually be done.

"How you feeling?" asks Chris.

Caleb turns to reply, but before the words can form he burps, then turns and barfs again with authority into the toilet.

Drifter's Loss

Cancer pushes his way to the center of the crowd. I follow along with one hand on his shoulder, one hand holding both our beers like a club. The wide alleyway reeks of cigarette smoke, testosterone and stagnant cologne, and all you can hear is the constant ringing of cell phones. The crowd is growing anxious, lusting for something—anything—to happen, and they won't be disappointed. Cancer makes his way to the middle and confronts the instigator, some buff Indo-Canadian dude dressed far too young for his years. The guy instantly looks intimidated. I hand Cancer his beer and without hesitation he gives the bottle one swift controlled yet violent shake. The beer squirts all over the East Indian guy's face and the crowd pushes in eagerly, their wish granted at last.

Cancer wastes no time getting the guy to the ground, forcing him to turtle as Cancer rains fists down upon his skull. The sound makes you clench your teeth, because you know what it feels like to be on the receiving end of one of those things. The guy tries to stagger up, his friends try to intervene, but the majority of the crowd is against them, and the lopsided fight continues. I see flashes of blood pooling on the pavement and cringe.

Cancer now has the guy pressed against the side of a black car with tinted windows. The overhead streetlights give everything a pale amber glow as he slams the guy into the window again and again, breaking the side view mirror. The guy struggles to block Cancer's punches with his forearms, but it's no use. His white shirt is ripped in countless places, and his face is bleeding from various points. Scuffed with asphalt and dirt and God knows what else, he's no match for this behemoth he's faced with. The owner of the car tries to get involved, but no one listens to him, and for his troubles he gets knocked aside by someone's fist. I take a long pull from my beer and push some other guy, but he shrugs me off. So then I make my way over to Cancer, who now has the guy in some strange headlock, both of them squirming to retain positions on the asphalt.

"Yo, Cancer. Yo. That's enough."

I wrap my arms around his shoulders, but he gets an arm free and starts pounding the guy's face again, whipping the crowd into a frenzy once more. The sound of fist on cheek, then on bone, then on cracked cartilage of the nose makes me want to scream out loud. One of the shots seems to finally stun the guy, and he goes limp. Cancer tries to finish him off, but I pull him off with one giant thrust. The guy is out cold. He'll tell his friends the next day he's never been hit that hard in his life, and he's right.

I pass Cancer my beer as we back away from the scene, hoping to avoid the police who must surely be on their way.

"Thanks," he says, taking a good long pull, wiping the blood from his knuckles onto his pants. "Fucking pussy fights like a figure skater," he growls.

We make our way to a 7-Eleven a few blocks down from the strip, this one frequented primarily by junkies and fags. Cancer is talking a mile a minute, still pumped full of adrenaline. No one even seems to notice the blood on him. We're not the weirdest thing these people have seen. Cancer cleans up in the bathroom while I flip through issues of *GQ*, *Rolling Stone* and *Cosmopolitan*. He comes out looking somewhat refreshed, but he still has that look on his face, not to mention someone else's blood on his skin.

We decide it's time to head back to Caleb's house. We contemplate running on the cab, but our driver turns out to be a young black dude who looks like Tiger Woods and boasts that he's a long-distance runner. So we just pay instead.

Perched on the porch outside the back of the house, Caleb is rolling a joint under the light while I sit admiring his work in a dilapidated lawn chair. Cancer is back inside, licking his wounds. He broke a few fingers, and will need to go to the hospital at some point. Bets have been placed as to how many splints he'll be wearing this time tomorrow. Caleb is dressed in his usual striped golf shirt, tapered jeans and gelled mess of hair. He's just had an argument with Cancer which escalated to the point of separation. Meanwhile, Ryan and Chris are inside with a small group of people collected over a long night of club-hopping. It's crunch time, and the guys are jockeying for position, trying to see who will get laid in the two open bedrooms. It's quite a sight to behold.

Hours have passed and it's become an early morning instead of a very late night. I've been drunk now for close to seven hours, and the intoxication has left me in a state of utter stupor. My body has assimilated an astonishing amount of alcohol, with which it's now operating is some strange symbiotic fashion. I'm also extremely tired, hibernating awake on the porch with some vodka and a Blackstone Cherry cigar, waiting for a sign to call it a night and throw in the towel.

Caleb has now finished rolling his joint. He knows I don't smoke pot, but offers me some anyway. I turn it down, nursing my cocktail instead. I will, however, have another cigar while he smokes himself into oblivion.

I watch as he smokes and talks, inhaling what must be an almost insurmountable amount of weed. "Its funny, man. I bumped into Amy tonight at the Canucks game," he says, referring to his ex-girlfriend. He blows smoke up towards the light. "And then like two hours later, I bump into Erin at that pizza place just off Granville by the bridge."

"No way."

"Yeah, but you know what the really fucked up thing is? I mean it's been blowing my mind all night." He pauses, smiles, and looks over at me nestled in my lawn chair, sipping my vodka. "The fucked up thing is, and I mean fucked up, is that the first time I met Erin was at a Canucks game, and the first time I met Amy was at that same fuckin' pizza joint."

"Whoa."

"Exactly. It's like someone's trying to tell me something, but I have no goddamned clue why or what they're trying to say."

"Either that or God's just fuckin' with you," I say.

"Yeah, I mean it's just a goddamn coincidence. But at the same time, what are the fuckin' odds, hey."

"I dunno, man, it's shaky. I think we like to see coincidences in life in order to make ourselves feel special. To give our lives meaning. I mean there are thousands of coincidences that go by every day unnoticed."

"No, yeah, I totally agree. But it's different when it happens to you. It's like last year when my brother had his car broken into. I mean the fuckers pretty much ripped his dashboard apart getting the CD player out, and stole a whole bunch of his burned CDs which are pretty much useless to anyone else. And they also stole his registration and insurance papers, like just random shit that has no value to anyone."

"Fuck."

"Yeah. And I remember he moped around the house for like days because his deductible didn't do shit for him, and I felt for him, but then again I didn't really feel for him, you know?" He pauses. "Anyway, a couple of months later what happens, *my* car gets ripped apart. And you now what? I knew exactly how he felt."

"No doubt."

"I mean did you ever hear that story about that major who used to live in Vancouver?"

I shake my head. Caleb takes another large pull from the joint.

"It's fucking nuts, man. Completely true story. My Grandpa told me, and I checked it out online because I thought for sure he was lying, but then sure enough there it was."

"So what's the story?"

"Kay, there's this British army guy named Major Summerland or something—can't remember his first name but he was a major—and when he was fighting in Flanders during the war he was struck by lightning and paralyzed from the waist down."

"Ouch."

"Yeah, so he moved to Vancouver after the war, I think the first one, and he was out fishing by a river when lightning struck a tree beside him. Tree falls on him and paralyzes his whole right side."

"Jesus Christ."

"Yeah, but it gets better. So like a few years later he's out for a walk, he's recovered from his injuries and all that, and the poor bastard is hit *directly* by lightning, paralyzing him permanently."

I look over at Caleb as he smiles, blowing smoke out his nose. I shake my head in bona fide astonishment.

"And then, to top it all off, the guy dies a few years later and is buried in that cemetery over by Boundary, and lightning strikes and destroys his tombstone."

"No fuckin' way."

"Yeah, I mean if that's not divine intervention or whatever, then what is? The guy must've been a raging pedophile in a previous life or something."

"Or he just got struck by lightning a bunch of times."

"Yeah, it's all in how you look at it, I guess. . . . I mean what the fuck though, hey."

A short silence ensues as Caleb relights his joint. He's stoned now, I can tell. It's time to head back inside and convince Cancer we should catch a cab or start walking home. Caleb leans back as I pass him on my way to the door. He blows smoke straight up, then coughs, then coughs again. Then he bends over, spits, and coughs once more.

"You want anything?" I ask. "Glass of water perhaps?"

"Naw, I'm good," he tells me with a yawn.

Hours later, having returned home, I stagger out the front door pulling my pants up and dragging my flip-flops on as I go. I walk down the pathway to the front lawn, feeling the morning dew between my toes. A dusty black Chevy truck is parked diagonally across the grass. I make my way to the driver's side to find Ryan hunched awkwardly against the window. I cock my hand back and slap the window right by his face as hard as I can. He bolts awake, shrieking. He looks at me, still half asleep, turns the ignition on which starts blasting *A Tribe Called Quest* and rolls down the window, seemingly almost in protest. Then he turns the CD player off and looks at me, half stunned, half asleep, and completely confused.

"Seth, what's up?" he says. He opens his eyes fully, then blinks and squints a few times. Then he notices he has a bottle of Jose Cuervo tequila right beside him. He snatches it up and proceeds to take a good long pull.

"You parked your truck on our lawn," I tell him.

He scans forward over the dashboard. "Shit, sorry, dude."

"No worries," I say, reaching for the tequila and taking a drink. The warm sting tastes like liquid rust and gives me the shivers all the way down.

"You wanna come in and crash?" I ask.

"Yeah, sure. Got any perogies?"

I nod.

"Well shit," he says, scrambling free of the truck. He stands there on the lawn a moment, his hair a messy heap of dirty blonde. Then he wraps his arms around me in a big bear hug. "Seth, did I ever tell you you're a really great guy."

I smile. "No."

"Well you are. I like you."

I put my arm around his shoulder and lead him towards the apartment.

"Thanks, man. Just go chill. I'll move your truck in a while."

Ryan and I start to walk, then he stops. "Fuck that," he says, "I'll move it. You can't drive stick, and I don't want you grinding my gears to shit."

And with that he turns around, leaving me alone on the lawn.

Seth & the Rhinoceros

Somehow, finally, I've talked Cancer into washing his jersey. The guy can be way too superstitious sometimes. He got cut just below the chin a few games back by a deflected puck, and bled all over his jersey as a result. But then, for some inexplicable reason, he proceeded to score a natural hat-trick.

Now I'm not one for superstition, but for Cancer, well, the blood stays until the run of good luck is done. Problem is, after about three or four games, the thing has really started to smell. In fact it smells so bad it stinks up the entire dressing room. Good luck or not, the guys want it burned.

Eventually, though, he was talked into washing it, and so we headed out to pick up our freshly sharpened skates, eyes still burning from the bleach that spread about the apartment.

Upon our return, we spend a good half hour packing up our stuff. We tidy up the apartment a bit too, so that when we come back from the tournament all sore, tired and depleted of essential fluids and vitamins, we won't have to walk into a stinky, dirty house. It's the most foresight we've exhibited in weeks, and are justifiably proud of our accomplishments.

Our team has been waiting for this tournament all year, the pre-Christmas Senior Men's tournament in Kamloops. It's the best of the best in terms of hockey, booze and escapades, and it's where all the guys who weren't good enough for the show—the best of the rest—end up battling for their version of the Stanley Cup. And this is where I am, pissing away my days, looking for some type of redemption I know will never come.

I pack my toiletries, my collection of prescription medications, some Extra Strength Non-Drowsy Claritin and the half bottles of ephedrine and methamphetamine I have left. We pack a cooler with ice for the four-hour drive, then stuff it with a twelve-pack of beer, probably close to a litre of vodka, a dozen Red Bulls and some bananas for colour. When we hit the highway the air is warm enough to keep the windows cracked, and by the time we pass the exit signs for Chilliwack the two of us have already gone through most of the beer and two or three Blackstone Cherry cigars. Most of the time has been spent in silence, something Cancer and I are entirely comfortable with. We can go hours in a car without speaking. It's just that comfort level you attain when you spend entirely too much time with someone.

Cancer smiles and glances over at me.

"What?"

"I was just thinkin', remember the circle jerk?"

"Of course I remember the circle jerk," I reply, taking a pull from a Red Bull and sucking on my cigar.

"Remember how Jonas used that excuse? How he said that because his magazine wasn't lesbian porn he was at a disadvantage?"

I smile. "And?"

"Well I was just thinkin' about it. There's some merit to it."

It was our rookie year with the Sicamous Eagles in the Kootenay International Junior Hockey League three seasons ago. Cancer and I met there and became friends, then somehow ended up living together in Vancouver, quite by chance. A few phone calls and some coincidental encounters at pubs put us together. Still, we'd always gotten along pretty well. I respect the fact he's bigger than I am, and he respects the fact I'm smarter than he is. Other than that, we needed little to feed our compatibility. Anything of depth usually went unspoken, but we thought the same—relaying it to the other seemed wholly unnecessary and quite possibly gay. We didn't want to get too close. We were two guys who lived together, that was all.

We were at some cheap hotel in Golden when the captain came in to officially break the news. The hotel was like something out of *Fargo*, one of those Best Westerns with the porn channel semi-scrambled, so that if you watched it hard enough, and long enough, you could just make out what was going on. Catch a nipple or a cock pounding into a pussy.

The premise is simple. When Junior teams head out on the road, there is always an extra room booked in which to store the gear. Spread out over every available surface, it airs out overnight in this makeshift equipment room. However, it's typically referred to as the "fuck room," because if you happen to pick up some local girl who thinks you're a potential NHL star, you take her there. Because no one would ever sleep in there, if she's willing to put up with the smell, you can have your way with her then send her packing without having to spend an extended amount of time with her.

And so it was that all the rookies including Cancer, myself, some weird little guy named Jonas and the backup goalie were stripped down to our boxers, handed a porno mag and a piece of white bread, and led into the fuck room. We were told to knock on the door once we'd "filled" our piece of bread. Cancer and I had already been given the heads-up, probably because we were the two most promising rookies, so we were at least somewhat prepared. I had been getting myself hard in our hotel bathroom with the aid of one of those little courtesy Shampoo/Conditioner bottles, while Cancer pulled a tuck because he'd been pulling it prior also, watching the scrambled porn on television. The boy exhibited an extraordinary level of concentration when he wanted to.

Once in the room I moved right to the window, placed the magazine on the bed centerfold out, and went to work on myself. I was able to place a healthy squirt onto my piece of bread in no time, though I remember trying diligently not to enjoy the experience at all. Once finished, I knocked on the door to uproarious applause, and exited the room like a conquering hero. My piece of bread was checked, and then immediately discarded, and I was given high-fives and accolades while still semi-hard. A somewhat surreal experience, that was.

Cancer came next. Exiting the room with hands in the air, cock still rock hard and poking out of the hole of his underwear like a bald ferret.

Then there was silence. And more silence. Jokes were exchanged as to why the backup goalie, whose name was Marco, happened to be so apprehensive.

"Dude, I've seen that guy in the shower," said Gill, a twenty year-old forward. "He's lucky if he can get a grip on that fucker with all that bloody foreskin he has there."

After a few more moments there came a sudden rumbling, some screaming, and finally Marco emerged from the room victorious, with Jonas on the floor behind him wailing away on himself. Marco displayed his piece of bread, and then celebrated by flinging it at some of the players, who scattered to avoid its contents.

"Jonas, take your time, man. No rush now, you be eatin' semen," said Gill to thunderous applause and laughter.

Eventually Jonas emerged with a vacant look on his face. He asked that no pictures be taken, and we all solemnly obliged. After all, any evidence of the ordeal was completely unnecessary. The guy was going to go through enough. And then, without hesitation, he rolled up his piece of bread and shoved it in his mouth. Everyone exploded in laughter. He chewed furiously, gagged once, then gulped it down and opened his mouth to show everybody it was gone. He was immediately handed a water bottle, which he proceeded to drain as everyone patted him on the back and applauded, some laughing so hard they were soon crying and complaining of chest pain.

"Welcome to the Eagles," said Gill as he smacked Jonas on the back.

A yellow sports car whips by on the right. I adjust myself in my seat, one hand on the wheel and the other wrapped around a Red Bull. Cancer has already polished off six beers and we've only just hit the Coquihalla highway.

"Cancer, pace yourself. We have to play tonight."

"I'm good there, Seth. Why don't you wipe off your vagina and pick up your end of the deal."

"Funny," I say, reaching back to grab another beer.

"Where are we?" he asks.

"About an hour from the toll booth."

"Fuck. We'll need to make a beer run in Merritt."

Cancer is drunk. But he plays better when he's drunk. He loses his nasty edge and calms down to a point where anger and frustration don't taint his play. He plays terribly when he's sober, always pounding poor bastards into the boards, running amok, and finishing off unnecessary hits and racking up penalty minutes. But when he's liquored up, even just a little, he smoothes out and his soft hands emerge. Add just a bit of booze and he becomes calm and collected on the breakout, which is crucial for a defenceman. Cancer has always been a defenceman. He got put back there in Atom because he was as big as a house by the age of ten. He's an excellent defenceman too, just fast enough to keep pace with shifty forwards, and big enough to rub anyone out in the corners.

Actually, he can't skate worth a damn, but he can keep up on a rush. Get him the puck on the fly and he'll knife the most beautiful pass to you in front of the net you'd think the bastard was Gretzky himself. He was also blessed with a wicked snapshot, as most big men usually are. He'll just curl his wrists and let 'er rip. If it doesn't go top corner, it rattles off the glass, spooking the goalie in the process, which is sometimes just as good. Then the next time he comes flying down, you can be sure the goalie is petrified, bracing for what will either be a goal or a giant welt somewhere on his body. But that's when Cancer will knife that sliver of a pass between the defence-man's legs, and all you have to do is keep your stick on the ice and then put your hands in the air when you score like you knew what you were doing from the get go.

Or maybe tonight he'll just decide he wants to fight the entire game. Or pick on some poor eighteen year-old still wearing a cage, acne all over his face, who just got cut from Junior A. Either way, I just stay out of his way, pick up the puck from the wrecks he creates, and make sure he doesn't get too wound up on Red Bull, ephedrine and speed in the dressing room between periods.

By the time we hit the toll booth the sun has started to set, melting a soft glow across the Thompson plateau, the commencement of the Rocky Mountains. The sunlight is bathing the tree line in amber and yellow, melting the remaining snow, and meanwhile my passenger and closest friend is either sleeping or passed out, quite oblivious to it all. Once we go through the toll booth I pick up speed, averaging between 120 and 130 kilometres an hour. The car hums with wind resistance as I nurse a Slurpee cup of vodka chased with Red Bull and smoke the last of our cigars. I figure if Cancer keeps sleeping, I'll just slide through Merritt so we can get to the hotel, meet up with the team, and maybe get a shower and a nap in before the game.

When we reach Kamloops it's dark and cold. We stumble into the hotel, situated nicely between the rink and a liquor store. While I check in, Cancer wanders the lobby with bed head, periodically scratching his nuts. There we meet up with the rest of the team, all of whom have been here a while and are going to head out for a quick bite to eat prior to the game. Cancer just wants to sleep though, and so we check into our room instead. It looks like every hotel room I've ever been in with its two tidy beds, TV, white bathroom with plenty of white towels, and the usual assortment of stained wood dressers and cabinets. I wonder how long it will take to ruin this one.

We decide to watch TV until it's time to leave for the rink. Cancer is out within five minutes, trying to sleep off his intoxication. I flick through the channels, looking for something interesting. It's always aggravating coming to a new town, where the channels are different than at home. I settle on a *Simpsons* episode, the one where Homer becomes the Beer Baron, and before I know it I've dozed off as well. I wake up just before it's time to head to the rink. Cancer is curled up in his version of the fetal position, pillow tucked neatly under his head. He snores quietly as I slowly push my index finger up his nose. Then suddenly he wakes up, startled and dazed.

"What the fuck?"

"It's time to go, asshole."

We stop at the gas station on the way to the rink to purchase some more Red Bull and energy bars. When we arrive at the rink the crisp cold air comes as something of a shock, but then it always does. The beer garden is full and a game is on. We stop and chat with some of our teammates watching the game under the heaters, then weave our way to the dressing room through a hallway of little tykes playing hockey with broken Synergy sticks and a tightly rolled ball of sock tape. Cancer playfully rubs one of them out, who quickly returns the favour by butt-ending him in the ass.

We enter our dressing room. The voices are recognized even before I can see inside. We're greeted with the usual barrage of "Hey what's up?" and "Fuck you" and the token stick in the nuts courtesy of the goalie.

You become acclimatized to the stench of hockey gear after a while. That smell of sweat-soaked fabric fermenting away inside a bag of canvas. This dressing room smells normal to me, but I'm sure anyone unfamiliar with this world would gag immediately upon entry. A hockey dressing room could be called a number of things, but none of these guys really give a damn what you call it. It's a place where men can be as uncensored, self-absorbed, sexist, racist and homophobic as they want to be without fear of repercussion. The dressing room is where a man stops trying to be polite and is free to air the dirty laundry of his life. Though most of the time he just talks about hockey.

Apparently we're the team to beat in the tournament, or so says our captain, an older guy named Jeff who used to play semi-pro somewhere on the East Coast before he blew one of his shoulders out. Now he not only runs a small roofing business, drinks and plays hockey, but has like seven or eight kids last time I checked. He's a great guy though, an all-Canadian male, or whatever the hell one might call a man like him. He lets us know immediately that being named the favourite in this tournament isn't something we can rely on. A few players nod in agreement. Still, most of the team seems distracted by his pre-game talk, probably because it feels like he could quite possibly repeat the performance afterwards, thus cutting into valuable drinking time for all.

Our first opponent is the hometown team, the Kamloops Ice Dogs. It takes me a couple of shifts to get my legs going, as it always does. I get caught out on a late change and chase the puck around for a good minute in our end, which, if nothing else, serves to clear my head and shake the rust off my legs. Halfway through the first period we spend the better part of a minute in the other team's end, and I get a great feel for the puck, ringing a wrist shot from the slot off the crossbar in the process.

The beer garden has already started heckling. Luckily, and quite arbitrarily, they've decided to pick on the opposing team's goalie, rail thin and sporting some weird Billy Smith mask.

With a few minutes left in the second period, I catch an errant pass between defencemen just inside the neutral zone and find myself on a breakaway. I cut my blades into the ice and make a B-line for the goal. My mind starts to scramble with possible scenarios. Shoot? Deke? How far behind me is that quick defenceman with the blue blades?

Everything happens so quickly in hockey you never have time to think, only react. I find myself coming in slightly from the left, so I fake right, go left and the goalie follows, then I drag the puck across to the right and wait him out, neatly sliding it into the open net. I turn around, smile, pump my fist and wait for my teammates to catch up. I'm surrounded in jerseys and smiles all at once.

We head back to the dressing room up 1–0. With our rock solid goalie, the strategy now is to play more defensively, something I completely ignore. The third period goes a little differently too. Apparently the other team isn't accustomed to playing from behind, and starts to get chippy after I net another goal. This leads to a penalty box parade, and we net two more with the man advantage, Cancer grabbing two assists and me, one.

Cancer drops the gloves with a few minutes left in the third, and the referee decides to send them both for early showers. No matter, we're already up 4–0, and to add insult to injury I score an empty net goal, picking off a breakout pass with less than a minute to go. We're already looking like a well-oiled machine, ready to face-fuck anything and everything that stands in our way at this tournament.

By the time I hit the dressing room, mind buzzing, adrenaline pumping, the beer is already pouring down throats. Within five minutes the cooler's contents have been decimated, and we spend the rest of the time talking about number 3, who was a fucking asshole, and the breakaway I scored, and how Dale clipped Chris on the bench afterwards, ripping a big gash under his eyebrow. Dale pays for his beer. "It's all good," as they say. Cancer is way ahead of everybody of course on account of getting chucked early for fighting. He's half cut in no time and seems hell-bent on hitting the peeler bars before the clubs, his traditional post-game ritual.

By the time we leave the dressing room I'm quite smashed. Cancer can't drive however because he's even more drunk than I am. When we arrive at the hotel, with me behind the wheel, Cancer staggers around the lobby in his flip-flops and hits on a group of young Asian girls. They're fifteen, maybe sixteen at best, but that won't stop him. He doesn't subscribe to the same restrictive moral code you and I do. Afterwards, we pass by an open door on our floor, the room inside filled with women our age. Cancer stops in his tracks, mingling without hesitation. I quickly join in. They look absolutely gorgeous. But then again, any girls rooming down the hall from a hockey team would look absolutely gorgeous.

We order pizza, and I pop a Celexa and an Ativan to bring myself down from all the ephedrine I took earlier. Then I grind up some Valium and mix it into my drink. I take a shower, blasting myself with cold water in an effort to calm those few remaining nerves still trying to sort themselves out from all the medications running through my innards. Cancer takes the battery out of the smoke alarm so that we can puff away with impunity on our cigars. Once the pizza arrives, we take it directly to the girls' room. Two other guys from our team are already there. The room is full of volleyball gear. No fuck room for them apparently. No matter. I suck back some vodka mixed with Mountain Dew. I'm dressed in my white Polo shirt and my light brown khaki jeans, and I feel great. On top of the world and totally together. All the illicit drugs at work inside me are having their desired effect. There's a champion in the making here, I can feel it.

Cancer is pulling this woman-baiting routine he's been perfecting for years. They ask him his name while checking out his tattoos—the arm sleeves, the tribal blazes that cover each shoulder—then he tells them. Cancer. They say, "What the fuck, you're lying." And he lets them think he is for a while. Eventually, though, they ask again, and you can tell they're half confused, half intrigued by now. My name is Cancer, he says. I was named after the astrological sign. Or if he's really drunk, he lies and says he was conceived on a red-eye flight over the Pacific, somewhere above the Tropic of Cancer, or else other shit like that.

Then there comes a point when they just think he's messing with them. So then he pulls out his wallet, which always contains three picture IDs: his driver's license, his old student card, and his bus pass which he only got because it had his picture on it. He's never been on a bus in his life of course. They read his name, and he pulls out his birth certificate to seal the deal. I've seen this routine so many times now I've lost count. But I still love it because it actually increases everyone's chances of getting laid.

After they realize his first name is actually Cancer, usually one of them—and there's always one of them—just can't help herself. And then he pounces, and I simply swoop in and clean up the leftovers. They're thinking Cancer's friend must be really unique and cool too, so I try my best to live up to the hype.

I meet this girl named Alys, the setter on the volleyball team that's also in town for a tournament. We talk a while, feeling each other out, and exchange glances across the room from time to time. But we're both still somewhat sober, so that's as far as it goes, for now. I've decided to take it slow, and ease my way into her.

Eventually the guys scatter back to their respective rooms to get ready to hit some bar, the same bar, it turns out, some of the girls are heading to. Apparently we're going to ride along with them. Ryan, one of our other centers known mostly for his Perreault-like faceoff skills, has brought a massive amount of coke with him. He's keeping it under wraps though, and simply whispers into my ear at one point, "You in?"

"Yeah, fuck it."

Here it comes. A powerful sniff, violently up the nose, like the start of a *Death From Above 1979* song. Cancer and I, along with Joe, Mike and Aaron, each do a few lines off the bathroom counter. We sniff it, rub it on our gums and lick it like we've seen it done in movies. I'm still not sure to this day if any of that actually does anything, but I'm sure as hell not going to ask these hooligans.

By the time we arrive at the club I'm riding high on the first wave. It's some dive in downtown Kamloops called the Max, located at the corner of a large industrial lot, only a few feet from the town's main train route. We pound back some shots to get going, then check out the place, and before we know it we're out on the dance floor with the girls, these same volleyball-playing girls who suddenly look much better and smell much nicer than any girls I've met in years.

Alys is all over me. We dance with the group a while, playfully exchanging partners, but soon she focuses in on me exclusively, grabbing my belt once and running her hand across my stomach, which I quickly flex in order to hide any bulge I might be sporting these days.

Eventually the guys retreat to the bathroom to do some more coke. I find Alys in line at the bar waiting to get some beer. I'm just drunk enough and high enough that the staggering noise of the club has become little more than a hum in my ears. A loud deafening hum, true, but soothing, in my mind. We do some Fuzzy Navels together, Alys and I, and talk about where we're from, cramming entire life stories into small vignettes and anecdotes. Alys reminds me of a girl I knew in high school, or so at least I tell her. She's like a sexy, younger looking Shania Twain too, I hear myself say. But the best thing she's got going for her is her skin apparently. Is it amber? Or simply golden brown. I'm all over this girl in my mind, but playing it cool on the outside, and by the time last call rolls around we're making out on the dance floor, inhaling each other.

Then things get a little blurry. Drinking beer in the parking lot followed by some holding hands and flagging down a taxi. Stumbling into the 7–Eleven to get some snacks before making out in an alley. Talking Cancer into crashing in someone else's room so we can have some quiet time alone in the hotel. I take a deep breath, trying to quell all the liquor running through me. I'm so ridiculously drunk even standing proves difficult. We have a good go at it, and afterwards both pass out.

Eventually I shift over and stand up, pulling the condom off and dropping it to the floor. I use my hands to guide myself down the pitch black hallway, cock still rock hard and leading the way. I turn the bathroom light on, catching a glimpse of myself in the mirror. I suck my stomach in, checking out my somewhat dilapidated physique, my forehead littered with beads of sweat, my face a patchwork of red. I pull the toilet seat up and bend way over so I can piss properly. I get most of it in the toilet, and clean up the rest with a towel. I wipe the piss off my hands as I walk back to the bed.

"Okay, I'm good," I tell her.

Alys is sprawled across the bed, legs crossed, her hair a violent halo against the mattress. There is nothing left of the bedding but one solitary pillow. We've been quite busy, I think to myself. We have sex a few more times, she gives me head, and then we fall asleep in a tangle of sweaty limbs and her hair. In the morning she leaves the room early, kissing me on the lips as I help her get dressed. We decide to meet up again after our respective games. She gives me her cell phone number and then quietly opens the door, peering out into the hallway before slipping out unnoticed. I wonder who else got laid.

A knock on the door around eight o'clock wakes me up again. I stagger up, squinting at the sun ripping through the curtains.

"Is she gone?" Cancer whispers through the door.

"Yeah, she's gone."

"Well let me in then, fag."

Naked, I open the door to find Cancer sporting the biggest grin I've seen in years. He punches me in the stomach. "You motherfucker," he says, stumbling past. He takes stock of the stripped bed and the collection of used condoms and wrappers strewn across the floor. "Fuck, okay, that's your bed."

I crawl back onto the mattress, covering my genitals with a pillow. Cancer plops himself onto the bed beside me.

"You'd better clean that mess up."

"Yeah, in a bit."

"Fucking Christ, I got seriously shut down."

"By whom?"

"You know that girl I met at like midnight? The one with the huge rack? I bought that bitch Denny's and everything and all I got was her number. I mean fuck, what's a guy gotta do."

"It's a mystery," I say. "Hey, when did I lose you? I can't remember much after the bar."

"Yeah, we figured you were set after you were making out with her on the dance floor. I figured we'd just let you do your thing."

"I did have to go at you to get you to sleep somewhere else though, I remember."

"You woke me up, you cunt. What, you expected an invitation?"

"I just remember you babbling on about tag-teaming her. Very suave of you."

He laughs. "She didn't like that one bit, did she."

"Ya think?"

"Whatever. I think we better find out where Ryan is. I heard he ended up at some broad's house like fifteen minutes out of town."

"Seriously?"

"Yeah, he tried to call me like an hour ago from a Subway. He was like, 'I'm getting a cab, but I have no idea where I am. Send help.'"

"Oh so you didn't talk to him."

"Naw, I was asleep. He left a message. I think he'll be okay. We don't play for another couple of hours anyway. And hey, how big could this town be anyway?"

Cancer hops in the shower, and then hits the hot tub with a few warm foamy beers to nurse his hangover. I feel great, probably because I've sweated most of the poison out of my pores and onto the mattress.

Eventually I head down to the lobby for the complimentary continental breakfast. I sit alone, dressed in only my boxers, and a family of four takes time out of their Kamloops vacation to quietly scorn me for my dress code violation. I couldn't care less. I stuff myself with raspberry muffins, pulpy orange juice, some generic fruit loops and a banana, then make straight for the hot tub to find Cancer deep into his third beer, mingling with some of the volleyball chicks from last night. I am quickly introduced. There's Katy, Ashley and Veronica. I ask where Betty and Archie are. She's heard that joke a million times apparently. Cancer is putting in valuable minutes here, for it's well known women will be more inclined to hang out with you if you organize something in advance and don't just show up at their room with a boner in the middle of the night.

Later, I head back to the room and, before I know it, I've nodded off and Cancer is waking me up, telling me we've got to get going. He's got an ice bath already in progress, a pre-game tradition in which he fills the tub with ice cold water, then dumps a garbage bag full of hotel ice in. You spend ninety seconds in the ice bath and it supposedly purges all the lactic acid from your legs. Now I'm not sure that's actually what it does, but it definitely does wake you up and make your legs feel better. It does do a number on your cock and balls however.

After the bath we head over to the rink. I don't bother to wait for the windows to defrost, but scratch as much of the ice off with my fingernails as I can instead, driving while peering through this small, somewhat ineffective hole I've made.

We suit up while talking about the previous night. Apparently Ryan was getting head in the hotel stairwell some-time before he vanished for the night. Tristan walked by and saw them, which spooked the girl who in turn fled on foot. We all laugh hysterically because Tristan's first reaction upon finding them there was simply to stare until the girl took notice. Ryan said Tristan stared at them the way a dog stares at you when you're trying to jerk off or take a dump—with that blank look of intrigue on its face. The dressing room is jovial because, for one, we had a great night, two, three guys got laid, and three, the team from Chilliwack we're playing evidently sucks. I get my gear on early and head out onto the ice to get some blood pumping in my legs.

Our opponents turn out to be as awful as advertised, and by the time the first period is over we're up 5–0. Cancer is absolutely massacring the opposition, hammering them into the boards at every opportunity, punishing them for having the audacity to even show up here. He's having a great old time just running around clobbering guys, knocking their helmets off, sending them to the dressing room in limping pain. I on the other hand am more worried about padding my stats. I've netted a goal and three assists by the time the third period rolls around and we're up 9–0.

A guy on the other team has taken a liking to harassing me however. He's a few inches shorter than I and probably a bit lighter—he doesn't look like much, and sports a half-visor, one of those faggy bubble ones—so I think I might take him on. After a whistle in front of the net he gives me a good cross-check to the chest, trying to push me away from his goalie. I smile, come back slowly at him, cock my right hand back slightly and crack him square in the jaw. He staggers a bit, and by the time he rights himself I've tossed my gloves, connected with a good right jab and grabbed his jersey. My heart starts to race, as it always does when I'm in a fight. I've never been a great fighter, but have learned enough through trial and error to know where I stand on the ice. The best thing to do in a full-blown fight is keep moving, keep throwing punches, and if all else fails, yank the guy to the ice with you and pray the refs break it up before you absorb too many fists with your face.

And always aim for the lower part of the face too, because fingers and knuckles tend to break like eggshells on a guy's helmet or visor. And forget the body shots—it's not boxing—stick to the face, don't try to go southpaw or anything tricky like that, and pay attention to what he's got a hold of, and what you're holding onto. It's like judo—grab the right part of his jersey and the guy can't throw, let alone manoeuvre out of the way of your incoming fist. And as I say, keep moving, don't stand still, don't let him get a clear picture of what he's aiming for, your face.

I hit the guy in the jaw again, and the feeling of knuckles against bone excites me. He tries to pull me in close, but I won't let him. I feed him an uppercut to the chin, then miss with the second one and catch my hand on his visor. Then the refs come in and break it up, telling me he's had enough. His face, and his faggy visor, are splattered with blood. I must have cracked him in the nose at one point, though I don't remember. When I get to the penalty box, I look at my right hand. The knuckle on the middle finger looks as though it might be broken, sticking abruptly out of place. I can move my finger fine though, so maybe it's only dislocated. I try to pop it back into place, sending bolts of pain all the way to my shoulder in the process.

My middle finger is broken. Meanwhile, the guy with the visor finds his way to the penalty box. He sits down, and wipes the blood from his face with his jersey. He takes a sip of water and spits it out, then looks over at me like he wants me to say something.

"What the fuck is your problem," I oblige him.

"Fuck you, buddy. You're killing us. Show some respect."

"Hey, don't dish it out if you can't take it."

"Can't *take* it? What the fuck is your problem. I was just clearing the net!"

"Eat shit."

One of the two timekeepers jumps in. "Hey guys, settle down."

I finger my opponent and smile. He fingers me back.

"I'll see you on the ice in five minutes," I tell him.

The timekeeper tells me to shut up, and I shrug as if to say, "What's up?" In the meantime my opponent stands up and puts his helmet on.

"Yeah, that's right," I say. "Put your visor on, bitch."

When our five-minute majors end we both skate to our respective benches. I'm overly angry at him, but don't know why. I bark at him and his bench a bit more, grinning and waving at them like a madman.

I tape up my finger and head back out with my line, but the game ends much quicker than I would have liked. I don't even get another healthy scoring chance, let alone an opportunity to fight visor-boy again. He heads to the dressing room after a few shifts, apparently to get his nose fixed. He got off easy, considering I could be the one stuck with the broken finger. By the time we hit the dressing room, the adrenaline and ephedrine have worn off and my finger starts to hurt like hell. The guys tell me to go to the ER and get it set properly, which I consider, but then decide if I just tape it up I'll be fine. Meanwhile, Cancer is loving the fact I fought the guy, visor and all. While he recounts the struggle in play-by-play style, Jeff comes over to reset my finger. He cleverly distracts me by asking me about my night with Alys, and right after I tell him about the great head she gave me he cracks my finger back into place.

We only have two games' rest before our final round robin tilt, so the team decides to hit the beer garden at the far corner of the rink for a spell. Cancer and I put back five or six while watching the games, filling the remainder of our bellies with fries and burgers from the concession stand. Then we head back to our dressing room where everyone's gear is airing out. It stinks like hell, but I have a quick nap under the bench anyhow, and before I know it we're suiting up against a team from Kelowna.

This team is no better than the first two, we can tell by their warm-up. You can always tell by watching a guy in warm-up if he's good or not, and none of these guys look decent at all, a few younger players even sporting full cages, fresh from Midget rep no doubt. Their goalie sprawls all over the place in warm-up too, also a good sign for us.

I recognize a few of them from the beer garden, meaning they're probably just as drunk as we are. I get Jeff to tape my finger, and I feel fine handling the puck in warm-up. Finally the game gets underway and we waste no time in taking it to this team from Kelowna, dressed in their black and yellow jerseys. They call themselves the Bees. We call them

fags. They're also mainly older guys, and their backend is bru-
tally slow. About three or four minutes into the game I steal
the puck off one of their defencemen around the red-line
and start making for the goal. I can feel the other defenceman bearing down on me from the right, so I take my right
hand off the stick, lean in and drive to the net as hard as I
can. He makes contact with me just after I flick the puck over
the goalie's blocker, popping the water bottle off the top of
the net. The three of us come crashing together as I soar into
the net, the goalie ducking under me at the last second. The
ref is pointing to the goal as I lie there smiling at the mess
I've created.

Later Cancer scores a beautiful goal from the point, a high
slap shot that beats the goalie clean. We pot another goal the
very next shift in similar fashion, and the floodgates are officially open. The game ends 7–1, as Glen gets lazy and lets in a
weak one late in the third. Afterwards the mood in the dressing room is extremely upbeat, even more so than before. Guys
are cracking beers at an alarming rate, joking and laughing at
the slightest provocation. Our team is tops in the tournament,
and rightly so. We're solid all the way through our line-up and
know it. We feel invincible and probably are.

I take my time undressing. It's only about seven so there's no
real rush to get going. I crack a Pilsner in the shower and slowly
wash up, paying special attention to my groin with the soap,
knowing it might be getting some more attention at some point.

Back at the hotel the team gathers in the lobby. We're
going to hit Boston Pizza for dinner then maybe head straight
to the bar after. Cancer and I are the two youngest guys on the
team, but everybody else isn't much older—late twenties, early
thirties. Jeff must be pushing thirty-five, but everybody else still
has that youthful asshole exuberance about them. We're a nice
mix of beards and baseball caps about to run amok on the
town of Kamloops.

Our waitress at the pizza place is stunning. She has a clean face, long eyebrows and a healthy tan. It's always the tan that gets me, and I begin to give her my full attention. Dora is her name. I make sure Dora knows I'm interested, but I don't gawk. The entire team is ogling her, and she takes it like all waitresses do, with a grin and a grain. These guys would fuck a bean bag chair if it had a nice rack on it.

She makes her way over to our side of the table where Cancer starts it off, as he always does, not giving a damn one way or the other. "So what's there to do around here tonight?" he asks as she passes our table a fresh jug of beer.

"Umm, usually Cactus Jack's is pretty full tonight," she replies, taking a quick glance at me.

"Is that the cowboy bar?" I ask.

"Yeah."

"Anywhere better, like something a little more modern?" Cancer asks.

"Well, River's is pretty modern. I like it there," she answers, one hand on her hip.

"So you heading there after work?" I ask, taking the reigns from Cancer.

"Me? Tonight?"

"Yeah."

"I dunno. Maybe."

"What time you get off?"

"I get off at eleven, I think. Yeah, eleven."

"And then what are you doing?"

"Well, a bunch of my friends are going to be heading out somewhere, so I might meet up with them."

"Well I think we're going to Cactus Jack's. You should ask your friends if they maybe want to meet up with us there."

She looks at me. "Yeah that might be an idea. I think they might end up going there if I can talk them into it."

"That would be great," I tell her.

Cancer jumps in. "So you gonna save me a dance?"

She smiles. "We'll see, big boy."

Dora walks away, and as soon as she's out of earshot I reach over and drop my fist on Cancer's nuts like a sledgehammer. He jerks forward and lets out a yelp.

" 'You gonna save me a dance?' What is this, *high* school, you fuckin' retard?"

He leans back, in obvious pain. "I think you popped one of my genitals open. I'm serious. I think I have a busted nut."

"I don't care. She's absolutely smashing and I won't have you ruin this with your asinine conversation."

As much as I loathe his ridiculous comments sometimes, they're also something I truly adore. Cancer's the guy you're always waiting for to say something stupid, and he rarely, if ever, disappoints. You can see it coming sometimes. You just look at him, and you can see those tiny toy-like wheels clunking around, ready to spew out something that will further and irreparably isolate you from any sort of intellectual conversation. But then again I also enjoy it, watching the fostered squirms and silence linger. I enjoy watching any and all boundaries fall, even if they fall on account of a racist or homophobic remark from a lug-headed ape like Cancer. It's my secret way of enjoying his friendship on a level he'll never quite understand.

I take a long pull from my beer. Meanwhile, Cancer is still bent over in his chair. "I so fuckin' owe you one," he says, trying to sit up, his face red, his eyes shut.

Wade, our token assistant captain and stay-at-home D-man, turns to me and says, "I knew this guy, Gary O'Shea, crazy as shit, he'd get drunk and when he'd meet someone he didn't know, he'd ask them what the capital of Thailand was, and if they got it wrong he'd kick them in the nuts as hard as he could and yell 'Bangkok!' "

Everyone around the table laughs.

"I remember this one time," Wade continues. "The fucker got lost in the woods up by Prince Rupert at a bush party, and so there he was walking around with a fifth of whisky when he fell down a ten-foot sewer drain and broke his hip. Man that guy had class."

Everyone laughs again, and the stories roll out. Like the time when Glen pulled the fire alarm in the hotel of the team we were supposed to be playing the following morning. He was so drunk, when he came running back to one of our rooms with a fire extinguisher, he emptied the entire canister on Mike and Bill. Or the time Sam had to run naked across the ice for rookie initiation, and fell because he was so drunk, splitting his head open, requiring a trip to the ER on a stretcher, naked, drunk and bloody. Glen talks about the time he was getting head from a stripper in his parked car in Penticton. While in progress, she inadvertently shifted the car into neutral, causing it to roll back a good fifty feet before smashing into another car, at which point she bit her lip. Glen laughs heartily as he tells us how he thought he was having some sort of spiritual reaction to the blowjob, and didn't know the car was actually moving.

After we finish up the food and the beer, we begin to make our way back to the hotel. Before I go though, I make my way up to the till to chat with Dora.

"So Cactus Jack's is good, eh?" I say, trying to appear calm and collected as I punch in the numbers on the debit machine.

"Yeah we usually do a bit of drinking there first, if the line-up's not too long."

"It would be cool if we could meet up later," I tell her, and she takes my receipt from dinner, to which I've added a ten dollar tip, and writes her name and number on the back in long loopy letters. She hands it to me, and our fingers touch.

"So then I guess I'll see you later."

"I think you will," she says, and my dick flinches ever so slightly at the insinuation. I make my hand into a pistol and fire a quick bullet at her, then turn to leave. As soon as I do though, I realize the pistol thing was probably gay, and wince accordingly. I can see some of the guys outside the front window dry-humping each other and mimicking the pistol thing, which makes me wince that much more. Meanwhile Cancer is pressed against the glass, licking it like a porn star, disturbing a nice quiet family of four. My wince is complete.

Outside, I hold up the piece of paper with Dora's number to everyone's delight. I raise my hands in the air in triumph, and as I do, Cancer whacks me in the nuts with the toe of his shoe. Everyone bursts out laughing. I drop to the ground, at which point Cancer mounts me and proceeds to dry-hump my face. I dart up with fist cocked, sending him reeling back.

"Don't be jealous, you cunt," I say.

"Jealous? I gave her to you, man. I assisted. I'm like the unsung hero of the entire operation."

By the time we reach the hotel, shower and change, the entire team is drunk. Naked men and curse words fly every which way and Jim, our backup goalie, is running up and down the halls with a sock over his dink and a hockey sock over his head like a toque. He's tripped up full-stride, and has to tend to disastrous carpet burns as a result. I decide to bust out my nice black dress shirt and dark blue jeans, as I want to make a decent second impression on Dora. My cell phone rings.

"Hello," I say, motioning to Cancer to turn the TV volume down.

"Hi."

"Hey what's up, Alys. I tried to call you earlier," I lie.

"Really. I must have missed it."

"Yeah I figured I was getting the blow off," I counter, putting her on the defence.

"Na, I wouldn't do that. Not after the night we had."

"Yeah that was good, huh?"

"Not bad."

"So where's your team going tonight?" I ask.

"I think we're going back to the Max."

"I see," I say, putting together a backup plan. "I think we're going to CJ's, some cowboy club, and then we might head over to the Max after. You wanna meet up?"

"Yeah, I don't think we're going to get to the Max until at least one. We still haven't even gone out for dinner yet."

"Well I'll probably be at the Max by one. And if not, I'll call your cell and we can meet up."

I glance over to see Cancer waving his index finger at me and mouthing the words, 'You're number one.'

"Sounds good," I say.

"Kay, I'll see you later."

"Later."

I hang up and Cancer jumps in. "You're on a roll, my friend."

"Yeah when you're on, you're on," I say, brushing some imaginary dirt from my shoulder.

"So looks like the guys do want to go to CJ's first," he says, "so that'll be good."

"Yeah I can go to CJ's and check out Dora, see what's up with her and how drunk she is, and if things go well I'll head out with her and her friends to River's, and if she's all stand-offish I'll just bolt to the Max by one."

Cancer gives me the thumbs up, then gets distracted by some rap video on television. He knows I hate rap with a passion, so he turns it up and starts singing along into the remote, even though he only knows about half the words, if that.

I head into the bathroom to gel my hair into its usual mess of locks. I take the tape off my finger, which has healed nicely, or maybe the alcohol has simply numbed it into submission. Either way it feels fine, a little stiff but good enough for now.

"Fuck this song is kickin'!" shouts Cancer.

"I can't believe you, man. Here's the guy who can't even watch a football game on account of all the cocky black players, and you're bobbing your head to this guy."

"Hey, I like the beat."

"Yeah, well, it's just funny this so-called music made by black people is listened to mainly by middleclass white kids."

"Whatever. A good beat's a good beat. Kayne's got it goin' *on*!"

"The hypocrisy is sickening. I mean sing about something other than bling and cars and pussy and champagne."

"Yeah but listen to that beat, man!"

Everybody hops into cabs and cars at about eleven to hit CJ's. The place is packed, but somehow Jeff, our pretentious yet lovable captain, has managed to get us in VIP. I'm worried Dora won't be able to get in because of the line-up. Most of the guys congregate around the bar, pouring back shots of whisky and 151. Cancer and I plough through some beers while walking around, scoping the scene. We talk to a few girls, and Cancer chats up some cougars in a corner. He tells them he likes his women like wine, aged and sour. They just blow him off. I keep checking the time on my phone, and at about eleven-thirty head upstairs to bum a smoke and call Dora. I have to plug my ear and hide in a corner in order to hear her. She's just met up with her friends and doesn't think they can get in because of the line-up. I ask her how many of them there are. Four. I tell her to wait outside the side door, away from the line-up, and then I go find Jeff. I ask him how he got us in VIP, and he tells me his cousin owns the bar, which stuns me. Why hadn't I known this before? Apparently he'd been telling everyone all weekend. I ask him if we can get four girls in the side door. He looks at me.

"That chick that worked at Boston Pizza?"

"Yeah."

He smiles and leads me to the main bar where he motions to a tall dude with neatly trimmed sideburns and a dark golf shirt. Jeff leans in and speaks into the guy's ear, but I can't hear a single word they're saying. I can see Jeff pointing to the side door. Then he turns to me and smiles.

"Yeah that's fine," he tells me.

We walk over to the door, and Jeff leans in to talk to the bouncer. The big man listens, then looks at me, then calls me over. "Which ones," he yells, cracking the door. I peek my head out, and see Dora with her three friends off to the side, huddled together in their short skirts, tank tops and puffy jackets.

"Dora!"

She looks over, surprised, and leads her friends towards the door.

"C'mon in."

The four of them scamper past the bouncer, Jeff and me. Dora wraps her hand around my hip briefly as she passes, and Jeff flashes a huge grin and gives me the "OK" sign. Even the bouncer looks impressed.

Dora returns once they're all inside and leans into my ear. Her perfume intoxicates me. "How'd you do that?" she asks.

"Trade secret," I wink. "Can I buy you a drink?"

"Of course."

We turn around, and Jeff and I are introduced to the three friends. Sherri, a tight little blonde with full lips. Jessie, a short brunette with a beaded necklace and hair done up in a bun. And Jackie, another brunette with light skin and slender, almost catlike features. It takes me about four seconds to forget each of their names. Cancer comes over and leans into my ear.

"You are a god amongst men."

I smile as we make our way back to the bar. Cancer and Jeff are chatting up Dora's friends, all three of which look very interested in these big city boys. I can see Cancer shaking their hands. Then words are exchanged as he pulls out his wallet to show them his ID. Meanwhile Dora and I head up to the bar, her hand on the small of my back as we shuffle forward in line. She tells me she works part-time at Boston Pizza while attending the University College of the Cariboo where she's taking sociology.

She lives with Jackie and Jessie in a house in Sahali, which is apparently fairly close to our hotel. She's thinking of going to Australia next summer with some friends, and plays both soccer and volleyball. She's a striker. She's not sure what she wants to do after she graduates, and she has a cat named Tucker, named after Darcy Tucker of all people. She's a Leafs fan. I tell her I'm a Leafs fan too, and that I have a poster of Tucker in my apartment. And apparently I'm in my second year of engineering at UBC too. I also play for the university hockey team, and am thus merely a pick-up for this team here. A ringer, if you will. And no, I don't work.

We do a shot of whisky and I buy her a beer. She leans in close when we talk, her fingers lightly grazing the top of my back now and then. Things seem to be going quite well. I check the time.

The girls seem to know a few people at the club, but not too many. They mingle with our team, and Cancer sets his sights on the blonde with the lips. After a while the four of them tell us they're going to dance. Dora tries to pull me out onto the floor, but I tell her I'll be there in a minute. Cancer and I need to chat.

"So," I say.

"Did you see her lips? Man, those are dick suckers if I've ever seen—"

"Shut up a second," I say. "So I'm taking engineering at UBC, and I play for the T-birds."

"Are you fucking serious?"

"Quite."

"Crazy," he says, shaking his head.

"What?"

"Well I just told lips there I'm taking engineering too."

We both keel over in laughter, and Cancer gives me a low five as I head out onto the dance floor. I can't get him to come just now, but he and Jeff follow along after a while. Some other guys from the team are already out there, grinding with some cougars. Filthy guys, they are. Fucking killers. Dora and I start dancing. She gets in close fast, wasting no time, making her intentions clear. The music is mostly country, but I'm too drunk to care and find myself singing along to Tom McGraw, or whatever the fuck his name is. Meanwhile Dora is getting closer and closer. After four or five songs she retreats with her friends to the bathroom, at which point Jeff, Cancer and I head back to the bar. Our home base of boys has diminished substantially. Seems everybody is out playing playboy. Cancer and I lean against a banister and assess the situation. He asks me what I'm going to do about Alys. I figure if I can get to Dora's house I can just make up some excuse if I happen to bump into her the following day. Cancer is pretty sure the blonde one doesn't live with Dora, but both of us can't remember her name for the life of us. Jeff is no help either.

When a two-stepping country song comes on, a stout, somewhat fuckable girl with a cowboy hat comes over and asks Cancer to dance.

"Sorry, my legs are broken," he says.

She looks confused. "Your legs are broken?"

"Yes, broken legs, can't dance," he says, staring at her blankly. She walks away with a bewildered look on her face. Jeff and I start screaming with laughter. We all clink our beers together. Jeff is quite drunk. I'm sure he doesn't get drunk as much as we do because he's all over the place, but surprisingly less annoying than I would have expected. Two of the girls come back and we talk a while, and then Dora returns and I get the blonde's name off her, playing dumb for Cancer. I mouth her name over Dora's shoulder when they're not looking. Cancer looks confused, so I draw an 'S.' He looks even more confused. Then I ask Dora if she wants another drink, which she does. I motion for Cancer to come with me. Once we're out of earshot, I tell him her name. Sherri.

"What the fuck is this?" he says, making a squiggly line with his finger.

"That's an 'S,'" I say.

"What, are you having a seizure when you write it? Fucking idiot."

Things get blurry from there. We decide to take some shots back to the group. I've burned through close to a hundred bucks by now, buying drinks for Dora and her three friends. Jeff seems to be hitting it off with the slender brunette, who lives with Dora. The other brunette is nowhere to be seen. I tell Cancer he ought to take the blonde back to the hotel room. He agrees, at which point I carefully explain the Alys situation again.

One time, when we're up at the bar getting a beer, Dora kisses me on the cheek. I check the time on my cell—it's one-thirty and I've missed two calls. I turn my phone off. Before I know it it's last call and Dora, Jeff, the brunette whose name is Jackie, and I have left the club and are heading to the Pita Pit, a couple of blocks down the road. We're outside the club when Cancer comes wandering over, looking gravely concerned. He's forgotten the blonde's name again. So have I.

"Fuck, she's so down with coming back to the hotel room too," he says, suddenly giddy with excitement.

"Yeah I think Jeff and I could score too."

"Dude, what's her fuckin' name?"

"I dunno. Ask her her age, and when she says it be like 'I don't believe you,' and then ask to see her ID."

And with that Cancer is off, never to be seen again. The air has warmed up remarkably, making jackets voluntary, and Dora's nipples press hard against the fabric of her shirt. She's got an ass that winks at me every time she takes a step, and legs like scissors that might cut me in bed. The four of us decide to split a cab because they live close to the hotel, and before we even get rolling, plans have changed and we're invited over for drinks. Jeff and I keep catching each other's eyes, both of us sporting big, catlike grins.

We're inside now, and the two girls are dancing around the house making drinks while Jeff and I mosey around, trying to appear relaxed and cool. Actually I'm drunk, so I don't really give a shit. The girls dance to rap music, grinding each other, and I do a shot of tequila out of Dora's cleavage on a dare. Then Jeff does a shot, taking a lime out of Jackie's mouth, and the two start making out right there in the living room. I start clapping.

"Él Capitan!"

I glance at Jeff's hand. His wedding ring has disappeared. And so it's not long before Jackie asks if he wants a tour of her room, leaving Dora and me alone. I move in for the kill, letting her press close to me as we talk. I can smell her again. I start to get hard, my blood picking up speed. Her breasts touch my chest and we kiss softly, my hands moving onto her hips. We remain this way for about a minute, and then she heads towards her room, leading me along by the hand. Once we're inside she closes the door and turns on a lamp, revealing a typical girl's room of beet red paint, a variety of black and white stock photos, a hair straightener and plenty of makeup cluttering a desk in front of a mirror. It smells like the Body Shop in here. I stand there in the middle of her room and watch as she removes her earrings. She looks at me. I smile, then start unbuttoning my dress shirt. I'm too drunk to attempt verbal foreplay, so I just go for it. She comes over and helps me. I like this because she's silent. I can't stand girls who talk too much in the bedroom.

Once my shirt is off she examines my tattoos, asking what they mean while she runs her hands over them. Then she notices the train track of stitches running down my left arm, and a few raised but fading scars across my torso.

"Car accident," I tell her.

She runs her fingers along the scars. "I guess it wasn't just a fender bender," she says, glancing up at me.

I look at her, and the memories start to come pouring back. But I scramble and turn the faucet off before they're able to do any real damage. Regardless, she picks up on my discomfort, and in turn pulls off her tank top to reveal a black bra. She moves in close and we start to kiss again. Then we're on the bed, naked, and I'm inside her. She never asks if I have a condom, so I don't bother with the formality.

She might not be a talker, this Dora, but she's a biter, and she likes to dig her nails into my back. She moans rather than screams, and her breasts are firmer than most girls' I've been with.

We go at it again and again, and eventually she cums, digging her nails into my chest. I cum inside her but keep going. But now that I've blown my load it becomes increasingly difficult to remain motivated. She keeps going though, and eventually I get hard again. Then I think she cums again because she stops and nestles up to me, moaning quietly, almost purring. We lie there in a sweaty mess a while, adjusting ourselves and exchanging few words. Then she gives me a blowjob and I reciprocate, which is great—except for the fact she mashes my face right into her pelvic bone when she cums a third time.

She tells me later she cums really easily, and I'm not sure if that's entirely a good thing. We fall asleep and I have a dream I'm playing golf with my grandfather and some guy I went to high school with. Then I'm on a bus with some of the guys I worked with up north and we're driving to Seattle, but we get lost along the way. Then I'm racing down a hill on a bike and can't seem to get the thing to turn.

Eventually I awake to Jeff shaking my shoulder. "Seth, hey, we've gotta go."

He's already dressed. I roll over, but Dora is still asleep. "What time is it?"

"Fuck, man, it's nine. We play in like half an hour."

I sit up. "Shit. Fuck. Okay, let's go."

Jeff and I dart out of the house, finding ourselves somewhere in Kamloops. Christ, we could be anywhere. But Jeff says he knows the way to the hotel, so we start running. I'm pretty hungover and can really feel it after a few blocks. I turn my cell phone on and call Cancer.

"Where the fuck are you?" he blasts.

"Jeff, where are we?"

"We're coming up to Columbia right above the TV station. We're on Kant Drive."

"We're on Kant Drive."

I can hear Cancer shout our location to someone.

"Dude, you're lucky," he says. "We're on our way to the game, and we've been trying to call you and Jeff for an hour."

"Did Alys stop by?"

"Fuck, yeah. She showed up at our room at like quarter to three, and I answered the door and said I had no clue where you were. She got all weird and said if I see you, to get you to call her."

Cancer tells me he's getting a ride with Wade and that he's got our gear and sticks in the back of the truck. They pick us up in Wade's huge black Dodge Ram, and we stop at 7–Eleven where I get a banana, a Red Bull, an energy bar and a hot dog, wolfing them all down before we even get to the rink. Meanwhile Jeff is filling Wade and Cancer in on all the dirty details of our night. Apparently he got laid too, and on top of that had anal sex, something he seems particularly proud of.

A t the rink, I throw up in the toilet just before I'm about to hit the ice. I feel like shit, so I take an ephedrine and a Claritin Extra-Strength. Then I have another Red Bull, and gulp down loads of water in the warm-up. My gear is soaked and soggy because I never had the chance to air it out, but after a while I get used to the slimy cold feel of it. I belch and taste banana and hot dog. I spill a bit of puke onto the ice, and one of the refs skates by with a bewildered look on his face. I just smile and shrug it off.

Cancer skates over while I'm stretching. He tells me he got laid, and we joke about Alys showing up. He tells me he might have asked her if she wanted to come in and have a threesome, but he can't remember. He was pretty drunk. He tells me he's pretty sure Alys hates his fucking guts.

The pills kick in after my first shift. I don't even touch the puck, but just skate around chasing on the forecheck. The team we're playing is from Calgary, and they're dressed in actual Flames jerseys. Still, they're supposed to be okay, and they did finish second in their pool. If we win this game we're off to the final, and if we lose we're in the bronze medal match. I'm pretty sure we'll just head home if we lose this one though, as everyone looks pretty pale and hungover. Besides, no one likes to play for the bronze medal.

After that first shift, for some reason—perhaps it's the drugs— the puck keeps finding its way onto my stick. I get two quality shots on goal, one ringing off the goalie's cage. After a whistle, a mêlée occurs in front of the net. Everyone jockeys around as the refs try to instil some type of order, but it's not working. I grab a guy from the side, and he turns and starts to yell profanities into my face. He's built like a boulder, and his face looks like it's been dragged across gravel. He drops his right glove and cracks me in the cheek. I try to block his second shot, but only manage to divert it to my ear. Then he pulls me in close and lands a few more punches, and before I know it I'm getting beat up.

He tries to pull my jersey over my head, but I'm having none of this shit now. I yank both of us backwards and try to toss him under me. We fall almost side by side, and the refs are on top of us quickly. I can taste blood in my mouth as the four of us flail around on the ice. Jerseys and limbs are everywhere. We break up and I stagger to my feet, and pull my elbow pads back on.

The ref only gives the guy two minutes for kicking my ass—roughing, technically—and I head to the bench and wash the blood from my face. I demand I stay on because this is my power play—I earned it. Nobody seems to object, probably because I'm yelling and bleeding and angry.

Setting up in the corner on the power play, I get the puck just as a lane opens up to the net. I dart towards it, and as soon as one of their forwards starts to reach for me with his stick, I let off a quick snapper that somehow finds its way in. The bench is energized by the goal, and then just before the end of the first period we score again, the end result of a beautiful two-on-one by Jeff and Tristan which sends our bench into a fever.

Next shift out, before I can even get my bearings, I catch a puck in the face. I'm split wide open, my eyebrow bleeding heavily. I can tell it's bad by the steady stream of blood painting a messy trail on the ice as I move. The referee blows his whistle and I look up, tasting the blood. I spit a flurry of blood across the ice, disgusted by both my luck and myself.

The period ends right after I leave the ice, and one of the tournament medics tapes me up with a butterfly bandage. You need stitches, he says. I just look at him.

"That will have to wait, I'm afraid."

At the start of the second, I'm off to the side of the net when a point shot comes in and the puck just rolls right out to me with a wide open net for the taking. Today seems to be my lucky day, one way or the other, and I snap the puck in with authority. Soon, though, the other team scores, and they seem to rally. We spend the rest of the second staving off their counterattack and killing a few penalties. Cancer is playing terribly and throws his usual temper tantrum when he gets to the bench, whipping a water bottle around and banging his stick against his helmet repeatedly.

A few shifts into the third I find myself on a three-on-one with Cancer and Tristan. Cancer is trailing the two of us and I cut left as soon as I cross the blueline. For some reason the defenceman keys on me and I slid a drop pass between my legs. Cancer steps into the puck and rips it past the goalie. But they respond immediately, scoring another unanswered goal to close the lead to 4–2. They pull their goalie with just over a minute remaining, but I manage to steal the puck at the redline and pot an empty netter for the win and the trick.

After the game the guys are buzzing, and the dressing room is bombastic as we scream and swear and wrestle with one another. We're off to the final and we've got a great chance at taking the tournament, something completely unexpected at the beginning. We've got four and a half hours before we're supposed to suit up for the final. Cancer and I jump in the back of Glen's truck, and I call Dora on my cell. She's still in bed. I tell her I've got a game at four-thirty I'd like her to come watch. She says she will, and she'll bring her roommate for Jeff too. I remember Jeff is married, but don't dare bring this up now. Things could get really messy if that got brought up now. My phone rings right after I hang up with Dora. It's Alys.

"So where were you?" she asks.

"You're not going to believe this," I tell her. "I got thrown in the drunk tank at around midnight, and didn't get out until like nine in the morning."

"What? Really?" she says. "Why didn't you phone me when you got out?"

I think she's buying it, but can't be sure. Maybe she needs some reassurance.

"Well my cell phone was dead and I had to charge it back at the hotel room, and by the time it charged up enough to call you we had to go play. We won by the way. We're off to the finals. I was just going to call you to tell you the good news."

"Are you okay though? What happened?"

"Ah, nothing. I was trying to convince the cops to let me call you, but. . . . Ah, those fucking pigs. Cancer said you stopped by."

"Oh geez, that's terrible. Why'd they throw you in though."

"Get this. I'm crossing the fucking street to come down to the Max to meet you, and I cut a cop off and he tells me to go home. Naturally I don't, but then of course the very same cop sees me a few blocks later taking a piss in an alley and he hauls me in."

"That's awful."

"You're telling me. So you wanna meet up? I'd really like to see you. How'd your game go, by the way?"

Cancer is waving his finger in my face. Then he sticks his entire upper body out the truck window and shouts at the pedestrians on the street. People look at him with perplexed and silent stares. It's Sunday morning, and we drive past a church just finishing morning service. "Don't pray to that God," Cancer yells at the families dressed in shirts, ties and dresses. "God is right here, right inside this truck. You've got the wrong guy!"

I meet up with Alys in her room. They lost their game and they have to head out on the road. She looks tired and we decide to watch TV together. I can sense maybe she knows I'm lying, but then don't really care all that much to be honest. I'll just hang out with her until she's gone. She gives me her home number—she's from Vernon—and I give her my phone number. We also exchange emails. She kisses me on the cheek as she packs up her gear, and then heads out to the team van in the parking lot. I'm getting steady glares from most of her teammates, who don't seem all that convinced by my wild and crazy drunk tank story.

After she leaves I fall asleep on my bed almost immediately, my morning drugs having long worn off. Eventually I'm woken up by Jeff and Cancer watching TV, eating stale chips and drinking beer in their underwear. It's almost time to head to the rink apparently. Cancer fires up an extra chilly ice bath. While I wait for the tub to fill I head down to the buffet, which still offers some leftovers from breakfast. I take one of the wicker muffin baskets and load it up with as much food as it will carry.

When I return to our floor, the ice bath is eliciting loud shrieks from our room. After we've all had our treatment, we cram the remaining food into our mouths as we pack our gear, leaving condom wrappers sprinkled across the floor and empty beer cans hidden around the room like Easter eggs. I check out, we pay up and split the bill, then jump in the car and head to the rink.

The team we're playing is from Prince George, and supposedly pretty good. They've won all their games handily so far, just like we have. Prince George is a shithole, says Jeff before the game. If we get beat by Prince George, God will surely punish us, he maintains. He seems pretty fired up, and since I've popped some methamphetamine, a Claritin and downed a Blue Gatorade, I'm pretty fired up as well.

I'm zoning in during the warm-up. A few of the guys skate by, telling me they want to see more of that shit. More goals, they mean. More fucking goals. That I can do, I say.

I see Dora and her friend sitting alone off to the left, dressed in sweaters and jeans. I wave to them. They wave back. Jeff skates over and tells me our puck bunnies are here. I say I

know already. I'm actually somewhat surprised to see them
here, on account of our literally vanishing from their house
earlier.

Both teams are pretty standoffish for most of the first period, and it seems like the refs are going to let us play. We
exchange a few chances, and at the end of the first things seem
fairly evenly matched. We talk about keeping up with our system—a tough forecheck, five guys up the ice, five guys back.
Jeff asks who's going to be the hero, which seems a bit cheesy,
but whatever.

The second period arrives and things get a bit shaky. They
score about five minutes in, but we quickly reply with a goal
of our own. I collect an assist on the play. Then there's some
rough stuff at the tail end of the second that gets the crowd
excited at what's been an extremely cautious affair thus far.
Before the period ends I ring one off the crossbar, and Cancer
joins me on the bench afterwards.

"You know, Seth," he says in all seriousness, "hitting the
post is a lot like finger-fucking a chick."

"How so?" I make the mistake of asking.

"Well, see, 'cause the post makes this cool sound when you
hit it, and when you're done you feel this kind of sense of
accomplishment. But then you realize afterwards that fuck, that
could've been your dick in there, not the same fucking fingers
you use to pick your goddamned nose with."

Everyone on the bench laughs. Tristan glances over at me.
"I think about half of that made sense," he says with a smirk.

"That's all that matters," I tell him.

In the third I feel pretty good considering, and do well on
the forecheck, making sure to mark up back in our zone. The
last thing I want is my check scoring the winning goal. As the
third winds down, both teams shift into a defensive posture,
waiting for overtime. I ask one of the refs before a faceoff what
exactly happens in overtime. He looks at me like I should

already know, then explains we'll have four-on-four for five minutes, followed by a shootout. Both teams get healthy chances as regulation time comes to an end. We huddle around for the start of overtime. My line is going to start.

Four-on-four is a different brand of hockey. The ice opens up tremendously and odd-man rushes are everywhere. But both teams are here for a reason, good goaltending and a solid unit. The goalies shine in overtime, Glen making some enormous saves. I keep thinking to myself I want to score the goal, but I only get two short shifts in and before I know it we're heading to the shootout.

Jeff and a few of the veterans decide the list. I'm shooting third out of five. Cancer is shooting first. The intensity inside the rink is palpable. Both teams don't want to make that long car ride home knowing what could have been. I look over at Dora and pretend to bite my nails. She smiles and pretends to bite hers too.

One of their flashy forward shoots first. I instantly hate him simply for the fact he's wearing number 99. As luck would have it, the puck flips up on end on him, and Glen easily corrals his weak shot. We all cheer and knock our sticks against the boards.

"Fucking ninety-nine. What an asshole," I say to no one in particular.

Cancer comes down on their goalie at a bit of an angle, fakes, kicks his leg back and throws the goalie the wrong way, roofing his shot home off the crossbar. Our bench erupts.

Their next shooter comes down on Glen, fakes, dekes twice, but Glen follows him and he sends the puck off our goalie's shoulder and over the net.

I'm starting to get nervous, knowing I shoot soon. Should I deke, try to pull him right and go five-hole, or come in on an angle and try to pick a corner with a snapper? The possibilities are endless.

Mike, a winger who plays on my line, is next. He comes down calm and slow and casually rips a wrister top corner, turning our bench into an instant madhouse. Mike saunters over and we all shower him with praise for his ridiculously cool goal. Then their third shooter comes down on Glen. He's a young defenceman, a big lanky guy, and he comes in and fires a quick shot, but Glen catches a piece of the puck with his blocker, sending it wide right. Our bench is raging with excitement now, and I'm nervous as hell.

I skate out onto the empty ice. All those in attendance stand up and voices erupt from both benches. The puck sits at centre ice. If I score it's over and we win. If I score I can end it all, and I'm extremely nervous but trying to remain stoic in the face of it all.

I'm going to deke and pull the goalie to one side. And I'm going to go in fast from the left on an angle, I've decided. The ref tells me to wait for the whistle before I go. I take a deep breath to calm myself. It's quiet now except for a few shouts of encouragement from my bench.

Finally the whistle goes and I burst into motion, skating in hard from the left. The goalie comes out to meet me, sliding to his right. I start to deke, but then I center off and so does he. I switch left to forehand, then backhand, and he seems to bite, so I pull hard right and he comes with me, dropping down into the butterfly. A flash of open net appears and I pull the puck back, flick it up, and it goes in over his glove.

Our bench erupts as I skate towards it, and the entire team comes barrelling towards me. The guys crash into me like a punt-return team, and I'm instantly crushed under their collective weight. My back is twisted and I can hardly breathe, but I don't care. All I can see is dark blue jerseys and all I can hear are screams of elation. Finally the pile starts to clear, and thank God because my back is killing me. Cancer comes over and we hug and fall to the ice. Glen lands on top of us. I get up and Jeff embraces me, screaming "You Motherfucker!" over and over in my face.

I hug just about every player on our team, and glance over to see the other team lining up along their blueline, looking exactly the way they should be looking. Defeated. Disgusted. Beaten and broken down.

I look over at Dora and her friend. They're up on their feet, clapping, and I smile and wave at them. In time we start to settle down and line up across our own blueline, gloves and helmets and sticks strewn across the ice behind us.

Each Prince George player is presented a medal, and has his name called out over the microphone. We clap for everyone, and especially for their goalie, who for his efforts has earned himself Player of the Game. The tournament organizer thanks the team and congratulates them for a great tournament. Then he announces the winner of the MVP trophy, and the guys grab at me as I skate over to collect it. Jeff gets called over to accept the cup, a huge bowl on a rectangular platform.

Jeff returns with the trophy and we all hold it up together, hands everywhere. Guys start screaming and I can't help but scream too, as together we tower above it all in this brief moment of true happiness.

Afterwards I chat with Dora briefly. She hugs me as I tower over her in my skates. She mentions something about wanting to come to Vancouver to visit me. I smile and say that would be great, even though, for some reason, I'm already beginning to doubt the truth of that.

Double Zero

I'm waiting at the bus stop, just past the Skytrain station by Science World. The sky is dark, but the city is still bright with sirens, and scattered shouts can be heard somewhere in the distance. A shopping cart slowly rattles down the street out of sight.

I've been waiting for Dora. She's come down to see me for a few days over New Year's. I was inside the depot when they announced her bus had arrived from Kamloops, so I darted out to my car to lean against the door and look tall, dark and mysterious when she came walking out the front doors. Small town girl looking for her big city boy-toy in the dark.

My stitches have come out and my broken finger resides in a small splint, but other than that I'm healed up and feeling fine. Dora walks out behind a group of backpackers. She's dressed in a sweater and those skin-hugging sweats young chicks wear. I haven't seen her since the tournament and she looks different somehow. Slightly worn-down maybe. Hollowed out. Still, the next few minutes are a blur of excited, uncomfortable conversation and a kiss on the cheek that escalates quickly into a series of awkward gropes in the middle of the parking lot. I touch her breast. She feels different, tastes different. My memory of her is somehow different than the real thing, which is a bit of a disappointment.

We get in my car and head for my apartment. She's come for the long weekend, having made the long trip down to cement herself in my heart, I suppose. But I could be wrong. She may simply be here to escape the boyfriend she has back home and never told me about. I haven't a clue and, to be honest, don't really care.

My cell phone saves me about ten minutes into the car ride, just moments after the conversation inexplicably dies. It's Ryan, and he's looking for Cancer who's supposed to be home. I tell him he's probably sleeping. It's Friday night and we were supposed to meet up at Ryan's house about an hour ago. Ryan, expecting company, is already wasted, and I can almost feel the spit blast through the cell phone as he speaks.

I look over at Dora. She smiles at me and looks out the window, a sign she's trying to give me some privacy.

"How long will you be?" Ryan asks.

"I just picked up Dora, so as soon as we get home we'll shower and get ready, and then I'll wake up Cancer and head over."

"Oh yeah, fuck, Dora. I forgot about her. Cancer mentioned something about a Kamloops chick coming down to see you."

I know Dora can hear my side of the conversation, so I make sure not to say anything stupid. Ryan, however, has other ideas.

"Cancer said she's a tall bitch?"

"Yeah, pretty much."

"Fuckin' A, man. Has she let you stick your finger up her ass? That's a sure sign she's into you."

"Ah no, man. I don't think so," I say, trying not to smile. Ryan knows she's right beside me, but doesn't care.

"You know what I've always wanted to try?"

"What's that?" I ask.

"See if she'll let you piss on her. I'm serious. Golden shower, man, R. Kelly style. Just piss all over her, then do the helicopter with your dick while you're pissing."

"No, yeah, good idea. We'll consider that for sure."

"And if she's really kinky, she'll be like—"

"Okay, later," I say and hang up quickly. I smile, turning my phone off.

"Who was that?" Dora asks.

"That was Ryan. Good guy. He plays in our league."

"Oh cool. I look forward to meeting him."

Every word coming out of my mouth is a curse word right now. I'm angry at myself, and desperately need to right this wrong. Fix this mistake I've created. Salvage some of the dignity I've negated.

I'm barrelling down Commercial Drive in search of Dora, my eyes darting left and right as I frantically search the night for her. I run a red light then cut off a bus, pull an illegal U-turn and start heading back. Dora suddenly appears there on the sidewalk, as if by magic. She's almost speed-walking, and I can see she's still crying. I get to the end of the block and turn around again, this time cutting off two cars. Both drivers honk their horns in disgust, but I ignore them.

I slow down once I get behind her. She looks back, sees me, then turns her head forward and picks up speed.

"Dora!" I shout out the open passenger window.

"Fuck off."

"Dora, look, you shouldn't be out here this late at night. This isn't the best part of town for a woman to be—"

"Seth, fuck off, okay? Leave me alone. Christ."

"Look, I know you're pissed, but can you just get in the car? I'll drive you to my place to get your stuff, and then I'll drive you to the bus depot and pay for a bus myself. And hell, if there isn't one coming, I'll pay for you to rent a fuckin' car and drive it home to Kamloops, all right?"

Cars are lining up behind me now because I'm driving so slowly. They honk and swear at me as they swerve left and zoom past. When we get to the end of the block, I pull onto a side street and get out of the car.

"Dora."

"Seth, fuck off."

"Dora, look, just let me get you someplace safe. I mean where the fuck are you even going?"

"As far away from you as I can get!"

I'm now walking directly behind her. People scan us as they pass, the whites of their eyes analyzing, considering, sceptical of all this noise we're making.

"Dora, please, it's not safe out here this time of night."

"Well why don't you get some of your engineering buddies to help us out? Or some of the university hockey team? Oh that's right, because it's all a fuckin' *lie!*" she screams.

I'm not sure how to respond to this, but try anyway. "Look, I'm sorry, okay? Please just let me get you out of here. I'll take you wherever you want to go, and we don't have to talk at all. I'll just drive you wherever."

She stops quickly and wheels around to face me, catching me a bit off guard. Her face is red and her eyes are bloodshot. Tears stream down her face. She asks me when I was planning on telling her, and her roommate, that Jeff was married, and had five boys, information Cancer managed to leak just about an hour ago. I don't answer. She steps up close and I lean back. The palm of her hand catches me square in the ear, sending me reeling back slightly off balance. She looks at me like I'm supposed to respond to this assault with a statement, but I just check my ear for blood and stare.

"What else did you lie to me about?" she asks.

"What?"

"I said what else did you lie to me about? Just tell me, for Christ's sake."

"Dora . . ."

"You know it's all bullshit. You would've said anything to get in my pants. You say all this shit and then think I won't find out? That somehow this won't all blow up in your face? My God, what a piece of work you are."

"I was going to tell you. Like at the right time though."

"The right time, huh. Tell me, when exactly is the right time to admit to something like that. It would never be the right time."

"Okay, please, settle down. Let's talk about this someplace else."

She just stands there and stares at me. In fact, she stares at me so hard and so long I grin ever so slightly at the absurdity of the situation.

"You think this is *funny*?" she hisses. "Fuck you, Seth!"

She comes at me again, and I let her have her way. This time it's a punch straight to the nose, followed by a kick to the groin that narrowly misses my balls. I stagger back and put my hands up to say "Stop," but she only cocks back again. I swarm her, corralling her arms in a bear hug. She starts to scream, demanding I let her go.

Some people walk by, stepping around us awkwardly. I apologize and move Dora to one side of the sidewalk, close to the store windows, and out of the flow of foot traffic. Meanwhile she's still screaming into my ear, and her nails continue to rip the flesh from my face and arms. I try to cover her mouth, but she bites my fingers, hard, and I let out a roar of pain. I take her to the ground, pressing her down with my knees. She's still screaming, but her voice is muffled by my chest and arms. We wrestle around for a few moments as I try in vain to calm her down. Then I hear the sirens, and soon the blue and red lights are flashing all around.

The next day, upon my release from jail, the boys and I spend New Year's doing what we do best, wreaking havoc anywhere and everywhere. We end up drinking outside the Pacific Coliseum, just for old time's sake, chucking beer bottles off the windows of the arena, cursing the '94 Canucks half-heartedly, wishing another riot would erupt tonight so we might do some real lasting damage to not only the city but to ourselves.

I think about Dora until I get drunk enough not to think anymore. Cancer and I end up walking home at about five in the morning, reeking of champagne and cigars, but no pussy. Neither of us really care, though, as New Year's is always a letdown. Kind of like your birthday, something built up simply because it needs to be smashed down. No, a new year was nothing special. Just another wobbling spin around the sun.

A few mornings later, a huge cigar burn greets me from the carpet beside my bed. My alarm clock is screaming at me. Upside down it reads 11:34. I roll over and realize I've puked all over my bed, which is just a mattress, a bed sheet and a pillow. This is nothing new though, and definitely not the first time either. I roll back over and decide to sleep a while before I get up. I have a massive headache running all the way down my spine.

I can hear Cancer in the living room, his filthy rap music blaring. He's getting ready to go out again, eager to drink the whole first week of the new year away. Ryan and some guy named James are over—I can hear them out there, baiting one another. I think Ryan lives here now, or so it seems. Whatever.

I stand up in bed, stretching back to loosen up and clear the cobwebs. I ache all over. Then I proceed directly to the fridge and crack the first beer I can find.

The phone rings in the living room. I hear someone answer it, then Cancer screaming at the top of his lungs, "Seth, phone, it's a girl!"

I stagger into the living room. The guys are watching the Canucks game, with rap music blasting in the background. There are beer bottles everywhere and fresh McDonald's in everyone's lap. Cancer holds the phone out in my direction. "It sounds like Dora. Don't be long, though, because we have to leave soon. Have you showered yet?"

I don't answer. Instead I take the telephone and walk back
to my room, away from the noise and confusion and smell of
overcooked meat.

"Hello?" I say, closing the door behind me.

"Seth?"

"Dora?"

"Seth, I'm going to be brief and make this short."

"Make what short."

"I feel I need to tell you what I've done—for closure."

"Uh, what? Closure? Closure from what?"

"Seth, please just listen, okay?"

"Okay . . ."

"Seth, I had an abortion two days ago. You're the only guy
I've been with in the past while, since I broke up with my ex."

I stand there, phone pressed against my ear, staring at the
wall.

"Seth?"

I don't answer.

"Seth?"

I stand there.

"Seth, did you hear what I said."

". . . Yeah. Yeah, Dora, I heard what you said."

Both of us fall silent. I'm trying to piece it together, but with
a million questions running through my brain, bouncing around
like lottery balls. I can't seem to ask any of them however.

"Seth?"

I don't answer.

"Seth, please acknowledge you heard what I said."

I wonder, briefly, how much alcohol Nicolas Cage's char-
acter in *Leaving Las Vegas* had to drink in order to kill himself.
Then I hang up and head down the hallway into the shower.
I sit down in the tub, lean forward and let the water pound my
head. I just sit there and think, until the water goes cold and
I'm forced to get out.

Back in my room, standing there amidst some scattered clothes and empty beer cans, I mutter to myself, "This is it. This is finally it and I've had enough. This is it," I repeat as my fists clench up. I can feel myself pulsating. It's time to get this over with.

I walk over to the wall, place my palms against it, and start breathing heavily through my teeth. Spit spurts out as I start to twist my neck, the muscles in my arms tightening up, and then I cock my head back and slam it into the wall, top of the fore-head first. The drywall crumbles under the impact, and my nose stops my head from going completely through. I whip my head out in a flurry of white drywall dust, and cough several times in order to clear my lungs. I stand there, looking at what remains of the wall. Then I repeat the feat until I collapse from exhaustion.

Eventualizationship

Day 1

My cell rings, waking me up. It's 1:20 in the morning, according to my alarm clock.

"Hello?"

All I hear is bar noise, muffled voices and music woven together in a tapestry of sound. I can hear one group of people more clearly, but can't distinguish any of the voices. Then a female voice separates itself from the confusion and says, "Hello? Seth?"

"Yeah?"

"How's it goin'?"

"Who is this?" I ask, lying back down in bed.

"It's Jill."

"Jill." I scan my memory quickly for a Jill, but draw a blank. "Hey Jill, how's it goin'."

"Good, how are you? We're at the Roxy, and you should come down. Cancer says you guys know one of the bouncers."

"Yeah, some guy that plays hockey with us lets us in sometimes."

"Cool. So you should come down here then."

"What time is it, Jill?"

"It's like close to closing. So you gonna come down? I'd really like to see you again. It's too bad we didn't catch up more after that night."

"Yeah, it is."

"So, yeah, come down and we'll catch up."

I hang up the phone, then turn it off and try to go back to sleep, the muffled bar voices echoing through my skull.

Day 3

I scribble something on the wall of my room, a joke told at a family dinner that, as far as I remember, everyone laughed at. It's always stayed with me for some strange reason. *I don't know why I filled out an organ donor card. No one should be forced to live with the burden of my liver.*

It's time to realize I've just jumped into the exact middle of the ocean and I don't know how to swim.

Day 5

This is really painful. Not a physical pain, mind you, but another kind of pain much more difficult to explain, let alone pinpoint to one extremity or region. It's inside the very marrow of my bones. It's in my blood. My brain hurts too, and it hurts to think about her—to try to rationalize what might happen if she calls, what I will say, how I will react. I've become obsessed, overanalyzing everything to death. But the funny thing is, now, if I had the chance, I wouldn't go back. I needed to be stripped of my ego and shown the error of my own ways. I needed to have something essential taken from me to realize yes, I can be an asshole, and yes, people can be just as cold as I can be. I needed to be shown I'm not invincible. I needed to be shown that someone can change *my* life without due care. That someone can take a life I created and crush it without so much as consulting me.

I was fighting the shakes last night. Fidgety, sporadic movements of flesh and head. Like a tick, or an inconsistent twitch. When I spoke to people on the phone, I was always moving, rubbing my jeans with my fingers, back and forth, over and over. I feel lighter. Things look different. The gas station sign outside my window seems a more vibrant yellow than before. Things are starting to change, but then again this is just the start of it all. The real battles lay ahead.

Day 6

I wonder what she's thinking. Does she know how powerful that phone call was for me? For me to finally hit rock bottom and start my long difficult climb back to being? She has to tell me why she did what she did. Why she had to wash me away in her kitchen sink of memories, cleansing me from her life.

I keep picturing her in my head. I picture her making the decision, planning how to wipe her mistake—which was me—from her life.

I think I know why relationships don't work for me. I want comfort. I want to be taken care of. I want someone to love me. Feeling love myself is irrelevant. If someone lives and dies by my happiness, I know I am in control. I have serious power over their emotions and I'm fine with that. I toy with peoples' hearts. I'm a destroyer.

I feel new and fresh, but at the same time I'm in constant pain. My brain is churning, working at full capacity. My mind is trying to rationalize what the hell just happened. I'm trying to formulate the perfect response should she call for some reason, even though deep down I know she won't. Many situations have been worked out in my head but I'm sure if they ever happened, I'd totally fuck them up. I'd destroy them. I'd do the only thing I'm good at. I'd attack.

I'm trying to remember the blur that was the last six days before I went sober. I thought I could go for longer, to be honest. I thought I could sabotage my body better. After day three I couldn't stop. I didn't want to face the hangover. Day four I slept in my car, eating nothing but 7–Eleven and McDonald's the entire time. I've lost over thirteen pounds, according to the scale in the bathroom. My skin is pale, and my knuckles and joints are beet red from a lack of sufficient protein.

I remember vague impressions of people, places, events, a cowboy hat, a brawl outside a club, pissing in the sink at a bar, puking in the pool at UBC before jumping off the 10–metre diving board, sending my body screaming into the water, a drunken missile in khaki shorts and a faded *Rage Against the Machine* T-shirt.

I remember Cancer trying to fight some guy he thought might have been his English teacher in high school, and then calling some fat chick who tried to intervene a "stunned cunt." As I recall, she responded by karate-kicking him really hard in the thigh, which only made him want to get at the teacher that much more. I remember jokingly calling Cancer a Jew because he wouldn't pay my cover at the Roxy, and then the bouncer telling us we wouldn't get in after hearing that. Fuck him. I remember crotching a bottle of Corona out of a pub on Commercial Drive and nursing it with Cancer as we stumbled towards my car. I remember having sex with some girl, without a condom, who had amazing breasts and an open sore on her vagina. And I remember the phone call, the one I received to start the past six days. It wasn't so much what she said, but what her words allowed me to do. She gave me a plausible reason to dig until I hit bedrock. Dig as deep as I could go.

I smile because I went out on my terms. I went out the only way I know how. Not through the back door, not through the front, but through the bedroom wall, head first and balls out.

Day 7

This feels like the last night in my body. My soul is seeping out of my skin, sweating its way out of my pores. The shakes—as I have dubbed them—are not slowed by the Celexa, and Valium, and Ativan, and anything else I can get my hands on. These shakes are my addiction moaning for a resumption of bygone days.

There is a sense of something. A beginning. This will be a place I have never ventured before, a place completely foreign to me. I'm scared of this new place, but without it now I would surely die. I'd suffocate if I went back now. I've tasted and sucked a full breath of a new kind of oxygen, and the old air simply won't do anymore. The old scents, the old tastes, the old feelings aren't me anymore. I have a short time to either right this ship and survive, or go down once and for all.

If I fail, everyone will abandon hope. They will grow cynical ears, and become tired of my hollow promises. I have one chance to live and a million chances to die.

Day 7½

I sit up in my bed, naked. I haven't so much as ventured past the Blockbuster down the street this last week, but now I'm getting ready to go out into the world.

I decide a forty minute shower might help. I sit in the tub, thinking, before heading down to the bank to attempt to increase my credit card limit which has recently been maxed out a second time. My car insurance is huge now, on account of the crash. I was the only one involved that didn't receive a huge payout from the government for the accident, albeit I lived. ICBC said I was still partially at fault, even though I was actually under the legal limit. Drunk, but not technically drunk. Whatever. They had good lawyers.

Rent, prescription medications, telephone bills, lawyer fees and retainer, parking tickets, credit card overdraft fees, ATM withdrawal surcharges—everyone wants money from me, even though I don't have any, and my employment insurance is now under the $1,000 mark. Even EI takes money from me for being on EI. What the fuck.

In retrospect, all I had to do to get out of this funk was get a job. But I couldn't do it. I didn't want to work another single day of my life.

Day 8

It's amazing how much you notice booze when you stop drinking. It's everywhere.

I've thought about getting absolutely wasted. Going to the liquor store, picking up some vodka and some beer, and just pounding it back until I throw up.

I keep calling people on my cell phone. I don't know why I'm calling them. I tell them what I'm doing and for the first time in a long time I feel like I'm saying exactly what I'm thinking. Saying exactly what I want to say. Everything is coming directly to them. No ulterior motives, no back-alley scams. Just me. Coming at them. Telling them what the hell is going on and why.

Day 9

I could really use a drink to help me get through this sobriety thing.

Day 10

Today I was offered my first drink, which I turned down. Beer is everywhere—on the counters, in the fridges, in the coolers, in liquor stores—everywhere. I've realized at least one conversation I hear or am involved in each day involves the idea of the consumption of alcohol. Bars are spreading like the Avian Flu since I've gone sober.

I'm not sure what to call myself. Recovering? Sober? Stupid? I just feel different. Like I've wandered into a deep forest and have no clue where I am or why I even came here. But somehow, if I wanted to go back the way I came in, I'm sure I could find it.

Day 11

I don't know why I tried to call Dora. Today seemed like the best day, and I was starting to get over her and what she told me. What a mistake.

Day 12

Jeff and the other team's captain are on the other side of the rink with the two refs. One of the refs is yelling something, gesturing with his hands at both players, but I can't quite hear what he's saying. One of our guys got viciously cross-checked from behind in front of the net just after the whistle blew, a blatant cheap shot, and Mike retaliated with a good solid punch to the face. Then one of their guys sucker-punched Mike in the side of the head and the battle was on. Chances are it might end up being a four-on-four or four-on-three for us when all's said and done. Still, we're up 5–2 midway through the third, and things look like they could be about to get out of hand.

Jeff skates over to the bench and says it's going to be a four-on-three for us, for two minutes. This means more open ice than Alaska, and a chance for me, hopefully, to get out and really stretch my legs.

Sure enough, I'm sent out with the three fastest guys on our team. I line up and take the draw in their end, and manage to lose it cleanly. Cursing myself, I rush the defenceman with the puck. He's able to fire it down the ice though, prompting Glen to leave his net to retrieve it. We dangle around in the neutral zone a while, until I cough up the puck and their two forwards head in on a two-on-two. I'm angry at myself now, as I know the bench probably didn't like the cough-up, let alone that fucking faceoff.

We intercept a bad pass and I'm sent in on a two-on-one with Gary, one of our fastest forwards. I'm a few steps behind him, without the puck, and I'm cranking full speed to catch up. Gary pulls across the blueline and the defenceman dives, sliding backwards to block the pass. Gary, ever patient, waits a few moments for him to slide clear before sending me a perfect saucer pass. I one-time the shot, which the goalie gets just enough of to send it ringing off the post. I hear the crowd and both benches jump at the sound of the 'ping.' The puck rattles around the boards before our third guy in manages to corral it. We cycle a while until one of their guys catches our defence-man flat-footed, and intercepts a pass to put himself on a breakaway. I'm still tired from the initial rush, but find myself closest to him, and therefore stuck chasing from their blueline.

The guy is fast, but not too fast, and I'm able to get close enough that I dive stick first, catching the puck and taking him down with me. We both go piling into the end boards in a per-plexity of sticks and snow. He gets the worst of it, cushioning my impact against the boards, and his bench screams for a call that won't come. He takes his time getting up, obviously a bit rattled, which puts us right back on a three-on-two the other way, with myself as the trailer. I'm once again in full stride, screaming down the center of the ice.

Gary has the puck and decides to split the defence, which he does with relative ease just inside the blueline. But he fum-bles the puck and gets only a weak shot off, which their goalie smothers easily. Play slams to a stop in a spray of ice, and with the whistle I immediately return to the bench. The small crowd in attendance is clapping, and both benches hit their sticks against the boards in appreciation of the last few rushes.

I'm so exhausted I feel like I'm going to throw up. I'm try-ing to suck in air as rapidly as possible, but as soon as I sit down, the contents of my stomach make a B-line for my mouth and I puke all over the floor. This goes relatively unno-ticed, except for Tristan, whose skates are now covered in vomit. He turns to me.

"Jesus Christ, Seth. Not on the Bauers."

He grabs a water bottle and cleans his skates off, then pro-ceeds to dilute the remaining puke with water. I lean back and let out an exasperated "Sorry."

Tristan smiles and squirts the water full force into my face and all over my jersey. "Atta boy, good shift," he tells me.

Before I can clean up the rest of the vomit, our bench
erupts. Cancer has scored a goal with a point shot off the ensuing faceoff.

"Fuck," I yell. "That's my plus-minus."

When I return to the ice, I decide the rest of the game
will be spent pestering their top scorer, who's currently tied
with me in league scoring with only a handful of games
remaining in the regular season. He's all flash with his gold
necklace, bubble visor and neatly trimmed mullet, all of
which, taken together as an ensemble, pisses me off to no end.
The bastard's also sporting a pair of those old white Nike
skates and white gloves, which is inexcusable, and so every
time I get near him I give it to him with my stick—hacking
him, hooking him from behind, making sure to rub him out
at every opportunity. He tries to deke me out a few times, but
I'm planted properly and stand him up. He's getting frustrated. I'm pissing him off.

The next shift, off the faceoff in their end, I push the puck
through his legs and dangle past. I get a good shot on net
which the goalie manages to steer aside. I head into the corner
to retrieve the puck and come out behind the net with my
opponent right on my heels. Before I can turn to feed the
puck into the slot, though, I feel my left leg lifted out from
under me, abruptly and blatantly. My face slams into the ice as
the puck is collected by their defenceman and shot out of the
zone off the glass.

No call. Our bench is furious. "Are you fuckin' blind!" I
yell at the ref. He just looks at me with a confused smirk, sig-
nalling he missed the call. "For fuck's sake, open your eyes!" I
continue.

Cancer hits the ice. And before I can even catch up to the
ensuing rush, he comes streaking across and catches my opponent admiring his own pass. Cancer ploughs full force into the
guy's face and chest with his shoulder, then falls on top of him

with all of his weight. The play continues as my opponent lies
there in obvious pain, face up, staring at the lights. I skate by
quickly before joining the counterattack.

"Fuckin' pussy," I say as I cut by. "Now you know how I've
felt the last week and a half."

Day 13

I stare into the mirror. I stare hard, at my features, at the familiar face I see there. I stare into my own eyes. I see the same
face I've seen every time I've ever looked in the mirror. I know
this face. I know this asshole.

I'm now seeing a girl named Melanie. A long, blonde-
haired girl, a graphic designer I met at a pub sometime during my six-day bender. She doesn't excite me the way
women usually do. Then again, nothing excites me the way
it used to. And she has nothing to hide, and no bruises to
conceal.

I met her two nights before I quit drinking. She only really knows the new me, which kind of excites me. But I also
know she knows the other guy, who is still very much inside
me, and wants to be inside her. She ought to steer clear of me,
but won't unfortunately.

Day 20

I'm sitting in a comfortable leather chair, rubbing my freshly
shaven face, speaking for the first time to my drug and alcohol counsellor, after a long time spent on a waiting list. I suppose addiction support is a popular thing these days.

"So, for you, having one drink would ruin this whole
thing?" she asks.

I adjust myself in my chair and think. I keep having dreams
where I have one drink, accidentally, and then regret it.

"Yeah, it would taint everything. It wouldn't be a failure,
but if I'm going to do something, I do it full on."

"That's a lot of pressure to put on yourself without a significant support network, to say the least."

"What can I say," I smile. "I thrive under pressure."

"Things are very black and white for you aren't they, Seth."

"Definitely."

"And do you think that's a good thing or a bad thing."

"I think it has its positives and its negatives."

"Right, on the one hand it will probably be the one thing that gets you through this. But then it will also take its toll on you because that type of mindset is so demanding."

"I don't know any other way, to be honest."

"Personally, I don't think you're in any position to try and tackle this any other way, Seth. But you need to be able to see the huge amount of pressure you're putting on yourself, and realize it will bring both good and bad things into your life. Like it has in the past when you were drinking too much."

"Yeah."

"So let's get back to that analogy you used of the wedding car with all the tin cans dangling behind it as it drives away."

"Okay."

"So basically you're of the mindset that, for you to move on with your life, you must cut all those strings entirely."

"Yeah, I think so. I think I feel as if my past life is following me, like it's right there over my shoulder, reminding me of what I could slip back to if I'm not careful."

She scribbles something down.

"So this girl you've been seeing, this Melanie, you have to cut her off because she's a product of your life before you went sober?" she asks eventually.

"I think so. I just feel as if that's almost a different person she knew, and that she's a reminder of the life I used to live."

"So what are you going to say to her?"

"To be honest, I really don't know. I think maybe I just need to see her and see where this is going," I shrug. "But I dunno."

"Do you think she feels the same way?"

"That's what's really puzzling. I really don't have much of a clue as to how she's handling this situation."

"Do you think you could carry on a meaningful relationship with her now that you're sober?"

"Perhaps."

"Do you think she's more involved in the relationship then you are?"

"I thought I knew the answer to that question, but now I'm not sure. To be honest, I'm not really sure about anything. I might be completely wrong about everything."

"I think you should definitely explore that relationship, even if it does look like it's going to end. You need to re-evaluate all of your relationships now, because as much as we like to think we stay the same, truth be told things have changed—you've changed—and your relationships with your friends and your family have changed."

"Yeah."

"It's a very interesting stage you're going through right now, Seth."

"No shit."

Day 25

For the past two days I've been hibernating in Chapters, mostly in the corner of the quiet and little used philosophy section on the second floor. I'm thinking of going back to start up my degree again. College sober would be good. A chance to refocus. A chance to regroup and try again.

Or maybe I'm just here to find an excuse to look for that one epiphany, that one line that will leap from the page and hit me right between the eyes, leaving me to emerge completely transformed, a revelation of a man. So I read the books, sometimes skimming quickly, other times drinking them in slowly word by word, jumping around from book to book. I scan through *The Essential Erasmus* by John P. Dolan. I read most of *Thus Spoke Zarathustra* by Friedrich Nietzsche and then take a well deserved break and get something to eat. I come back to read a select few chapters of *Leviathan* by Thomas Hobbes, realizing Hobbes from Calvin and Hobbes is *that* Hobbes, so I go read *Something Under the Bed is Drooling* and *The Essential Calvin and Hobbes* by Bill Watterson. After a long stint in the bathroom followed by a trip to the corner store for a Pepsi and a cigar I throw myself into *The Art of War* by Sun Tzu, but somehow end up in the kids' section reading *Where's Waldo?* and *Find Waldo Now?* by Martin Handford. After finding the stupid fuck in every picture I return to the philosophy section and read the first few lines of selected chapters of *Being and Time* by Martin Heidegger. I start reading *Meditations on First Philosophy* by Rene Descartes but I can't concentrate enough and decide to go home.

I rent *Spartacus* and *Tombstone* from Blockbuster, and Cancer joins me for part of the latter.

Day two I start out much more determined by reading most of *Republic* by Plato, but I find it much less exhilarating now that I've read it with intent, much like when I saw *The Godfather* for the first time and was rather disappointed. Then I start *Il Principe* by Niccolò Machiavelli, quitting after the first paragraph and jumping right into *The Nature of Judgement* by G.E. Moore. I take a long break for lunch, wander around and listen to some CDs at Virgin, then head back into the bookstore after it starts raining heavily. Surprisingly no one has noticed I basically live here now, probably because most everyone is a shift worker and it's so bloody busy all the time. Not with readers of course, but with people buying knickknacks for their home.

I read *The Twilight of The Idols/The Anti-Christ* by Nietzsche word for word, the whole way through, then head to the magazine section and start reading *Time*. Somehow I end up scanning the UK edition of *Maxim* for topless women, and then lower myself to poring over artsy photography mags for skin. I contemplate hitting the Erotica section, but decide to walk home in the rain, my hoodie off, trying to soak up as much water as possible. Drowning in a way.

Caleb comes over with a few joints and we watch *Apocalypse Now: Redux*. I get really stoned for the first time in years and swear I see a Mexican samba band playing in the trees, then get all wigged out at the Napalm explosions and drift off to sleep around the time they end up at the French Plantation. No real loss there. They ended up cutting that part for the cinematic release anyway.

Day 26

I'm back with my counsellor, feeling bored and boring. I tell her this.

"So how does that make you feel?" she asks, leaning back in her chair.

"Bored," I respond with a smile.

The office window is open, but the air isn't cold enough to affect us in here. It's nearly twilight, still light out in the city, but the streetlights have already come to life.

"But how does that make you feel?" she repeats.

"Better, I guess."

"In what way?"

"Well I guess I'm not hungover as much, that's for sure."

"And how does that make you feel?"

"Better."

"What are some of the external benefits you're seeing?"

"Well I have more money, I'm not drinking and driving, and I'm not drunk or hungover all the time."

"And how does that make you feel?"

"Christ, lady. Like I said, a bit bored to be honest with you."

"So do you think you might slip back into drinking?"

"No."

"You seem pretty adamant about that."

"Yeah."

"Why?"

"Because I know I won't go back on my word. I wasn't brought up that way."

"What way were you brought up?"

"To do something if you say you're gonna do it."

She adjusts her position in her chair. "Seth, don't be afraid to say you're scared or you're depressed or you want to turn back. It's natural, you know, to have feelings like that."

"I know. I'm just starting to feel like I've woken this beast, that's all. This deep beast of depression. It's weird because I know where it's coming from."

"What sort of depression is it exactly?"

"It's like this hard stuff at the bottom of a glass that's gotten sticky. You've cleaned and washed the rest of the glass, but there's still this hard stuff down there."

"That's an interesting analogy. So you feel you've come down to the last nitty gritty parts of your depression."

"Yeah, but this one feels weird. It feels mundane, but then it also feels extremely powerful. It feels dormant, but I also know it's always there. Waiting."

"When is it at its worst?"

"Sometimes it comes and slowly builds and just hovers and keeps me in its grasp. Usually when I'm distracted or preoccupied I'm fine, but when I'm alone it can be tough."

"So what can you do to preoccupy yourself?"

"I'm not sure I want to simply mask this or try to ignore it. I just want to make it go away. I want to fight it and beat the living shit out of it, to be precise."

"And how do you think you can do that?"

"Honestly? I don't know. It seems like I have no control over it. It's not like a light switch where I can just turn it off or something. Besides, I think it's controlling me more than I am it."

"Are you still taking your medications?"

"Yeah. But maybe I should switch or look into getting something stronger."

"Well you could, but it may have mixed results."

"Pills have done it before, and I'm sure they could do it again."

"Well, yes, but you have to make sure you're not relying on them to make you happy."

"To be honest, I'm perfectly fine with that. I'd rather rely on science than some blind faith I'm going to get through this one day and be better and happy and not depressed."

"Is that your goal, Seth?"

"Isn't that everybody's goal?" I say.

"So what is blind faith to you?"

"Faith in something with your eyes closed."

She smiles, but barely. "But what do you mean by that?" she asks.

"I think when you take what could be a supposed truth for granted, and just accept it for the truth, well then you're relying on blind faith."

"So having faith in something that's not absolute?"

"Well, yeah. I mean faith isn't absolute anyway, is it?"

The air is thick. It feels dead. I sit against the wall of my room, my stained mattress I call a bed beneath me. I'm slightly dishevelled in my wrinkled black suit with my tie undone, my shoelaces untied and my shirt un-tucked. My hair is a rat's nest of auburn brown, still glued together with day-old hair gel. I sit with my back against the wall, cigar in hand,

and I stare. I lean there, staring, waiting for nothing. Something is happening to me. I run my hand through my hair. I lean my head back against the wall and close my eyes. I close my eyes and sit there in my suit and think about all that's become of me of late. All that's brought me to this very exact point in my life. To this nothingness.

Just as I lean in to take the draw in our own end, I see the referee glance over at Glen then blow his whistle. We turn to watch our goalie hurry over to the bench. We're up 2–0 with just under a minute remaining, and the other team has pulled their goalie. We all skate over to the bench, and Jeff comes out onto the ice.

"Why the timeout?"

Glen pulls up his mask. "Seth, you wanna win the draw back to me a bit on the side?"

"What, you gonna try for a Hextall?"

"Yeah."

This acknowledgement elicits a lukewarm response from the rest of the team. Glen is good with the puck but, unlike this team we're playing, not exceptional, meaning two goals in under a minute isn't too much of a stretch for them. But Glen has always said he wants a goal before he dies. The guy has never played a single game outside the crease, even way back in Atom, and since he's long past his days as a back-up in the AHL, he wants something to remember the last few years of his competitive career by. Wade pipes in.

"Fuck, if you can get it to him, Seth, give it a shot." He turns to Glen. "Other than that, fuck if I'm going to pass it to you."

Glen scrunches his face. "If Seth gets me the puck off the draw, I'll go for it."

"No pressure on me, eh?" I say, slapping Glen's pads with my stick.

Gary leans in to talk, water bottle in hand. "Fuck, Glen, if you score I'll buy you an Asian hooker tonight."

"As long as she's not Filipino. Fuck those Filipino girls are vicious. I had one steal my wallet and camera in Thailand while I was sleeping. Fucking cunt."

We all laugh, and the whistle blows. The faceoff is in the right circle, my strong side to pull the puck back to the corner forehand. The guy I'm up against is a good draw man. He likes to do the Gretzky and turn his whole body right off the draw. I figure I'll counter with a full turn of my own.

I can see he wants to go back to his defenceman on his right for a shot from the point. I'm going to have to stick my ass through his thigh if I have any chance at winning this draw.

The ref drops the puck and I turn, and as luck would have it the puck finds its way onto my stick. I'm now facing Glen, who's already got his stick ready, and I hit him square with a pass. Then I grab their centre around the elbow and dig my skates into the ice to block him. Glen doesn't hesitate, and the puck saucers through the air. Everyone seems to stop moving, even their defencemen, who should be chasing the puck. But we're all frozen as we watch. Somebody lets out an astonished "Motherfucker!"

The puck drops just before their blueline, seemingly right on target, and cheers erupt. It looks to be going in. I put my hands in the air and start to shout encouragement along with the rest. The puck looks like it's on a string, almost as if it's being pulled in.

Earlier this evening, Melanie came out to watch one of my games. It was the first time anyone had come to see me play since Dora, and before that, Sarah. I usually play terribly in front of such a personal audience, too wrapped up in trying to impress my one-woman fan club to be good with or without the puck.

Tonight is no different. I try to look tough by fighting some guy who's had my number all year, only to find out the guy can definitely throw. Punch after punch lands on my face as he pummels me with impunity. I get lucky though, as the only real damage done is to my ego. Well, that and to my nose. I end up back on the bench with the guys tapping me on the head. "Nice show, Seth. Way to take the shots," they say, snickering. I feel like an idiot now, thinking all my goal scoring meant I could throw punches with anyone. All I want to do is find somewhere to lie down so I don't hurt myself anymore.

To make matters worse, at Melanie's house after the game I end up ejaculating prematurely. And it's not the first time either. Now that I don't have drunk dink and masturbate incessantly, I can hardly last a minute. Melanie understands however. She says it's cute, kind of like we're back in high school. She says at least I'm not on the other end of the spectrum, unable to get it up in the first place. Very little consolation this is, I tell her.

I want to tell her my secret. I want to tell Melanie all of my secrets. But I know how much it will hurt us both. I don't want to hurt her. It's the last thing I want to do. I want to fall in love with her. She has been there for me, and she has stood by me in a way true friends will always do. They accept the fate of their friends and walk the journey steadily alongside. I want Melanie beside me in my journey. I want her to love me the way I love her. I don't want her, I *need* her. She's been good to me. She's been there and willing to change with me, without addressing me as if I was something that needed to be fixed. I just hope my secrets don't destroy what we have and what I want with her. I pray to whomever I can, hoping things will work out, and my lies will be erased and won't taint this portrait of myself I've drawn for her.

I hope she understands. If not, I don't know if I can take the hurt again. I don't know if I can go through all *that* again. I feel so stupid and childish for the things I've done. She deserves more than I am. Certainly more than the false image of myself I've given her. It's embarrassing that I keep this from her, and dangerous because I feel caged. The pressure is slowly increasing. I hope and I pray she will find a way to understand my stupid lies were only to keep her here. But I don't want these lies anymore. I don't want to be a liar anymore. I want to change, all at costs. I want to tell her I lied, but know deep down I am too much of a coward to do so. I will mask lies in lies, covering lies with more lies, trying to make things seem more truthful when I know the damage has already been done from the get go.

Day 30

Nursing a cigar and Pepsi, I park the car and pick up my cell phone. I turn down the volume on the CD player, then dial the number I've know since I was young. It rings three times before my father picks up. I can tell what type of mood he's in instantly by the way he says hello. It's all in the greeting. He will let you know how he feels right away, no questions asked.

"Hello," he says.

"Hey."

"Hey, Seth."

"How's it goin?"

"Good."

"So I wanted to talk to you about something," I say.

"What would that be?"

"About me being sober now and my drinking problem."

"So what do you want to talk about?"

"I want to talk to you about *your* drinking problem."

"Okay," he says, and we slip into our usual uncomfortable silence.

"Dad?" I say eventually.

"Yeah."

"I want you to tell me about your drinking problem."

"What do you want to know?"

"Everything."

"What does 'everything' mean?"

"Like when did you start?"

"I started about the same age as you."

"And?"

"And what?"

"Dad, I don't want to pull teeth here. I'm trying to open up to you."

"I don't know what you want me to say."

"That's exactly it. I don't want to make you say anything. I want to talk to you, you're my father."

"Okay."

Silence.

"Fuck," I say in a long, drawn-out breath.

"What?" he replies.

"You know what, Dad? Fuck it."

I hang up and take a long drag off my cigar. He won't call back and I know it.

Driving now, but in no particular direction, somehow I find myself heading back home. I don't feel like heading home. I decide to keep driving until I figure out what I want to do but, in the end, just end up heading back home. The city is asleep now and I don't feel like waking it up.

The streetlights cut throw the windows, running across the dashboard in lines of yellow and white. The city is watching over me—the linear lines, the lights, the windows. The black sky fills the background in completely. I feel safe in the city. I feel connected. I enjoy the comfort and the security these buildings offer me. I enjoy artificial light more than I enjoy sunlight, though something about that concerns me.

By the time I get home I think I might be able to sleep. Cancer is already in bed, having spent the better part of the day there after a long debilitating night of debauchery. I thought I heard him having sex with someone earlier, but I'm not entirely sure. He might well have been alone in there. The house is surprisingly clean. Cleaner than usual at least. Someone did the dishes, and the living room has been organized and tidied. This must mean Samantha was over. She's the one who will come over and do our laundry, clean and cook, all in the quiet hope Cancer will finally fall for her. But he won't, and in the meantime he'd be stupid not to string her along. He's always saying to me, "I like to pursue, not be pursued" in this silly Shakespearian tone.

I'm starting to realize some things about our friendship. True, we accept each other's faults along with our assets, but I realize now I've assimilated his faults to such a degree they've become mine somewhere along the line. We've become bad people by letting each other drag the other down with him. We are the same, Cancer and I, and that scares the hell out of me.

Day 31

I'm wrapped in my black suit, this time with a white tie. I'm standing in front of a judge. The courtroom is empty except for two moderately priced lawyers and a handful of Sarah's family. My counsel has already told me what is going to happen today. It seems my sobriety, taken together with my regimen of medication, means the law no longer wants anything to do with my rehabilitation. I guess they think abstinence and prescribed drugs in my system means I'm rehabilitated. Maybe I am.

My treatment via a mental health counsellor and clinical psychiatrist is ending, though I still have a few appointments with each which must be kept. I've paid the six hundred dollar fine for the DUI, completed my sixty hours of community service (picking up garbage along the highway in Surrey) and served my yearlong probation. Technically, and legally, I have paid for my sins. Technically and legally, I am a free man. And I am a rehabilitated man apparently, though one who broke all kinds of stipulations of his probation and sentence and got away with it somehow. I beat the system, and for the first time in my life I feel horrible about it. I feel like I should have been caught.

According to public record, which is all that really matters, I was driving a car while intoxicated along Highway 1 just outside of Langley when I lost control in the rain. Although I was drinking and driving, I was technically not at fault for the accident. The rain had collected in a grade in the road, and I just happened to be the first to drive through it. I was abiding by the speed limit. I was exercising due care. There were two people in the car, but I am the only one alive. I've told you all this before. Still, if Sarah's mother only knew the truth. What would she think if she knew her daughter was actually driving the car? What would she say to me? How would she look at me? Would she even be here? I look over at her and feel like blurting it out, but I don't. This is the best lie I've ever told and it will die with me. I will die with this lie inside me. I will die for what ought not to be.

The courtroom door clicks open, breaking my trance. The judge has finished, and I walk outside to my car with my lawyer shaking my hand, as if in victory. I feel like I'm walking through a dream. I see members of Sarah's family leaving, and they don't make eye contact with me. I am that monster again, the one who lives in the basement of their lives, shunned completely.

I feel like I've stepped outside my own life. The legality of the situation is over, but my suffering—and more importantly—the questions I still have, remain. The wound has festered and healed wrong, and now it's here to stay. A permanent affliction.

The judge commended me for ceasing my alcohol intake and going sober. I couldn't care less. I'm sure he'll tell his wife, while sitting beside a fireplace with scotch in hand, just how remarkable I am for doing what I've done. Well fuck him and fuck that.

Cancer is at home when I return. He didn't bother coming to court. Neither did my parents. I think they're sick of sitting behind me in court. Can't blame them, really. The guilt rising off me and settling onto them. They are tired, and they want to move on.

"So," Cancer says, coming into the kitchen as I take off my jacket and loosen my tie. "Everything go okay?" he asks.

"Yeah, fine."

"Cool." He pauses. "I bet you feel good getting all this shit behind you, huh?"

"Yeah, I guess so."

"Anyways, whatever, it's done. All you can do is work on yourself, man."

"Yeah."

I head to my room, take my clothes off and go to sleep. I don't want to think right now and the only way to do that is to sleep. Cancer still hasn't acknowledged I'm sober, or that he even knows this. It gets tougher each day we don't talk about it, and then he goes out and gets annihilated and goes to work and comes home drunk and drinks in front of me. I don't know if he wants to talk about it. I don't know if he *can* talk about it. And to be honest, I don't really care.

I'm walking down the street I used to live on. Lower middle-class houses with small front yards, no fences and the odd tree or bush line the road. Most of the paint on the houses is fading, and each one looks slightly neglected in its own way.

Cancer is here. We're heading to my friend's house to watch some porn because it's been banned, and then I realize how the government arbitrarily decided upon all this, but when I try to express my viewpoint it all comes out of my mouth the wrong way. "You know what I've just realized? I can only watch porn with the sound off," I say.

Cancer looks at me with a confusing smirk. "Are you okay? You stoned?"

"No, I don't think so. You?"

Cancer looks at me, and his eyes close. I awake. I'm sweating slightly. Trucks hum by in the distance. The room is dark except for the red numbers of my alarm clock—a hard, beating red. I roll over and try to go back to sleep, but it's futile. I am awake.

Day 32

This is only getting harder. And I am only growing weaker. Thoughts of ending it all are seeping in. The depression is at war with my sanity, and it is winning. I am withdrawing from the world. The life is being sucked out of me. I am no longer happy or sad, just numb. I want the high of alcohol. I can take the lows if I know the highs are coming again at some uncertain point.

These pills do nothing for me anymore. They stop my brain from overheating, but they do nothing for my depression. Is this it? Is this as happy as I'll ever be? Will I face this feeling the rest of my life? When will I be free? When will my pain go away? I just want it to go away. I just want to feel normal, to feel as if I can be of this world and be productive in it.

I need something stronger than this. Pump me full of medication. I don't care anymore. I don't care if I'm not me anymore. I just want this feeling to end. I don't care if I'm medicated. I just don't want to care anymore. I need a vacation from myself. This depression is killing me, and all I know how to do is sluggishly fight on. I don't know how to give up. My stubbornness shall be my salvation, and my ruin. I'm like a boxer who keeps getting up after he's been knocked down countless times. Everyone just wishes he'd stay down, for their sake if not for his own, but the stupid bastard insists on dragging his ass up off the canvas only to get pummelled once more.

I am losing this fight. I am too stubborn to quit and not good enough to win. So I just keep getting pummelled, and dragging my ass up off the canvas.

Day 49

I've switched prescription medication from Celexa to one of its sister drugs, Effexor, less commonly known as venlafaxine hydrochloride, an antidepressant/anxiolytic. Plus I will also be taking Bupropion, or Wellbutrin, at night. This is all under the guidance of my physician, who claims such a cocktail will work wonders. I did some research and suggest the natural remedy hypericum perforatum, also known as St. John's Wort. He dismisses the notion with a slight air of sarcasm, as if it is pure nonsense to him.

I've been weaning myself off Celexa, which whisks the physical body through fiendish cycles of deprivation. The body experiences uncontrollable rushes of blood, like quick sprays and leaks which leave the veins momentarily depleted. It's known as discontinuation syndrome. Like an ultra-fast wind rushing through the skeleton, unfiltered. You get light-headed and feel as if your body is scanning ever so quickly for something it can't find, and it's warning your brain of the deficiency in real time. Mentally you feel great. You feel calmer, clearer and much more opaque. You feel, in a word, un-medicated. But then your body begins to yearn for that pill again.

I'm lost somewhere. Somewhere between my nerve cells
that are receiving dopamine and trying to replace or find
cohesiveness with the serotonin already there. It's mass transit.
It's rush hour traffic. It's a swerving between happiness and sad-
ness prescribed and picked up at your local drugstore for
$13.46 a month, tax included.

No one else can see this transition, but it sends out a quick
splash of pins and needles every time it happens. You lose all
mental momentum as you're swept up in this rush of blood,
chemicals and a searching for something that just isn't there.

You realize your body is wrong, and you are broken and
you need daily medication to survive. Without these little pills
you would unravel into something dreadful, something chaot-
ic and constantly out of line. You feel weak and extremely
unhopeful knowing you rely on a clutter of fine particles
called N-methyl-3-phenyl-3-[4(trifluoromethyl) phenoxy]-
propan-1-amine hydrochloride stuffed inside a half-inch
digestible container for your happiness, for your general well-
being. For life, liberty, love, and the ability to carry on with
anything. You feel taken for granted, and completely fucked
over. Someone, or something, has got your number, and it's not
giving it up anytime soon.

Sleep while you're tapering off these pills becomes a constant quest, an exhausting journey into half-awake, half-slum-
bering nightmares. No longer held back by gravity, the blood
rushes to your head, and you are forced to constantly adjust
your neck and windpipe to keep the rushing tolerable. You
fidget and paw, and your mind does whatever the hell it wants
to, as though it has a mind of its own.

You become something of a ghost inside your own body,
silently watching yourself. And the really frightening thing
about all this is you are now clean. You have only a small
residue of prescription medication inside you. You are as pure
as you will ever be, and there would be no way you'd even last

the weekend in this state. You are a bunch of scribbles on an Etch-A-Sketch, a Ralph Steadman portrait scrawled to the sound of a racy Blood Brothers song. Cold breath on the inside of a car windshield and shivers running across the surface of your spine.

Anger. A slow simmering anger is in me all the time now. I don't know why or where it came from. I don't consider myself a violent person. But I can't stop thinking about all the violent things I've done. But I wasn't always the instigator. Like the time some chick on the dance floor split my lip open with a glass of Rum and Coke. Or the time I got the shit kicked out of me by an East Indian gang. Or the time I fought my father in the basement when my mother and sister decided to stay the night in a hotel, and got him in a headlock as the two of us ploughed through the wall. Pinning him to the ground and splitting his eyebrow open with one good elbow, though, that was me that time.

I'm sitting in his patient's chair. He's just finished telling me if we're going to continue on with our sessions it's going to cost me, because they're no longer a provision of my probation. He also tells me that for the next four weeks, starting next Tuesday, he'll be on vacation in Hawaii with his family. I will have to find a new psychiatrist for a while, and I will have to pay to see him apparently.

I feel like urinating all over his office and then strangling him with his tie. He'll probably try to reason with me in indistinguishable gasps as I wrap it around his esophagus and cut off his air supply.

"Hawaii, wow, you must be looking forward to that," I say instead.

"Well, yeah, we go every year. My wife is more into it than I am, and the kids enjoy it too. I just go for the golf."

"Golf, huh. Cool."

I wish I had a pitching wedge right now. I'd go to work on his face for a hole or two.

He opens up his notebook and has a gander. "So to your counsellor a few weeks back you described your relationship with women as 'terrible.'"

"True."

"Would you say that still applies?"

"Yeah, I think so."

"Why?"

"I've just had terrible luck. I think maybe I attract the wrong kind of women."

"What kind of women do you attract?"

"I dunno," I shrug. Then gesturing at the photo of his family, "The opposite of your kind apparently."

He pauses momentarily, then casually carries on, "Okay, another thing you said was while you had no trouble attracting women, you did have trouble keeping them around."

"Yeah."

"I take it you don't want to talk about that either?"

"Well I'm pretty sure I know where you're going with this."

"And where is that?"

"You want to find the root of my problem with women. How about my mother? Let's start with her. She was a very meek creature who always seemed like she was holding on by a thread."

"And you've carried the image of that forward into all your relationships."

"Yeah I guess I did."

"So are you willing to talk about the incident that caused you to stop drinking?"

I look at him. I know he wants to talk about the abortion. Of course he wants to talk about the abortion, the sick fuck. But then hey, why the hell not? What else can I do? Let's give him this and see where he goes with it. Let him carry my dead offspring all the way to Hawaii for all I care.

"How much has my counsellor told you?"

"Not too much," he says. "Just the basics."

"Okay, well, you know a partner, or girl, or girlfriend of mine—whatever you want to call her—recently had an abortion."

"Yes, I think that's pretty much all I was told."

"Well there it is," I say with a hint of derision.

"And she didn't consult you until after the fact, is that correct?"

"Yeah, that's correct. She forged my signature on the consent form or something. I don't know how it works."

"So I know you must have gone through a lot of tough feelings and emotions, feelings of anger and confusion, which obviously led you to stop drinking. Which is something I applaud, by the way."

"Thanks."

"And what are your feelings towards your ex-girlfriend now?"

I contemplate my answer a moment. "Well, first off, we weren't really even dating. And to be honest, now that I've thought about it as much as I have, I think she maybe made the right decision."

"But I'm sure it would have been nice to be consulted?"

"Yeah, it would've been. But then I guess it was her call in the end. . . . You know, something inside me broke when I found out."

"What broke?"

"Something—or things. I think the worst thing was that obviously she—Dora was her name—didn't see me as a suitable father figure, not that I blame her for that or anything. I mean I was and still am a complete fucking wreck. But, you know, I just feel like I was part of a murder that was covered up."

"Interesting. So you feel as if you have a secret with her."

"Yeah, not a lot of people know about it. But then I have a lot of secrets."

He looks at me. "When you say that, you seem to tense up. Are your secrets something that hinder you?"

"Yeah, of course. I've got plenty of lies and secrets stored up I'd love to have come out, but I'm sure the majority of them never will."

He looks at me, I look at him, and a long silence develops between us.

"So on the flip side," he says at length, "do you have any good secrets? Or are they always associated with negativity."

I smile, ever so slightly. "I have two good secrets. One I can tell you, and one I can't."

"Okay."

"The first one is a *New York Times* newspaper article I came across in a library archive five or six years ago about a dog that got out onto the lawn of the White House and was shot by a secret service agent. The first names of the dog, the agent, and the dog's owner, when taken together, formed 'John Fitzgerald Kennedy.' And I was born that day, just around the time it happened. And I think you're the first person I've ever told, to be honest."

He's smiling—I'm not completely sure why—and despite myself I smile too.

"Wow. That's definitely something I can see you cherish. What does it mean to you?"

"Honestly, it doesn't have to mean anything. I just like the fact I was born around the same time something as unusual and interesting as that transpired."

"I see. And the other secret you can't tell me about. Why don't you feel comfortable telling me about it?"

"Well, for one, I think you're obligated to report me if I implicate myself in a criminal act, correct?"

"Yes," he says, then hesitates. "Yes, but you can tell me the generalities, and how this is a positive thing for you, despite the fact you broke the law doing it."

"I didn't break the law doing it. I broke the law because I haven't told anyone I *didn't* do it."

He looks confused, and justifiably so. "So this was something you did, or *pretended* you did, out of the goodness of your heart."

"Yeah, I . . . I just needed to do something like that for someone else, someone other than myself. And to know that deep inside me I have something good there, something I could maybe reflect back on at some point. Something I know makes life better for others, if not necessarily for myself. I dunno," I shrug, "it was kind of a spontaneous thing too. Maybe I'll never know why I did it."

"So this was something you did for someone else as a favour?"

"Yeah."

"Do they know you did this favour for them?"

I adjust my position in the chair. "It's a she, and no, she doesn't know and never will."

"Because you don't want to tell her?"

"No, because she's dead."

A silence falls as he struggles for a response. Then the words come out of his mouth, and I can hear every one of them before they even touch his tongue.

"Are you referring to the female in the car accident?"

"Yes, I am."

"And is this something you'd like to talk about?"

"No. . . . Yeah, no, I'm pretty much one hundred percent sure I don't want to talk to you about this at all."

He looks at me like this was some kind of insult. "Okay, on another note then, are you willing to talk about the fact you're still exhibiting signs of post-traumatic stress disorder?"

"No."

"So what are you willing to talk about, Seth?"

"We can talk about hockey. How about hockey?"

"I'm sorry, I'm not much of a hockey fan. Haven't really followed the Canucks much of late. I'm a big Mariners fan though," he says, trying to be good-humoured about it. I don't like it.

"Yeah I kind of hate baseball," I tell him.

I'm in the counsellor's office for my last session. She says if we are to continue to meet, I'll have to go on a waiting list because my appointments are no longer court-ordered as part of my probation. I can go to AA meetings though, if I like. She says it will be at least a month and a half before I can see her again, if I choose to get on the waiting list and, in turn, start paying. Or I can try to see another counsellor. On top of this, my employment insurance is about to run out and I haven't even started looking for a job or filled out any applications for school. In a word then, I'm fucked.

"So I remember, in our last session, you said something about not taking any dreams you have literally?"

"Yeah, pretty much."

"So I guess you're not much for horoscopes either."

"I read mine once in awhile like everyone else, but it's essentially bullshit, yeah."

"So why do you think you read it?"

"Maybe there's a part of me that wants to believe something bigger is out there helping me through all this."

"I see. And in terms of the dreams you have, are there any recurring themes?"

I ponder this a moment. "Um, sometimes. . . . Actually I used to have this falling dream where I wake up just before I hit the ground, but then everybody has that one if I'm not mistaken. . . . The one I've been having lately is where I always seem to be running or climbing or trying to catch up to someone and my legs don't seem to work properly. It's like I can't push them fast enough, and it always feels awkward."

"So there's a theme of catching up and not being able to perform at the standards you've set for yourself."

"Yeah, sure, I guess so. They're just dreams though, you know."

"Any others?"

I pause. "Yeah, I have this dream where I'm always trying to get my hockey gear on for a game, and each time I try it's a different team I'm playing for, and guys I've played with before are there, and I can just never seem to get my gear on right. I'm always stuck in the dressing room while everyone is out there playing, and I usually wake up before I even get to hit the ice."

She raises an eyebrow. "Interesting. So what do you think that represents to you?"

"That I'm a raging homosexual?"

"Seth, please, be serious."

Actually, I keep having the same dream. I end up drinking, and I'm disappointed in myself. I don't tell her about it though. I do tell her I've lost count of how many days I've been sober though. She asks me if I think this is a good thing.

I tell her I don't know.

Automatism

I've taken to sleeping as my new hobby. Sleeping in, napping, going to bed early and waking up late. It's the only break I get. It chews up the clock on this long, drawn-out battle I've been waging with myself of late. And yet I'm sleeping away my problems. I know this. I'm ignoring my pain by avoiding it, allowing it to languish there unattended. I've become some-thing of a hypersomniac. A casket of flesh.

Drifting in and out of sleep leaves the brain trying to dis-cern what is real from what is not. Stories and memories cloud together with dreams in one long fogbank of semi-con-sciousness. Memories are called into question, their validity uncertain. What seemed like truth, an actuality, becomes something open to debate. After a while, more and more memories fall under the category of inconclusive. The past becomes a guessing game. A haze of thoughts fighting one another for legitimacy. Just imagine for one moment all you could remember about your life were the dreams you may or may not have had.

The long sheet of tinfoil over the one small window blocks all outside light from my room. I adopted this practice while working up north, so I wouldn't be woken up at three in the morning when the sun came up. I like it dark. It calms me, and gives me a sense of comfort. The light of day is now something to be avoided at all costs.

I'm trying to think back to the first time I ever got drunk. I'm at a table with my family for Christmas dinner at my uncle's luxurious house in Halifax, paid for by some nonde-script desk job at an oil and gas plant up north. Everyone is there—cousins, uncles, aunts, my grandparents—and I am so

drunk on white wine I'm wavering back and forth in my seat.
We bow our heads to say grace, and when I close my eyes I
lose balance and fall off my chair, taking a bunch of plates and
cutlery with me.

Everyone bursts out in laughter. My parents laugh too, but
I know they feel ashamed and are embarrassed of me. Their son
is already becoming the drunk he was always destined to be. I
get back up and excuse myself from the table to another round
of applause and laughter. I go to the bathroom, puke, lie down
in the tub and pass out.

Melanie moans ever so slightly as I pull the sheets clear
and press my naked body against her back. I rest my
head behind hers on the pillow, and she acknowledges me by
pulling me in close and quietly moaning once more.

My thoughts begin to drift, ebbing in and out on the
tide. I'm walking with Melanie along Kingsway holding
hands, and she pulls in tight. We're on our way to see a
movie, and she's decided walking to the theatre for a good
hour beforehand is a good way to clear our minds, a good
way to talk about interesting and important things. But all I
can think about is the fact my legs hurt and that I have to
take a piss.

Melanie looks at me and begins to talk. But every time
she speaks I can't understand a word she's saying. I'm frustrated because I can't comprehend what she's trying to tell me.
All I want is a word, one single word, to come from her
mouth I can grasp onto. But then she drifts away having said
nothing at all.

Other than the occasional tryst with Melanie, my life now
consists of watching movies, sleep, constant masturbation, long
shifts on the toilet reading outdated issues of *Maxim* and *Sports
Illustrated*, and going for occasional walks downtown. I've
become completely isolated from my friends, and I wander the

streets trying on clothes, listening to CDs and reading everything I can at Chapters. Then I return home to sleep, sometimes
for up to fifteen hours a day. It's the only way I can compete
with these extreme emotions I'm occasionally plagued with, by
becoming extremely emotionless otherwise. My life has
become one long lazy afternoon filled with mundane remedi-
al tasks broken up movies like *Heat* and *Reservoir Dogs*, and long
drives in my car. I'm nothing but a collection of flesh and bones
wandering around in search of a suitable place to collapse.

Lying in my bed at around one in the afternoon, I'm barely
awake. I've twisted my biological clock around so much it
feels like eleven at night. But I feel sober. I feel clean. I feel
something, which is better than nothing, and that pleases me.

When I finally emerge from my room, Cancer is in the
living room playing GoldenEye. He's sitting on the couch
crammed against his new bench press with old posters of
Mario Lemieux and Anna Kournikova hanging overhead like
some sort of weird propaganda. He's deep into a game but
takes the time to glance over as I stagger about the kitchen in
search of something to eat.

"Hey," he barks. "Don't eat anything, I just ordered pizza."

"What'd you get?"

"Hawaiian and pepperoni. It should be here any minute,"
he says. And then he's back to his game. I think it's Tuesday, but
it could be Wednesday or even Thursday.

"What day is it?"

"Friday."

Returning to my search, I decide to abandon it and wait
for the pizza. I flop down on the couch beside Cancer. He
moves over and looks at me.

"Haven't seem much of you lately," he says. "You've been
sleeping a lot."

"Yeah."

He returns to his game.

"How's work?" I ask eventually.

"Good. Called in sick today, even though they asked me to work on the weekend. I'm still burnt out from our game on Wednesday, and there's no way I could haul lumber all day today. I mean fuck it, I'm union now, so what can they do, fire me?"

"Good call," I say, getting back up and heading to the kitchen, once again in search of something to eat. There's some chicken flavoured Sapporo Ichiban in one cupboard, dried Cheerios in another, and a bunch of canned soup in the cupboard above the fridge. But there's a six pack of Pilsner in the fridge, I notice, still moist from the liquor store freezer, as well as a small serving of mystery food in a sealed Tupperware container. The kitchen is surprisingly clean. Either Cancer got tired of the fruit flies, or else Samantha came over again. Either way, it's in respectable shape for the first time in weeks, and I appreciate the state it's in.

I decide to go back to bed with the foolish notion Cancer will wake me up when the pizza arrives. He doesn't, and I end up sleeping all day and then heading to our game on an empty stomach. At the arena, outside the dressing room, Cancer and I stop at the large white board.

"See, look, what'd I tell ya."

I'm looking at the board, at the league standings, and at the top scorers in the Greater Vancouver Senior Men's League. The first name atop the list is mine. 35 games with 40 goals and 18 assists for 58 points plus 22 penalty minutes.

"What'd I tell ya. Jeff was right, you're gonna win the scoring title."

There are four others within a few points of me, but there are only two games remaining. Both our games are against the same team. Whatever happens, right now I'm atop the league, and I feel good. Hungry, but good.

"Forty goals. You've got the Richard trophy sewn up for sure," says Cancer, pointing the blade of his stick at the goals column. I stare at the board, knowing everyone in the league stops by to talk about the scoring leaders and the teams atop the league. At least I have this, however insignificant it may ultimately be.

We enter the dressing room, and before I know it I'm out on the ice. Things go well, I'm feeling good, but then at some point during the third period I'm knocked unconscious, and some time later a doctor tells me I've just received a nasty concussion.

"You've just received what I like to call a nasty concussion," he says, checking my eyes with his pen light.

"Well shit," I say.

He tells me my concussion is a possible grade-two, and that I may experience up to twenty-four hours of post-traumatic amnesia as I was out cold for close to ten seconds. He suggests I stop playing hockey. I suggest he fuck off.

"This is your fourth concussion, your teammate said. I think you need to re-evaluate your chosen form of recreation," he says, checking my ears with some sort of probe.

"Wow," I say, more surprised there was an actual probe-wielding doctor in attendance than with his somewhat downbeat diagnosis.

I sit back against the wall of the dressing room. I can barely feel anything. I can see a few people crowded in around me, including the team's trainer/equipment manager Jimmy who thinks he's some great healer and that he has to help everyone all the time, all because he's got his Industrial First Aid ticket. Standing there on the periphery, the dumb fuck already has his latex gloves on. I laugh, but it comes out wrong.

I feel blurred and slurred, as though I'm slightly asleep. The doctor tells me I'm going to the hospital and that an ambulance will be picking me up shortly.

"I'd rather not pay the fifty-three bucks they charge for an ambulance," I manage to say, and everyone chuckles, including the doctor, his rectangular glasses framing a pair of steady blue eyes. His neatly groomed five o'clock shadow crinkles up around his cheeks when he smiles. He's so close to my face I can smell his latest application of Tommy Hilfiger cologne.

"Can't we just take a cab," I suggest.

The doctor denies my request, and asks me to follow his finger as he moves it back and forth across my field of vision.

"I could probably follow it a little easier if you wouldn't fuckin' move it around so much," I say to more laughter.

I wonder if we're still winning. But more importantly, I wonder if Cancer beat the shit out of the big Indian defence-man who caught me with my head down coming across the redline. I'm sure Cancer messed him up good, and that makes me feel better.

I can smell my own sweat, and feel the heat coming off my body. I keep running the play over and over in my mind. Watching the puck knife between two of their players, softly connecting with my stick. That defenceman, though, he was waiting for me. He had it out for me all game, and got his wish this time, getting me back for deking him out and roofing the go-ahead goal late in the third. Getting me back for throwing my glove in the air and shooting it with my stick à la Teemu Selanne. That theatrical little display probably didn't help my cause, in retrospect.

I'm screwed, and when you've been knocked out, nobody listens to a word you say. So my skates are removed, and I'm wheeled into a fifty-three dollar ambulance ride to the nearest hospital.

By the time we arrive I've thrown up twice in the ambulance, and managed to further piss off the two paramedics with my non-sequential ramblings and insults. "You guys ass suck," and things like that.

Cancer shows up about an hour or so later to find me in a pale blue hospital gown, absentmindedly picking my nose. My CAT scan has just come back negative, which is apparently cause for celebration. Cancer's been drinking heavily already because we won, and has managed to smuggle in a bottle of lemon vodka to help further the cause. He takes sips whenever he thinks no one's looking. No one's looking. No one ever does.

"Yeah, I got that chug good," he tells me. "Cracked him three or four times right in the face. Blood everywhere. It was good."

"Thanks, man. I appreciate it."

"No problem," he shrugs. "Just doing what I thought you'd want me to do."

"You did, believe me. I owe you one."

"Your goal was the game winner, by the way. Everyone's at the bar doing shots in your honour."

Cancer and I chat until the ER doctor returns for another quick look at me. He hands me some forms, tells me I can go, and tells Cancer to wake me up every two hours, and to bring me back if I feel dizzy, nauseous or throw up more than once. Cancer tells the doctor he will wake me up by teabagging me, and if I puke on our carpet again he will cut my nuts off without a moment's hesitation. I'm pretty sure the doctor has no idea what teabagging is, but says that will be fine.

Cancer doesn't shut up the entire car ride home. He goes on and on about how my helmet flew all the way back to our blueline, and how he fucked the guy up good and we won and how he helped kill two late third period penalties.

"I was down blocking shots for Christ's sake," he boasts. "I never block shots. What a madman."

All I want to do is go to bed and pass out but Cancer has other ideas. Apparently we're going to the bar, because the Canucks played earlier and he wants to show up in full suits and pretend we're Edmonton Oilers—the Canucks' opponents—to see if we can pick up any puck bunnies. I politely decline, over and over, until eventually he gets the hint and heads out with Ryan instead. I'm sure he'll be angry with me tomorrow, but I'm more worried about him strolling in at three in the morning and actually teabagging me.

I hit the medicine cabinet for some T3s—acetaminophen and codeine—and end up taking two plus an Ambien for a good night's sleep. I'm out within a half hour and fall into a night of stark and troubled dreams.

I'm driving along a highway in the mountains somewhere. My father is with me, as well as my science teacher from high school. They talk about me like I'm not there, though I'm sure they know I am. We eventually get lost, and all the highway signs are blank.

I wake up, roll over, and fall back asleep. Blood and death are all around me. I'm trying to outrun some massive animal as it eats everything in its path. I keep losing ground as it nips at my heels and I awake again. I glance at my alarm clock, which reads 6:32, and follow the cord to the wall and yank it out. The red light disappears, and I pull the covers up to my neck and fall asleep again, this time for close to twenty-four hours. Now I'm wide awake, but feeling nauseous. I head for the bathroom to survey the damage. I actually don't look all that bad. I take two more T3s and head into the living room to watch some TV. Ryan is asleep on the couch, snoring voraciously. He's obviously passed out, because he's still fully clothed and a can of beer sits spilled on the carpet near his feet. I pluck the remote from his grip and turn on the TV. After some mindless channel surfing, I shove a sock in Ryan's mouth to quell the noise. But he just turns over, spits it out and keeps snoring unabated.

I'm not sure where Cancer is, but I'm betting he's asleep in his room. I wander down the hall to find his door slightly

ajar. It creeks open under the weight of my hand, and I turn
the light on to find a naked woman fast asleep on his floor.
She's tanned, and an indecipherable tattoo floats languidly
above her crotch. I stand there motionless a while, quiet so as
not to wake her. I begin to get an erection, and decide to come
back later to have another gander, but by that time she's gone.

Sweet revenge, I think to myself, sitting in the dressing room
before the game. Sweet revenge is going to be had tonight.
Tonight we are up against the same cellar-dwelling team with
the same big Indian defenceman, the same big chug who
knocked me cold last time out.

It's our last game of the season and I'm going to win the
scoring race. Meanwhile, our team is going to finish second in
the league, while the team we're playing isn't even going to
make the playoffs. This is a dangerous situation, and no one
knows it more than the referees—you can see it in their posture prior to the game. They're tense and alert, even in the
warm-up. I watch the Indian guy skating around. He must be
at least six-four, but probably under 195. He's big, but not too
big. He would fall hard if I caught him right. He could be hurt
if I caught him right.

I skate around, shooting the puck into the empty net, and
stretching up and down. The buzzer goes and I head to the
bench. This isn't going to take long.

My first shift out, he isn't. He isn't out on my second shift
either. But then as I jump the boards for my third shift midway through the first period, changing on a dump-in in their
end, I spot him, back there with his defensive partner. I hover
sideways just inside the redline. The puck goes behind the net,
and his partner collects the dump-in as he starts to cut left into
the circle. Then his partner shifts and zips him a quick pass. By
this time I'm already flying towards the blueline. He turns his
upper body backwards to collect the pass, and then starts to

turn back towards me. I lower my shoulder just a bit, but keep my elbow in. This is going to be a clean hit, have I the final say in it. And we collide.

I catch him right in the face with my shoulder, while the rest of his body I just manage to clip. I hear the air exit his abdomen as we both go down, his stick broken, his gloves off and his helmet whipped back so hard his chinstrap pulls up around his throat like a horse's bit.

As soon as I get my bearings, still sliding towards the boards, someone is on top of me, raining down punches from what seems like six different directions. I claw to get a piece of jersey, taking a good shot off the right cheek in the process. I feel my teeth cut the inside of my mouth as I stagger to get my footing only to be wrestled back down. Now we're on the ice, rolling around, and more bodies join the fray. I feel the guy start to pull away against his will, and he claws at my neck to get back at me. I feel his fingernails dig into my skin and I let out a noise. Then his grip loosens as he's separated from me completely, and I stagger to my knees amongst a furious line brawl. I look up to see Joey, a lanky winger, feeding the Indian fists as the latter tries to turtle ineffectively. Joey is too quick, and all the Indian can do is squirm and hide behind his forearms.

Then one of their players grabs Joey, and in an instant I'm on him from the side. We grapple as he turns to face me in a tangled mess of jerseys and arms. Then I catch him with arguably the best uppercut I've thrown in my life.

Teeth make a very distinctive sound when the crack. Reminiscent of thick glass covered in a layer of old paint breaking under impact. My opponent drops awkwardly to the ground and I move in for the kill, feeding him shots to the top of the head. The third punch I land hits him square on the top of the skull, sending a shockwave up my forearm. I hesitate, cock my fist back, and wait. He's turtling now, and I can see scattered blotches of blood collecting here and there on the white ice.

I stand upright to find one fight still in progress, as well as a large scrum which has two referees occupied. The other referee is simply watching the fight, and as soon as the scrum settles, everyone is watching the fight. The goalies have come over too. It's Wade, our hulking assistant captain, and he's trading punches with some guy of about the same size, with haymaker after haymaker connecting on both sides. I hear Wade's knuckles hitting helmet again and again, and it makes me wince. I look back to find the guy I fought still on his knees, his hands on his mouth, trying to stop the blood from leaking from his face.

Eventually Wade beats the guy to his knees and the referees move in. They continue to hold onto each other a while, wrestling as the two referees try to separate them, but then eventually their tempers die, and both benches hit their sticks against the boards in acknowledgment and appreciation. I look over to see the big Indian defenceman hunched over and retreating to his bench, two of his teammates attending to him. One of the referees turns to me and shouts, "You, out!"

"What the fuck for?" I say, raising my hands in innocence.

"You know what for. Hit the showers, pal."

"Fuck you."

I turn and skate towards the dressing room. I feel good, almost stoned, with the adrenaline still speeding around. I make my way to the boards where two young boys open the gate for me. They both just stare as I walk into the dressing room and out of sight. I sit down on the bench and take in a big pull of oxygen just as Wade bursts into the room, blood dripping from his eyebrow. He says nothing. He simply drops his helmet, gloves and stick to the ground and reaches into the cooler for a beer. I watch him drink, my head resting against the concrete wall. Then he bends over, grabs another beer, and tosses it to me. I crack it open and take a drink.

"Good hit," he tells me.

This is my last session with the psychiatrist. I can't afford the one hundred dollars he charges per session, so he's agreed to see me one more time for free. I don't like him at all, and seriously doubt he likes me. About the only thing I take from these sessions is the fact I get to talk to someone without them waiting to tell their side of the story.

"So how do you feel," he says, slowly removing his glasses, trying to appear interested in the life of a miscreant like me.

"You know, honestly, not a hell of a lot better," I say. I have a black eye, a nice gash running across my eyebrow, and a small cut on my lip from last night's game. I told my psychiatrist I fell down some stairs, to which he laughed his pretentious laugh.

"So do you feel as if you've failed?" he asks me.

"Yeah, basically. Whatever, though, I'm done. I'm so tired of getting nothing but shit from everyone. I mean it feels like I've been catching shit my whole life. I've been catching shit since day one. So what does it matter, I might as well go down in flames and be done."

"You know, you don't have to take that route. There is help."

"Yes, there is," I say. "At a hundred dollars a pop I've just found out."

He doesn't answer immediately. In time though he says, "You seem angry, Seth."

"Yeah, well, I am angry. I'm angry I've been getting the run-around for so long now. I mean I start taking these pills you pre-scribe for panic and anxiety attacks and depression, and those work for a while, at least until you tell me to go off them which I do, at which point the attacks come back and I get back on the pills, only this time they don't work at all. So I move to another kind of pill, which works a bit better but not a whole lot better, so I end up augmenting that pill with yet another pill, and I make my regularly scheduled visits to my psychiatrist and my drug and alcohol counsellor who tell me to go to AA and NA and other things of that nature, and when that doesn't work out they tell me to look into something else and then all of a sudden something happens in court and poof, my health is suddenly no longer an issue and I'm tossed out on the street. And then it's a hundred dollars a pop from here on in, kid. And now my employment insurance is about to run out, which means my medical bills for the pills I need to live are going to increase by three hundred percent, so yeah, I'm pissed. I'm really pissed."

He gestures for me to stop. "I know," he says, trying to calm me down.

"No you *don't* know. Bullshit."

He gestures again for me to settle down.

"It's bullshit. *You're* bullshit," I go on.

"Okay, let's change the subject," he says. "One thing I said that was important for you to have, once you stopped seeing both myself and your counsellor, was a solid goal to work towards, and you expressed some kind of interest in returning to college. And I know you can't afford it, but student loans or a bank loan might be something worth looking into."

"Money, money, money. It's all money."

"I know, but just looking at some of the reports I have here . . . I mean you seem to be able to get top marks whenever you want." He flips through some pages in a folder. "High grades in Social Studies and English in high school. Some impressive but inconsistent marks in Introductory Philosophy and Introduction to Critical Thinking at UBC. But then you fail your other classes. Actually, it appears you barely graduated from high school, even though you had over ninety percent in Social Studies, English and Sociology. I mean when you apply yourself, according to your grades here, you're a very bright young man. I might even say gifted. And I'm sure you've heard this before, but you've got an excellent analytical brain that seems to be going entirely to waste at present."

I don't say anything.

"In terms of philosophy, were there any ideologies you found interesting during your stint at college you might like to pursue further? Or maybe you could apply to your present situation?"

"No, not really. I mean I studied a lot of them, but in the end I realized something."

"What's that?"

"I realized philosophers are kind of like art critics. They can't decide on anything. The only thing critics and philosophers can decide on is they're smarter than you and I and they should be showing us as much as often as possible."

He laughs. "That's funny."

I smile. "No it's not, you fuckin' prick. It's not funny at all."

I'm sitting on the bench between my two wingers. The second period has just ended and we're losing 2–1. It's the first round of the playoffs, we're playing the seventh place seed, and we're losing. If we lose tonight, they'll sweep us. The team we never lost to once the entire season will sweep us. The guys are going crazy—Jeff is yelling and Cancer is shaking, ready to explode all over the bench. I can feel the sweat collecting in my sparse, week-old playoff beard, below my nose and beneath my bottom lip.

"Jesus Christ," says Wade. "Make sure you gain the blueline for fuck's sake. Icings are fine, but get that fuckin' puck out of the zone. None of this up the middle shit—it's killing us trying to make the pretty pass to Seth or Jeff to spring them."

Jeff pipes in. "Guys, the main thing is to focus on that next goal. It's simple, if we don't score we go home. We need to pull together here and play like a team, because we're all out there running around, hearing footsteps like a bunch of women. Seth has been taking a fuckin' beating all game long. I mean protect him for fuck's sake. Finish your checks and take the hit. No stupid penalties. No retaliation. Play hard to the whistle and that's it."

I'm huffing heavily, feeling my fat lip through my glove. The ephedrine is opening and closing my bronchial tubes at an exasperating speed, and I can barely keep up with my lungs' requirements. This team is running us. And they've been shadowing me all night, taking me out of the game in the process. The same two or three guys have been on me the entire time, pestering me, hacking me, chirping endlessly, and it's pissing me off. They're beating us physically, and that's all that matters. We're about to have our long promising playoff run cut considerably short.

My next shift out, I line up one of the guys who's been shadowing me and run him so hard into the boards his helmet pops off and I hear the wind leave his chest in a gasp. He falls to the ground and a scrum ensues. Their entire team is after me.

Next shift out, I take the puck wide on a three-on-two and run the puck, myself, and their defenceman straight into their goalie. I make sure the goalie's mask gets in the way of my knee, another scrum ensues, and I get two minutes for— something, I don't know what. I don't ask, and don't really care at this point. I want to run amok.

From the penalty box I watch as one of their forwards glides down the ice along the boards. As soon as he crosses the blueline, though, Cancer rubs him out with authority, and he doesn't get up. The other team says Cancer kneed him, and they complain bitterly to the referee but to no avail. "I didn't see it," I tell the timekeeper with a shrug.

Before I get out of the box, Cancer drops another guy right off the face off. He gets up and Cancer tries to fight him, but the guy just backs away with a smile on his face and points at the score clock.

Once my two minutes are up, I head for our zone, creep up alongside one of their players, and crack him as hard as I can in the face with my elbow. A huge scrum ensues, and I'm back in the box. They score on the power play and I'm out, this time relegated to the bench. As the final minute winds down, Glen scampers to the bench only to have them intercept a dump-in, turn it around, and throw it in our empty net. Their bench erupts, triumphant. Cancer is on the ice, and he cocks his stick back over his head like a tomahawk and smashes it over our crossbar in disgust.

Philosopher's Sins

Once I'm hidden from view in the alleyway, I slow the car to a stop. The gravel crumbles under the tires, making a loud sound that ricochets off the walls. I turn the ignition off. The CD player, playing "Looking Back Again" by Brand New Unit, stops abruptly, and silence fills the car. I open the door, take a puff from my cigar, and sit with my feet out the open door.

I stand up and pull my wallet out, closing the door behind me. I take out a small note written in pen on the back of a restaurant receipt. For some reason I still have the number Dora wrote for me in Kamloops. I've never been sentimental at all, but here I am with this piece of paper in my hand, so what the fuck. I take a drag from my cigar, straightening the receipt out and holding it between thumb and index finger. I hold the tip of the cigar to the corner of the note and nurse the fire until it burns on its own. Then I watch the paper disintegrate until what remains is too hot to hold. The ashes float through the air, lingering and weaving gently as the smoke from my cigar climbs into the air like a cancerous grey vine.

Someone nudges me with an extended hand. I look over to the driver's seat and find Ashley, though I don't recognize her for a split second. We're outside my apartment complex, that much I can see. I'm so drunk I have to close one eye to curb the blurry double vision currently plaguing me.

"What happened?" I ask.

Ashley assumes a confused and utterly pissed off face. "Well, you showed up at my house drunk as hell. I haven't seen or heard from you in over a *year*, and here you show up tanked and wake up my roommate. What the hell."

I suck in some air, trying to breathe properly.

"And now I'm across town with no money because I had to drive your drunk ass home," she goes on.

I hiccup loudly as she starts to get out of the car. I try to stop her but can't seem to grab her coat. "Ashley, at least let me give you some money for a cab ride home."

"You don't have any money, asshole."

"What? How do you know?"

"I checked your wallet. Trust me, you're tapped out."

"I'm sorry."

"For what?"

"For whatever I did earlier."

"You mean for showing up at my place, breaking the fridge door in search of beer, telling me all about all the lies you told me, then making a huge scene when I refused to let you drive home?"

I wince. "I did that? Really?"

She turns and leaves, walking out of view. "Bye, Seth."

I finally track down Melanie's number in Calgary. It's funny, but when she left, after I started hitting the bottle again and she pulled away from me, she didn't make a big scene. She's a mature woman, and she decided to move to Calgary for a graphic design internship for the summer. Did the failure of our relationship have something to do with her moving? I have no idea. But she didn't light my lawn on fire, or see me at the bar and throw a drink in my face. No, she just left, and she had every right to. I'm a disgrace.

I call, but get her roommate. Melanie's away for a few days on assignment apparently. The roommate says she'll pass the message along. I have every confidence she's lying.

This is the end of something. The end of everything and nothing, at the exact same time. Something which never

really began and now will never be finished. Inside this moment
I've found something. There is something here for me, something
to be clung to amidst the chaos of my life. I haven't quite grasped
it yet, nor am I completely sure what it is, but at least things are
clearer now. The fog has lifted and my eyes are no longer cloud-
ed over. It no longer hurts to look at myself and my situation and
at what may come, and it no longer hurts to let my emotions get
the best of me. My confusion has become my peace.

I'm back before this all started. Before her, and her, and
that other girl. Before that really bad thing happened, and I
went looking for something I knew I'd never find. I went
looking for her when I knew she was already gone. I went
looking, and found nothing.

I can still taste her mix of saliva and breath. I can still smell
her from time to time, a quick scent I'm not sure is real or
imaginary. The fragrance is familiar, and stays only long enough
to register. The touch, the feel of sheets reminds me of her. The
feel of skin against skin, or wet hair on my pillow, cast adrift in
a beautiful halo. I want to be with her, rather than simply
remember her. I ache for her.

I remember the way her face looks up close. The way her
hazel eyes look when they're staring directly into mine. Her
nose, her eyebrows, her lips. Her body held against mine in an
entanglement of limbs. We became something almost symbiotic, moving and adjusting together, talking about nothing, and
everything, at the same time. I can feel her heart beating, and
the way her chest vibrates with sound when she speaks. The
way her nose feels against my neck. The way she kisses me gently on the forehead, then pulls me in tight to her body, grip-
ping my waist with her hands. Our limbs work as one—inter-
twined legs, interlocked fingers, our brown hair spilled all over
each other. Saliva moving from one mouth to another. Her
breath inside my mouth, filling my lungs. My body inside hers,
as one.

Now all I have of every woman I've ever been with is a tombstone. All these women, all these encounters and memories and feelings and lust, they're all here, all one, and she lies beneath them, lifeless. And now I'm forced to wait for something I know will never come. My life, part of my life, has died and will never be reborn.

Thoughts come and go. What if I'd done this? What if she'd done that, or instead done something else? Even something so minute and mundane as turning left on a street we were supposed to go right on would have changed everything. Even a slight slip of the foot on the gas at the right time and I would've died with her, or she would have lived and I would have died, which would've been infinitely better.

Every time you come to the question of whether God chose you or not, you're left with this gaping hole you can't comfortably venture into. You can cover that hole with falsities, employing logic and reason as best you can, but you can never solve the riddle. That hole is here to stay. That hole is your life as it exists today.

I see her at the most mundane of times. She comes to me unbidden while I'm standing in line, or tying my shoes, triggering an almost physical response. And when the sensation fades, the memories, the smells, the sounds go with it as my mind tries desperately to recuperate.

I know she'd be so proud of me. Aren't you proud of me, Sarah? I've become the man you were waiting for. I'm sorry I'm late though. I'm so sorry for what happened. This chaos caught us, and tripped us up. At least we both have this image to hold onto. I know I was close to you. I know I was there with you when you were crying, and I know I made you laugh until tears welled in your eyes. I know I was with you at one time and no one can take that from me. We were one at one time, and that's all I have left.

I'm sitting on our couch, eating some perogies and watching the Canucks game with Cancer. The Canucks are going to miss the playoffs officially with this loss to the Oilers. Cancer is trying to pretend nothing has happened. However, the fact I've told him I'm moving out at the end of the month has definitely rattled him. To where, I don't know yet. All I know is I'm leaving. Chances are I'm going to get in my car and just disappear. For how long, I don't know. I can tell Cancer is searching for words, but trying to seem as though he's not.

"So do you want to talk about this?" I say at one point. He stares at the TV for a couple of seconds.

"I dunno, man. It's not like I can say shit like 'Well you didn't consult me' or something."

"It was a decision I had to make."

"I know. It just kind of leaves me in a difficult spot, y'know?"

"I know. It's just I have to do this. And I'm not saying it doesn't fuck you over. I mean obviously I'll try to help you find a roommate, if you want to stay here."

He pauses. "I totally understand that part," he says at length. "It's just . . . fuck . . . I dunno."

I clean my plate, picking at the cheese with my fingers. "Anyways, let's not talk about it tonight. Sleep on it or something."

"Sure."

"I'll be here until the end of the month. We'll have lots of time to talk about it before then."

I stand up and head to the kitchen, wash my plate off and place it in the dishwasher. Then, washing my meal down with a huge slug of Pepsi, I head into my room, wander a bit, clean a bit, then decide to lie down for an after dinner nap. I gently toss and turn for a good ten minutes, and contemplate jerking off, but then realize I'm really not in the mood for such extracurricular activity. I start to drift in and out of sleep while watching my alarm clock, watching the time jump as I slip in and out of consciousness. Finally the phone rings, and I sit up in bed, confused.

"Hello?"

"Hi."

It's Caleb, I can tell right away.

"You seen the snow yet?" he says.

"Snow?"

"Yeah it started snowing like a few hours ago."

"No shit," I say, standing up and looking out the window. "Fuck, it's April."

"I know. Weird, huh. Apparently Whistler's got like three feet right now. It's nuts."

I stare out the window, watching the flakes collect on the pavement. Our conversation pauses, something which rarely happens between us.

"What's going on, Caleb?"

"Not much, just sitting around. You know, the usual for a Sunday night."

"Cool."

He adjusts the phone and coughs quietly. "So I heard you guys got swept," he says.

"Yeah, we didn't do too well."

"Fuck, man, I heard they were shadowing you all series."

"Yeah, it was pretty bad. I took a lot of penalties, but I guess you have to give them credit for sticking to their game plan."

"Shoulda pounded the shit out of them."

"Yeah, we tried. But they just played really hard."

"Yeah, sure," Caleb coughs, and I can tell he's smoking a joint. "Hey, at least you guys made the playoffs. You did better than us and the Canucks, eh?"

"Yeah, but you guys'll be better next season. I heard we're losing some guys."

Caleb takes a big drag off his joint. I wait to hear him exhale before he beings to speak. "So, yeah, the not drinking thing didn't go too well, eh. I mean not that it was a bad idea or anything. . . . Oh and I heard you're moving out, is that right? Cancer must be pleased."

"Yeah it's been a little weird between us, no question. But then it wasn't like I was making any sort of post hoc conclusions about drinking because of him."

"What do you mean?"

"Post hoc? It means—"

"I know what post hoc means, but how does that apply to you and Cancer?"

"Okay," I say, "like if every time I hang out with Cancer I get drunk and do stupid shit, well then I must get drunk and do stupid shit because of Cancer. But I made it very clear to him that wasn't the case at all. I just think maybe he thinks he's an alcoholic now," I go on. "Because if I quit drinking because I thought I was an alcoholic, and if he drank with me pretty much every time, well then maybe it kind of labels him as an alcoholic, in his mind."

"Well he is an alcoholic. There's no question about that."

"I know, we both are, but maybe he just wasn't cool having someone else decide that for him. He wasn't cool not having control over the situation. I mean I heard his mom found out about me and that I tried to stop drinking, and called him all worried and he was like 'What the fuck?' "

"Yeah, well, I guess it's his problem in the end. I mean you kind of had a bit of an epiphany a while back, and so yeah, I guess now is as good a time as any to quit."

"You mean the car crash?"

"Yeah. I mean—"

"I've never really looked at it that way, to be honest. Coincidences are just coincidences. Sarah was insistent on driving, and we hit that—"

"What?"

"Huh?"

"You said Sarah was driving."

"No, I mean she insisted she drive, but then I talked her out of it. Either way, it's tough for me to draw any type of conclusions as to why it happened. There's no *reason* why it happened. It just happened. It's like how I blew my knee out. I mean I planted my foot wrong on a hardwood floor. That's it. At most there was probably a drop of sweat there that made it slip, and that drop of sweat could have come from anyone or anywhere."

"So you don't see a pattern in your life?"

"Well, maybe. I mean I kind of like the idea of synchronicity and some Grand Plan, but yeah, I think it's all just random shit that happens to a guy."

"Yeah, well, I don't know too much about that," he says, taking a pull from his joint. He blows the smoke out, then continues. "What do they call it when someone makes connections between two things, like strings together coincidences that actually have no meaning?"

"Apophenia?"

"Yeah, that's it. Maybe you're doing that. Or maybe *I'm* doing that. Or maybe God's just trying to fuck with you," he says. "How's that."

"No doubt," I laugh.

He pauses, then asks, "So are you going to come with us to get some leftover tickets tomorrow?"

He's referring to the fact Canucks' tickets go on sale tomorrow because they're out of the playoffs. The only good things about these remaining meaningless games are the fact there's usually plenty of fighting and we can go down to the penalty box and fuck with guys like Matthew Barnaby and Sean Avery while getting drunk on smuggled-in liquor. It's kind of a Canadian ritual.

"Yeah, Cancer wants me to go down because he has to work tomorrow."

"Box office opens at eight."

He takes a few quick pulls from his joint. Meanwhile my phone beeps.

"Hey, I'm getting another call. Can I call you back in like ten minutes?"

"Actually, I'm heading out, I think. Call me—"

"Hello," I say, having already switched to the other line.

"Okay, so what was this apology about?"

"Melanie?"

"Yes. It's Melanie."

I pause a moment, gathering my thoughts. "I just wanted to apologize for my behaviour in general," I say at length. "Just let you know I'm sorry. You know, that things got so fucked up."

"It's so very unlike you, Seth. It didn't ring true at all."

"Yeah, well, things are different now."

"Figured as much," she says. "But apologizing and saying 'I'm shit' over and over, it's just so . . . meaningless. I mean were you just using me for some type of comfort, or what."

"No, it wasn't that. It wasn't that at all."

"Okay, well, that's all I needed to know. If I can be sure of that, then it's cool."

"If I did, I wouldn't have felt like shit when you left," I go on. "I don't know where the fuck I was—or am, for that matter. I'm still lost, I think."

"Yeah, but you made it sound like you 'played with my heart' or some such crap. Screw that. I mean that everything got messed up is one thing, but what we had is quite another."

"I didn't play with your heart, Melanie. But then I don't think I was especially careful either—which I apologize for."

We both fall silent a moment. Then she continues, "Good luck with the move by the way. Sincerely."

"Thanks. I need all the help I can get."

"Well I don't know how I'd be able to help. But I do hope you make it work."

"I think I will. I'm just not looking forward to actually getting started. I mean it's getting pretty weird already."

"I can imagine."

"But in a way I like it, you know? I mean there's a whole new world out there."

"Yeah, change is good. You always say that."

"Change *is* good. But it's never easy."

"Nobody said it was gonna be easy, Seth."

"Yeah, I know. But I was kind of hoping it would be."

I look out the window.

"It's snowing here," I say.

"No way, really?"

"Yeah, really. Snow in April in Vancouver is just plain crazy."

We say goodnight and hang up. Then I stand up from my chair and scratch myself. It's dark out, and the snowflakes, like miniature magnesium flares in the night, twinkle through the glow of lamps down the street. I'm pretty sure Cancer is still up. I head out to the living room to find him slouched over on the left arm of the couch, his right hand down his pants. His left hand is holding the remote, and *Latin Lover* is on the television. I take the remote out of his hand and turn the TV off. Then I cover his shame with a pillow and head into the bathroom. As soon as I sit down on the toilet I hear my cell phone ring. I hesitate a moment, then decide to let it ring. After I finish, I brush my teeth and check out the long scar on my right arm in the mirror. It's now a light pink. The fifty or so stitches look like little train tracks running down my biceps. My bottom lip is still fat from our final game, still bruised some two weeks later, but now it's a thick dark purple with a few enduring bite marks for character. I'm still losing weight, and my stomach is completely flat. I can make out a few ribs, and my neck looks rutted when I flex it like that. I look like a recovering crack addict. But I don't really care. Good enough, I think.

I make my way back to my room, sit down on my bed, and open my wallet that's lying there on the floor. I pull out a twenty and move over to the desk, sit down in the chair and pull out a black felt marker. On a piece of paper I write, *Ashley, thanks for the ride home that night. Sorry for all the shit I've caused you. Seth*

I look it over, then ball it up and toss it on the floor. I take another piece of paper and start again. *Ashley, thanks for the ride home that night. Enclosed is the twenty bucks I owe you for a cab ride. Sorry for all the shit I put you through. Seth*

My cell phone beeps, telling me I have a new message. Ignoring it, I fold the piece of paper into thirds, open the top drawer of the desk and pull out an envelope, tuck the twenty into the letter, and then slide the letter inside the envelope. I seal it up, pressing the corners closed, then write *Ashley* on the front of the envelope. I stare at it a moment, then tear it open and walk over to the one wall of my room I haven't put my head through. I tack the twenty to the wall, and with the black felt marker write in big block letters, *Ashley, thanks for the ride home that night. Sorry for all the shit. I hope you forgive me someday. Seth*

I leave the room, shutting the door behind me, and turn the hallway lights off as I exit the apartment. I take the back stairs down to the front door of the complex, passing three empty beer bottles and a bag of trash along the way. I open the door and step out into the cold crisp air and the silently falling snow. A thin blanket of white covers everything now.

I walk down the lane to my car, watching my footing all the way. The first thing I notice, when I get in the car, is my breath fogging the windshield. I turn the keys, and the stereo blasts some frantic punk song at me. Cringing, I turn it down quickly, and flip the windshield wipers on and blast the heat. Only cold air comes out, and in the meantime I search for a quieter CD, settling on something Cancer likes to listen to when he's hungover and feeling melancholy. I pull out of the dead-end street, putting my seatbelt on as I go. The roads are empty, as everyone is either asleep or watching TV. I light my last half of cigar. Downtown is quiet, with only the odd pedestrian or vehicle making their way somewhere in the snow.

An odd serenity settles over me as I get onto the highway heading east out of the city. I see the lights of houses, and far above them the twinkling lights of ski runs seemingly suspended in the darkness. I drive a while, smoking my cigar slowly, then at the last second pull off and cut down below the highway. Once I make it through the light I'm fairly sure I know where I'm going. Two lights then left, one light then right, then all the way to the end before turning left at the T in the road. When I reach the house, the lights are off.

I leave the car running. I'm not going to be here long. I knock quietly but firmly on the door once, twice, three times, but there's no response. Then, suddenly, the hallway light comes on and a blurry figure appears in the open doorway.

"Seth? Is that you?"

"Hi, Christina."

"Ashley's not here. She's in Seattle," Christina says in a somewhat exasperated tone.

"I know. I just wanted you to let her know I left her something at my apartment."

She looks at me, confused. "Why didn't you just bring it over," she says.

"I was going to, but then decided it would probably be better if I didn't come here."

"Yet here you are," she says.

"Yet here I am."

She shakes her head and sighs. "Well, whatever it is, maybe you could give it to her when she gets back."

"But I won't be here—I'm leaving, that's the point. Can't you just tell her I left it for her?"

She looks at me anew, now thoroughly confused. "What's going on, Seth. It's like past midnight."

"I didn't wake you, did I?"

"That's not the point. You can't just come around here like this."

"I wasn't going to. Look," I say, "I don't need to see her. I'm cool with that. I was just wondering if you could pass this message along for me."

"That you left something for her. In your apartment."

"That's right."

"That you won't be at. Because you're leaving."

"Correct."

"Oh how mysterious," she laughs. "Well then what is it exactly?"

"A letter."

"Oh Seth," she winces. "I don't know."

"Look, can you just tell her? I don't need to speak to her again at all, and I won't come by again, I promise. Can you just do me this one favour and tell her?"

She stares at me a moment. And eventually she says, "I'll tell her."

"You promise?"

She stares at me again.

"Please, Christina? I'm not asking for a lot here."

"Okay, fine," she says. "But you have to realize, coming around unannounced like this isn't the best way to win her back. Not after all this time."

"I'm not trying to win her back. Look, I wasn't even going to come here. I knew she was in Seattle and I just sort of . . . came," I laugh, and she looks at me once more.

"I'll make sure she gets the message, psycho."

"Thanks, Christina. Thanks a lot."

I turn and walk away, hearing the door close shut behind me. Then I get in my car and make my way back to the freeway. Once I'm on the highway, cruising nicely, I light up what little remains of my cigar.

I sit and drive and smoke in silence. Then, when the cigar runs out, I just sit and drive. Eventually I take a pen out of the glove box and roll up my right sleeve, making sure to keep one hand on the steering wheel the entire time. I scrawl these words across my right forearm:

to whom it may concern

I start to speed up. The car begins to rattle at around 140, then settles in nicely around 150 before almost floating at 160. I look to the left, at the concrete divider whipping by, then to the right at the deep ravine running alongside. It must be at least fifty feet down that embankment. I turn back straight, take my seatbelt off, and pull the car into the right lane. And then with one steady pull of the steering wheel I crank the car right and send it sailing out over the ravine.

Conspectus Alibi

I can't hear anything. I can't see anything. I can't taste anything. I can smell ammonia. I can feel something, but I'm not quite sure where, or what exactly it feels like.

In the bathroom, with my best friend Nicky, our reflections partially blinded by the summer light. We're gelling our hair into Mohawks with gobs of Vaseline, still fresh faced and prepubescent. We rumble through the house on the stained wooden floors, long sticks carved into swords clutched in our hands.

Out back behind the large farm house is a huge grass field alongside a river. The trees, some of which hang out over the river, look like elderly fingers trying to dip themselves in the healing waters below. We sprint across the field, dodging cow pies. It's warm and muggy out, and semi-trucks motor by on the Yellowhead highway out of sight.

I run so fast I tumble face first onto the grass, my left arm breaking my fall. Nicky doesn't look back, but keeps running towards the river. I look at my hands—they're dirty, and bits of grass and crushed rock have been ground into my skin. Scrapes of blood that look like tread marks colour my palms. I get up and continue running, this time faster than before. I can see Nicky about fifty metres ahead, his Mohawk cutting and bobbing through the windless summer air.

We line up on the blueline. My helmet and gloves are off. I'm still breathing heavily, and adrenaline pumps heavily through my exuberant teenage veins. One of my teammates comes up from behind me and puts his arm around my shoulder, then messes up my hair.

"How's it feel, Seth?"

I look over at him. Both of us are smiling. The whole team is lined up along the blueline, eighteen smiles in a row. A stout man in a windbreaker steps out onto the rink with a microphone. Feedback scratches the air. "I'd like to thank everybody who came out today to watch the final," he says to the crowd.

I look into the stands. I can see my grandparents who came over from Halifax. And there's my mother. My sister. And my father.

"What a final," says the stout man, motioning to the crowd, and applause and cheers erupt once more.

"First off I'd like to thank the Burnaby Ice Hawks for a great tournament. They played extremely well. . . . And I'd like to present the player of the game medal to number thirty-two, Joseph Blackman."

Matt looks over at me. "Blackman? What the fuck kind of name is 'Blackman'?"

We all chuckle quietly as we clap. Their goalie skates over, still flush from crying.

"Now I'd like to present the Bantam AAA Provincial Title to the Langley Eagles. Could we have the captain come over, please?"

I try to appear as modest as possible, even though as soon as the final whistle went this was all I was thinking about, getting this trophy.

"We would also like to congratulate team captain Seth Wilhelm, our tournament MVP."

I skate over feeling like a king. My coach pats me on the butt on the way by. I stop at the guy with the microphone.

"Congratulations. Great game, son," he says, his voice low and so much more personal now without the microphone. I thank him and he hands me the trophy. It's lighter than I thought it would be. Two long golden poles with wooden ends bearing a voluptuous lady with wings. I turn to my team and raise the trophy over my head to a huge round of applause. This is the single happiest moment of my life. My teammates skate over and I pass the trophy to our goalie.

Later, I'm in the car with my grandparents, my sister, my mother and my father, and we're heading back to the hotel before we begin the long drive home. My father is silent. Everyone is talking about the game. My grandfather commends me for my hat-trick, including the empty net goal I scored with ten seconds remaining. But my father is silent. Why won't he say something? Something inside me breaks that night.

There's a feeling of utter vastness hovering above my head. Almost as if I'm lying on top of a skyscraper with only empty space above me. But I can't see anything, and don't feel fully awake. What feels like four or five different parts of my mind are shaking, almost vibrating with thoughts. They crisscross each other multiple times, like a superhighway with ideas, smells and feelings zipping by in little cars. Then more images start to flit in and out, faster and faster until I'm shot up in bed, eyes open as I pull myself to one side.

I'm in a hospital bed and it's pitch black outside. A dark figure sleeps on a chair in the corner, hunched over awkwardly. I puke down my chest, blood mixed with bile. My head starts to rush and I'm immediately out again.

Now we're in bed together, Sarah propped up against the bedboard, scribbling away in a diary as I lay across the sheets like a gunshot victim. I look up at her.

"What are you writing about now?"

She looks up from the page at me. "Nothing."

"Nothing?"

"Nothing, Mr. Nosey."

"Okay then, write away," I say, then start to work my way up her naked thigh with my stubble. She giggles a bit, and I wrap my arms around her and close my eyes.

"Yeah so there was this serious language barrier with her because she was Mexican and really didn't speak any English at all, so we get back to the hotel room and she starts giving me this hand job, but just like fucking cranking on my cock and I'm dying because it's so painful, but I don't want to say anything because, hey, it's a hand job, and she's looking at me all in pain and she's thinking I like it so she starts going harder and by this time I'm digging my fingernails into the bed, almost to the point of ripping the fucking bed sheets and she's just going nuts on my cock and finally I just have to stop her and put my cock in her mouth and say 'gentle' in as plain English as I can manage."

He takes a pull off his joint.

"Man, remember when you and Cancer were fighting on that guy's patio? Both of you were so wasted you couldn't even stand up. And fuckin' Cancer tries to throw you in the hot tub and you squirm out and bust a beer bottle over his head, and then you both go ploughing through a screen door and fall into some sixteen year-old chick and cut her up real good. And she's screaming 'I'm bleeding! Oh my God, I'm bleeding!' as the two of you get up and you throw up all over the kitchen floor when Cancer tackles you again. God, that was a great night."

I see him once again, my other self staring back at me like a mirror. Our palms are cut open, and our blood mixes together through the open wounds. He yells at me in my voice, "I don't owe you a fuckin' thing!"

Then everything goes white, and I hear the chime of church bells in the distance. I'm asleep but still very much awake. The ground is cold and my body feels like a slab of cooked meat. A constant pain courses through my body, from every joint in my hands to my knees and ankles, pooling in my legs. I'm tired and I've just woken up from a long sleep. I feel like death.

I sit up to what seems like a haze. Every sense feels muted. Strained. The sun is arcing across the sky at an alarming rate, and each building in the city appears as though it's leaning towards me. I stare directly into the light, until it trumps my vision and the white becomes too painful to take. It penetrates me with beams of white, throwing my body backwards to the ground.

The grass has a certain taste I can't quite place. And from this proximity the concrete reveals its various imperfections, almost like admitting a mistake. Its sandy surface rubs like the head of a matchstick on my skin.

I look slightly to my left to see a long line of amber streetlights. A sense of emptiness hangs in the air. My veins open up, and rainwater mixes with blood. I look down my forearms and see my hands just lying there lifeless at the ends. Two creatures whose time has run out.

I raise my head and let my cigar fall to the ground. It falls so slowly, as though it's sliding down a line. I rub it out with my palm, exposing tobacco flakes, dusting them over the pavement like leaves in autumn.

Something comes over me, clarifying my situation momentarily, like a faint tingling sensation in the left lobe of my brain. I blink, then look to my left again. It's quiet. Some sense I've never experienced before pours too much information into my head, filling the empty spaces with an all-encompassing light. A tingling feeling begins to gather in my torso, running down my right leg before appearing, quite suddenly, in my right wrist. I feel the numbness with my leg, the pins and needles when I press thigh against forearm. My mind crawls, slowly starting to wake. Everything

feels fuzzy. My vision is blurry and I feel numb all over. I try
to speak but can't seem to move my jaw. I try to lift my
arms, but they feel too heavy to possibly be animated.

I try to speak again, this time managing to get a few meaningless words out. I'm on a morphine drip, I can tell. I feel
drugged and weak. I try to think back to what happened, but
I can't quite remember. I try to move again, shifting over and
looking to my left to find I'm in a hospital bed and it's dark
outside. My head still feels numb, my thoughts aimless and
trivial. I can't remember anything and it scares me, sending
cold shivers throughout my body.

I let out a soft "Hello," which sounds more like a moan to
me. My mouth is filled with saliva. I drag my body up towards
the head of the bed, taking all the little suction cup monitors
with me. Machinery is all around me, surrounding me. Once
I'm sitting up in bed I see I'm the only person in the room.

My mind still can't seem to grasp anything. I'm really not
sure what's happened. Everything that's ever happened to me
feels like a story I've read somewhere. I pull two tubes from my
nostrils and sit up in bed, feeling light-headed. My legs fall to
the ground. I stand up, and as I walk away from the bed all the
monitors and their little suction cups pull away from me and
my hospital gown falls open.

The linoleum is cold, sticking to my feet. It's the first real
sensation I've felt. I look down to see my toes, pasty white,
pushing against the ground, which strikes me as amusing in a
way. Smiling, I walk out of the room to find a long hallway
to the right, and a shorter one to the left. I head left to find
an unoccupied reception area. I've yet to see a single soul, but
I can feel the presence of people all around me. I'm not
alone.

I stumble upon a waiting room where a single female body
wrapped in a blanket lies across three chairs. I stand there in
the middle of the waiting room, unsure of what to do. I'm still

light-headed and now tired from too much walking.

Just then a massive figure comes barrelling around the corner. "Seth? What the fuck?"

Cancer is holding a bag of chips and a Pepsi. His words wake up the body lying on the chairs. She rolls over and stands up.

"Seth," says Sarah. "Oh my God."

Something comes over me, clarifying my situation momentarily, like a faint tingling sensation in the left lobe of my brain. I blink, then look to my left again. It's quiet. Some sense I've never experienced before pours too much information into my head, filling the empty spaces with an all-encompassing light. A tingling feeling begins to gather in my torso, running down my right leg before appearing, quite suddenly, in my right wrist. I feel the numbness with my leg, the pins and needles when I press thigh against forearm. My mind crawls, slowly starting to wake. Everything feels fuzzy. My vision is blurry and I feel numb all over. I try to speak but can't seem to move my jaw. I try to lift my arms, but they feel too heavy to possibly be animated.

"Dude, you awake?"

My eyes open to the bright lights of a too white room. A round figure comes into view.

"Seth, you okay?"

I watch as the figure leans in close, then gently slaps me on the face a few times.

"Seth, wake the fuck up."

My vision begins to clear. The features of the room become more distinct. I'm in a bed and it's dark outside.

"Seth, how many fingers am I holding up?"

I try to focus in. Three slightly blurry shapes block out the light.

"Three."

"Close enough."

My vision clears further, and my limbs begin to respond to my commands.

"Am I in a hospital?" I ask.

"Motherfucker, I can't believe you."

"What?"

"Your fuckin' car went off the highway into a ravine."

I search my memory, but can't seem to recall anything of the sort. The last thing I remember is heaving some guy through a window at Denny's before pummelling him.

"I got a phone call like an hour after you left," Cancer continues. "Doctor said your car went off a forty-foot embankment into the snow. You're a lucky son of a bitch though."

"Why?"

"The paramedics said you weren't wearing your seatbelt. The car must've been going like at least one-twenty, and when it flipped you went flying out the driver's side window."

"What?"

"Yeah, your car is apparently ripped to pieces. Destroyed. You would've died had you had your seatbelt on."

I try to sit up. I'm dressed in a hospital gown, and there are pulse monitors stuck to me and tubes jammed up my nostrils. Cancer gently forces me back down.

"Seth, the doc said not to let you get out of bed. He said he put you on a drip just to be safe. Fucking insane shit, man. Paramedics said they've never seen anything like it. They got the call, found the car, and there you were, lying in the snow like a motherfucker. And you were fine, just a bit banged up."

None of this seems possible, as I have no memory of it. I shake my head in wonderment.

"Your parents are on their way."

"Great."

"Christ, you're one tough son of a bitch," Cancer chuckles. "That's two car accidents you've lived through now."

I smile, trying to remember the first accident. I remember Sarah, but I can't recall what happened, and it frightens me.

"So my car's totalled?" I say.

"Totalled," he says. "Apparently they found part of the dashboard like a hundred feet from the rest of the car, and all the wheels were missing. Fucking Christ, it scared the shit out of me when I got the call. I had to hop in a cab and come down here."

I shake my head, unable to comprehend the situation. "What?"

"Fuck, just wait right here, okay? I'll go get the nurse. She told me to come get her when you woke up. So stay here and don't get up, okay? Promise?"

Cancer wheels and runs from the room. I turn my head and watch him go just as an old man staggers past in a hospital gown and slippers, clutching an IV on wheels. He doesn't look over at me, he just keeps walking, and I keep staring at him until I can no longer see him.

I look the other way and out the window. I'm on the first floor of the hospital and I can see a parking lot outside where people huddle together, smoking amid the falling snow. I lie back down and wait for Cancer to return.

My family arrives shortly, my mother and father together with my sister. We walk around the hospital a while. I don't want to go back to bed, I tell them, so we walk around the hospital in the middle of the night. The next day I'm moved to my mother's house, where I spend the next few days sitting in front of the TV watching *Oprah* and *The Price is Right*. People call and visit. I nod and tell them I'm fine. Then I get a call that shakes the very foundation I once stood on. I borrow my mother's car and make my way across town. Sarah's mother stands in her living room. The fireplace crackles behind her.

On the coffee table sit six separate books, all with Sarah's name embroidered on the front cover.

Sarah's mother stands there, hands at her side, watching the flames. She stands there deep in thought, for what seems like hours, and could possibly be days. As far as she is concerned this is her life, she tells me, this endless period of mourning. I say nothing. Her daughter's diaries sit closed on the table. That whole world was waiting to be exposed, she says, but for the longest time she was unsure, torn between the idea of opening up a wound that was now only beginning to close, and letting it heal once and for all. She'd made progress, she says, and reading these diaries could have undone it all. Exposing herself to such things could have broken her down again, and she wasn't sure she was strong enough to build herself back up once more.

The phone rings. She lets it go. Finally the voicemail picks up and it stops.

"Do you want anything? Some coffee perhaps?" she asks.

"No thanks," I say.

She nods at the fire. "Seth," she says eventually.

"Yes?"

"My psychiatrist told me I should try to read her diaries for closure, but I just couldn't bring myself to do it. And I admit I was going to burn them, but then when I heard about your accident it just kind of forced me to read them."

I stand there silently, staring at the back of her head. Finally she turns around, and my eyes drop instantly to the ground.

"Seth, I read the diaries and there was one passage that struck me. How your father tried to teach you how to drive a manual shift, a manual car, and how you couldn't. And how he beat you because of it."

I stand there, staring at the floor.

"And then she talked about how one day she tried to teach you again, to try to help you—she's always trying to help people with their problems—and you couldn't do it."

"That's not true. I—"

"Seth, you couldn't even get out of the parking lot," she says, "and it was her car. You couldn't drive her car. And so I read this and I thought, How could you have been driving that night?"

I try to look at her, but I can't.

"Seth, I need you to answer this question for me. I want you to trust me. You know you can trust me."

I just stand there diverting my eyes.

"Seth, I want you to tell me what happened that night."

Acknowledgements

Mom, Dad, Max, I love you. Thanks to Chris.